Mothball Magic

Mothball Magic

Rena Rocford

Space Wizard Science Fantasy
Raleigh, NC
www.spacewizardsciencefantasy.com

Cover art by Moorbooks
Editing by Heather Tracy
Book Layout © 2015 BookDesignTemplates.com

Mothball Magic/ Rena Rocford.— 1st ed.
ISBN 978-1-960247-55-1

For my mom, who shared her love of reading with me.

CONTENTS

Chapter One

Inconveniently, magic returned in the middle of me cooking dinner, in the boring part where I walked away from the stove—watched pots not boiling and all that. The fire ruptured from the burner, spilling over the edge of the pot and spiraling up to the ceiling. I stood in the doorway to my bathroom, staring like a damned fool. As I stared, a creature rippled through the column of fire.

Only magic did that, but there was no more magic. I'd locked it away seventy years ago.

The stench of burning pasta wafted through the room, following the billowing furls of smoke, twisting to the ceiling in a pillar of undeniable, magical fire.

There aren't many things like magical fire. The way it breathed in the power, setting itself to the heartbeat of the person controlling it. Calling an elemental required something deeper than magic—more primal. Magical fire, in particular, only ever answered to desperate calls—powerful pleas into the ether of the between—and even then, only truly powerful mages could ever hope to see one, let alone call one. Without an anchor, an elemental would only have seconds in the material world. They needed power, a connection to a mage. That's why the column twisted in pain. No one controlled this fire creature. No one had called it.

It pulsed, the power of it growing suddenly and dropping, before spilling power into the real world like a light house beacon burning brightly into the night. Then it slowed and pulsed again, like a pulsing heart.

Oh gods. It *was* called by someone.

My heartbeat rushed in my chest. Who was still alive? And how had they called it? I thought everyone died when the council—

And then I saw it pulsing in time to my own racing heart.

It matched me. *I* called it?

But I hadn't made a desperate enough plea in decades, not since the accident that took—

Maybe it's a trick? I opened my channels, dropping the cup in my hand. It shattered on the ground, spraying my shins and slippers in shrapnel of porcelain and water. The power rushed in, spilling into my channels, like rain on the desert sand. So long. It had been so long since the power had been here. Seventy years without a drop. Seventy years watching the world move on without me. Thank you for your service, ma'am, but we don't need you anymore.

And here it was burning my dinner.

The weight of this reality settled in my mind as the power spilled through me like water wicking through a paper towel.

I had locked up magic. It was my spell that took away everything from every mage to walk this green earth. On pain of death, I had cast the magic. I'd been the only one powerful enough—dumb enough!—to think I could speak for everyone. For seventy years my spells had held the Source in place, in secret.

But somehow, amazingly, it had gotten out. Magic flowed through the world again.

And that meant The Winter Queen would be coming for my blood.

All this sluiced through my mind as I stared at the conflagration that used to be my dinner. Damn it all, I'd really wanted that ravioli, even if the doctor said it was bad for my sugar.

How was it here? Why now? Why hadn't the damn spell broken when we'd crashed the car? Why hadn't it come back when it could have done a lick of good? It comes back now? When I'm older than the dirt, my body twisted with age and pain? How dare—

The creature in the column blinked at me, turning toward me. The fire rushed up, taking the curtains in a terrifying hunger, transferring my anger into power and heat and a rage that only fire knows.

I held out my hand as I capped my feelings into a jar. Without hesitation, the little dragon slipped from the fire at my stove to my hands. It limped through the air, its hind leg not fully formed. Poor thing, not called here, but breaking through the ether between worlds, and barely with any help from this side. It would have to have a powerful need to slip the bonds of its realm and come here.

Hopefully for more than burning my dinner.

It purred when its nose hit my hand, heat followed with a thrill racing up my arm. Then the fire burned up it, as I hadn't cast any of my protective spells, and I felt like a damned apprentice with burned sleeves. At least it didn't burn my hair. The creature—no, the dragon—rubbed under my hand, nuzzling close to me, moving like a cat, but the scales hardened, pearlescent plates as she moved, twisting around my sleeves and trying to rub her head against my chest.

My heart sagged. I'd forgotten what it was like to hold a fire creature, a dragon.

Then the dragon shifted, a growl burbling up through its—her—throat, a threat from the business end, even if she was small.

I followed her gaze. Standing on my couch cushions, leaning toward me, stood Winter. Even in my apartment, she was confined to the old laws. She could not set foot here, being a creature of the air and the cold. None of the fae lords or ladies could stand on the earth that was claimed for mortals, but it didn't mean she couldn't be somewhere if there was something else to stand on. Her malice radiated off her like a tangible force. She might be a creature of air, but she could have been a walking malfeasance the way she despised humans. She wore her hate like a cloak, even as that side of my apartment crusted over in ice, blooms of crystals twirling through the air and spinning across the floor. The patterns could almost trick a person into believing the pale monster with the translucent blue skin could be beautiful. Her glacier-colored hair spilled around her, moving as if she were submerged in the ocean, rocking and pulling to some unseen current.

Of course, it was. Her hair ebbed and flowed with the current of her magic. Even though all of humanity had gone seventy years without so much as a lick of magic, that hadn't constrained either of the Queens. She looked just like the day we'd made our bargain: hide magic away from humans and in exchange, she would forgive the transgressions of the humans who'd held the Source of All Magic.

"What do you want?" I yelled, stalling for time.

"Your heart!" Her words hissed through the air like water spraying from a sprinkler, each sibilant breath spilling across my mind as her words hit my ears.

The dragon hissed at her. *Ha! That's right, sweetie, know your enemies.*

"It's not yours yet," I said cautiously. "Your Majesty." I hurried to tack on the honorific before her face could shift at the destruction of my manners. People have been slain for lesser slights with her.

She narrowed her eyes at me. "I am surprised to see you still able to walk. Doesn't that hip hurt?"

Pain flared in the old joint. Years of abuse and no more healing magic had done more damage than a single bullet from a stray Nazi. My dragon growled again, tensing her whole body as she prepared to leap at the Winter Queen.

<*Stay with me*, dragon,> I thought at the creature, desperate to give it an anchor.

<*But she threatened you,*> she whined back.

"I'm told human joints hurt more in winter," Winter said, trying to goad me into breaking hospitality first. If I did, she'd kill me right here.

I nodded. "I'm told we should stick to business." With effort, I measured my words. "The accords have a stipulation. I have a week or until the next full moon to rectify the terms of our agreement, whichever is longer. You can wait a whole week to plunge the world into snow and ice."

Something like a hot lance exploded across my chest, stealing my breath and dropping me to my knees. The dragon attacked the queen with a shriek. A flash of light exploded into the room, filling it with power and sound. The pressure of the Winter Queen's magic popped my ears, and I cried out.

The power holding the dragon in this realm gave way before the brute force of the fae lord, and the dragon unraveled like the string on a bag of rice, slipping from form and reality back through the gates from whence it came.

I put my knee up to push through Winter's power and stood.

"Enough!" I yelled, pouring magic into my voice, a simple thing to bring her back to attention.

She snapped up, caught off guard by my simplest spell.

Ha! Seventy years rusty but I still got it, you ageless bitch.

Smoke trickled into the air around us, rolling across the ceiling, and the alarm suddenly blared to life.

Winter ducked her head, holding her hands over her ears. "What?"

"It's a fire alarm!" I yelled.

"Is this how you call your reinforcements?" she hissed, twisting her head to glare at the alarm on the wall.

"Sort of? Firemen will be here soon!" I waved toward the door. "You should go before they see you!" I said, hoping she would take the hint. I hadn't made the noise, and she couldn't claim it was me breaking hospitality rules. And I'd warned her people were coming. All the truth, and all very hospitable. So far, so good.

She glared, her hatred freezing the air around her, but the fire alarm continued. Then she relaxed, standing straight, her head nearly to the ceiling as she stood on my couch. "I have changed my mind," she said simply. "I say you broke the terms, and I don't have to wait."

Ever so silent, slow and careful not to let it ripple, I gathered magic toward me. The Source of Magic spilled power into the great ley lines of the world, like some giant canal system. The lines, in turn, filled and sprayed everything in the world around them. But, as a mage gathered power into themselves to later be expended in a spell, the mage made waves in the power, detectable by anyone. A careful mage, or a mage with low capacity, like a small ship, doesn't cause much in the way of a wake. Other mages with greater capacity were like lumbering freight carriers.

I wasn't some dinghy, but if I siphoned the power slowly, she might not notice me building up my defenses. I held my expression still as stone. "It doesn't matter if you changed your mind!" I yelled over the alarm. "We have an accord. One written in blood!"

"It only lasts as long as blood pumps through your heart!"

As she yelled her response back, I wove the framework of a spell, ready to fill it with the power slowly—too slow, honestly. I'd be more likely to turn back the tide with a teacup than gather up enough power at this rate.

Careful is how you win, Ruth.

"Are you threatening me?" I asked, voice lower.

She heard my threat and turned her head to regard me with only one eye, as if monocular gaze could reveal details her second eye confused. "It doesn't matter if you're dead!" she hissed.

I rolled my eyes. "Do you really want to go through the whole song and dance? How much threatening is enough for you to agree to the accord we came to an arrangement on before? I have until the full moon to put magic back where it belongs, and you cannot impede me. I have it all written down."

Her smile sharpened to match her angular features. Fat flakes of snow started to shower down from the ceiling, coating my good sofa pillows in a fine layer of powder.

"Those are hand stitched!" I pointed at the pillow made for me by my wife, Dorothy, now in a plastic cover.

Even the thought of her name, even while staring down the Winter Queen, the loneliness etched itself across my chest, grabbing at my throat, a sudden lump of pain.

Damn her and her tricks. This was a charm. A manipulation.

I closed my eyes to gather my feelings and properly direct my rage. "You cannot trick me. I demand you abide by our agreement!"

She hissed at me. "Very well, mortal fool. You have seven days or until the moon is full and in the sky. I shall not impede you. I shall not slow your steps or block your passage. If you do not have the heart of that dead star cloaked by the time the moon reaches its fullest, I will suck the blood from your body, enjoying the dying warmth as you turn to stone in my hands."

My breath blew out through my nostrils as if I were a bull, reining my emotions back in. "Then the accord stands." My clipped words would have been a warning to anyone who knew me, but Winter just smiled as though they were delicious.

"Indeed, they do." She ran a finger across the top of my couch, and where she touched it, a seam split open, revealing the stuffing underneath. "Humans," she said absently. "You always think you're so clever with your words and your agreements."

I tensed, ready for anything.

She canted her head like a coy girl instead of a monster of ice and shadow. "You're free to move. I'm not blocking you. But we never agreed on the air."

Her expression twisted from someone playing with a charming toy to the hatred of foul enemies.

In that second, I unleashed my spell, a woven wall of protection, snapping up between us with a sudden glow, each strand of magic bracing and supporting the other. The power spilled from me faster than I could drag it into my reservoir.

As my power filled the space between us, the billowing smoke increased tenfold, filling every part of the room, blocking out all light. Shit, she was the queen of air and darkness.

My heart skipped a beat.

I could die right here, choked by the smoke from my own burnt dinner, and Winter could just eat me at her leisure. *Bad move, Ruth. Did you learn nothing from the Order?* I could ward myself against burns, but I had to breathe like everyone else.

First rule of fire: don't breathe the smoke.

I scrambled for the door, only to find Winter had coated the ground in ice. As my foot slipped out from under me, my thoughts gathered on curious ideas. Technically, ice could be considered a breach of the contract, but it had been snowing before. She could always claim innocence.

Something like an explosion lanced off the side of my spell, causing light to rupture in the billowing smoke like lightning rolling between clouds.

As my whole body sailed through the air, I couldn't help but stumble onto one thought: My daughter (technically granddaughter, but I'd raised her as my own) would be informed of my death by accidental smoke inhalation. They'd find my body on the ground and think I'd choked to death when I'd caught my dinner on fire.

All the noble ends I could have come to, how many times had I slipped through death's cold embrace only to die in my own kitchen?

Figures.

Chapter Two

My body made itself known by creaking, and aching, and generally hurting. I took a breath, and that burned my lungs. My throat was raw and dry, like someone had ground sandpaper down my windpipe. My nose burned, ached, and something rigid sat on my upper lip stuck to my skin.

Shit, Winter! What happened?

My eyes popped open at the thought, only to take in a sterile room, a television on the far end, a window to my right, and Jessica leaning against my bed, sleeping—well, as much as anyone can sleep in a hospital. Which is to say, she looked tired.

The soft beep of machinery behind me filled the room. An IV snaked out of my arm, and the stench of bleach and something else slithered through the air. Hospitals all smelled the same. I tried to take a full breath, but it felt like something weighed me down from inside. Of course, smoke inhalation. At least fire was my primary element, and it didn't hurt me as much as most people.

Winter knew that, though. Had she really tried to kill me, or was her stunt to make it so the humans would try to stop me? Damn that cunning bitch and her power.

I reached for the mask on my face, but it felt like someone had stuffed my skin with metal ingots, each muscle trying desperately to wrap around the inert, heavy lumps. Or just my arm was stiff. My elbow practically creaked, it had been so long since I'd bent it.

Oh gods, how long have I been here?

Light poured in through the window at a high enough angle that either it was morning or late afternoon. I reached for my power and found it missing. Damn it, damn it, damn it all to a frozen lake in spring. Was magic back or wasn't it?

Then it hit me. If my spell was faltering, it would flicker like this. It would desperately try to keep righting itself.

Would Winter count each time the power flickered off and on in the spell a breach of the contract? Did it matter if it guttered like a flame?

Too many questions, and all the answers were on the other side of the country. Why had I been such a fool to let myself get seduced by the ancient trees on the west coast? With a conscious effort, I wrenched my thoughts away from the self-flagellation. None of that mattered—okay, it mattered, but it was worthless to dwell on it. The arrow of time pointed one way and there was no way to regret my way out of this problem. I needed to get out of here, and I needed to be able to breathe.

I turned my focus inward, attempting to gauge how much magical power I still had in my reservoir. I traced the channels within me through my mind's eye. Like a waterway, some channels were lined with impermeable materials like stone or cement, and some channels were carved from earth or sand, and relied on the natural flow of water to direct it where intended. And so it was with people and magic. The more complex the channel network within a mage, the more complex the spell. Some mages had very simple channels, but the breadth of them allowed for vast amounts of power to pour through uninhibited. Those mages were always used for wars and battles, or at least they had been before the deal with Winter. Some mages could never build their inner network to more than a couple of channels and a pool or two, able to cast only a few, simple spell forms. Then there were those who were like me, middling. My channels were mostly impermeable, but they spilled into the equivalent of a sand-lined cistern within my soul. The sand could absorb magic, holding it against an emergency, but dredging up the magic-soaked sand within the cistern was spending a kind of cache that couldn't last long—that sand was a person's very soul.

Many mages died from overspending themselves. Many more had spent ruthlessly of their deepest reserves, forever changing who they were as they spent their very souls in a spell.

I had never been that reckless.

I had never been in a race against the waxing of the moon for which the prize was my life.

When I found the deep well within me, it was as I'd feared, empty, but the traces of magic clung to the bits of my soul at the bottom of the well. Ever so carefully, I measured out the barest amount I'd need. I had to be able to breathe. Every second in this bed was one I wasn't making my way to the broken spell. And having my soul intact wouldn't matter if I was dead. I needed to get up and out of this bed.

With the image in my mind, I drifted out of the real world and drew the spell into my inner focus, visualizing the effect I needed. Lungs healed, sacks filling with air and exchanging the molecules to enrich my blood. I held the image, feeding the tiny pieces of me coated in the precious bits of magic into the framework of my spell. Bit by bit, the magic filled the space I'd made for it, but it didn't flare to life. It coughed and sputtered like a car engine trying to turn over, but when I fed it enough of me, the spell caught.

The magic sizzled through me, all goosebumps and something I could almost feel. And then my lungs suddenly itched like mad. The room came into sharp focus and my drifting head resolved solidly into the place where the energy that made up me resided. I hadn't realized how far outside of myself I'd gone.

Damn Winter and her games.

Stupid to think that bint would play fair.

"Mom?" Jessica asked. She blinked, as if trying to clear a stray hair from her eyes. "Are you okay?"

"Depends on how you count okay," I said through the mask. It cut into the bottom of my nose, and I pulled it off. That brought the IV close enough for inspection and after just a moment, I figured out how they'd attached it and began the unsubtle process of pulling it.

"Mom! What are you doing?" Jessica asked.

"What does it look like I'm doing?" I finished pulling the tape off, and slid the IV out, cranking my elbow over my fingers to slow the bleeding. One by one, I pulled the leads from my chest and the machines behind the bed started to give off an annoying beeping alarm. I went to swing my legs over the side, but my hip informed me we had taken a fall, and it was no longer on payroll.

Whelp, there were two who could play that game, stupid hip. I rolled the other way, and my feet hit the cold linoleum floor. I almost followed that up with a faceplant but caught myself on the railing.

"Mom! Stop! This is madness!"

"Don't you understand," I said. "I have to get out of here."

Too late I realized that by rolling to the other side, I'd put Jessica between me and the door.

"No, you need to sit back down. I'll call the doctor over. You almost died."

I started searching for clothes, a phone, anything that might be useful. I finally found the bin that held my personal effects.

"They cut my shirt?" I asked, holding up the fabric. Charred sleeves and a jagged line up the back where someone had cut the shirt off my body. "Barbaric."

"You were dying!" Jessica yelled in some misplaced loyalty to an EMT.

"Did they really have to cut my clothes off?" I asked. "Really?" I gave her The Look and that shiver of guilty feelings squirmed down her spine in an almost completely invisible movement.

Then she gathered her composure. "Yes, they did. They really needed to get you out of your clothes before you died."

I leveled my best *MMMph-Hmmmph* at her. She let her head sway from side to side. "Okay, as soon as they gave you oxygen you started to get better! But they said they might need to operate on you today if you didn't get better."

I nodded. "And I got better. Now come on, let's go. I have to get somewhere before—"

"Before what?" Jessica asked.

"Uh," I said to buy myself an extra second or two. *How do I tell her? How do I tell my granddaughter about all of it? The lies? Worse, the truths. How could I tell her about magic as I was on my way to go lock it away again? Surely, my* casting had woken her up. She was definitely as gifted as my Anne had been. It wasn't something that skipped generations, not in my family. I'd come from a long line of mages, and the only thing notable about me was that I hadn't been nearly as powerful as my mother.

But was it worth destroying the life I had built for her? And for what? One week with spotty magic then never again.

The Order had cast themselves into oblivion rather than live without magic. What would Jessica do to have it yanked away again so quickly?

"Before they shuffle for my bridge game," I lied. "We have to hurry."

Jessica took a breath like I'd deflated her. "Mom, you almost died. Your apartment—it's— Well, you're lucky to be alive. They found you passed out inside." She choked up.

Yeah, I bet they found me passed out inside. Stupid Winter. She definitely won that round.

"It's important to me," I said in the tone that was supposed to get her on my side.

She nodded. "How about this. You sit back down, and I'll go get the doctor. They should be here already."

Yeah, in a normal situation there wouldn't have been magic, and their stupid machines would keep working just fine, but even the tiniest bit of magic had knocked out radios in the big war. I wasn't surprised that the modern stuff fizzled out just as quickly.

"Okay," I lied, and moved to slip one of my cheeks onto the mattress.

Her eyes narrowed before she went through the curtain. I listened for her footsteps. She paused just outside the door and waited for a moment. She probably thought my hearing was as bad as a normal elderly person, but magic had mixed too far into my blood. I'd been born in 1888 and been considered young when I fought in the second war. People who pooled magic in their bodies simply lived longer. If magic had continued to flow through the world, I might have reached a third century or even more, given modern medicine.

The bone-deep ache in my body informed me I wasn't going to turn back the clock any time soon. Alas.

Regardless, I had the hearing of a twenty-something who didn't go to rock concerts, and my patience paid off. She walked away, heading for some nursing station. I slipped around the curtain, took a brief look down the hall and made a choice. It didn't matter which way I went, I just had to get there. I headed right and hoped this ward would have another exit. I ducked into a linen closet, carelessly left open. People moved down the hall. I grabbed a sheet and twisted it around my waist so at least my derrière wouldn't be flappin' in the breeze. The indignity of a hospital stay could easily be summed up by the fact that gowns covered none of the important bits.

With the sheet tucked in like a skirt, I slipped farther down the hallway, edging toward the exit sign.

"Where'd she go? Mom? Mo-om!" Jessica's voice rang down the hall.

I hurried my steps, limping as my hip caught. Getting old sucks.

Chapter Three

I hit the main hallway as close to a run as I could manage. The damn place was a complete labyrinth, but they hadn't changed the layout since Mary's Henry had gone through chemo. These halls were an old nemesis, worn with time and hate, but still a known entity.

I took half a second to orient myself at the next intersection, picking my next step. I turned toward the ER and hoped for the best. As I came upon the waiting room, I cased the area. Families waited in clusters, spread around the room so they could all politely ignore each other. Each group lazily watched phones, talked in whispers, or read magazines from the dubious selection on the scattered tables. One family crowded the nurses' station, making a fuss about something.

Then I spotted it, sitting like a gold nugget waiting to be pulled from a river: an unattended jacket. As smoothly as I could, I reached down as I walked past, slinging the fabric over my shoulders in one smooth motion.

A teenager with too long legs looked up from his phone at me and pulled his legs back up. I winked at him. His eyes grew wide and he averted his gaze. Poor kid.

I tried to swallow the limp in my gait by smoothing out my stride, making it deliberately even as my hip screamed in protest. I'd need to take an extra aspirin when I got home.

Crap, I wasn't going to get to go home.

My home had a smoke smear across the top, and if I didn't make some serious progress, someone was going to notice that the tubby old lady was wearing a gown, a sheet, and a stolen jacket. And not a single phone to use. There wasn't even one in the pockets of my purloined jacket. Dammit, I needed a way out of here.

I weighed my options. I could steal an ambulance, but that would be quickly traced, and I didn't want to have the authorities on my tail so soon. It was clear Jessica wasn't on board, but how much help could she muster in a few minutes? A whole lot more if I stole a rig full of gear, medicine, and sirens. I could steal a phone—there were over a dozen in this room alone, but how to unlock them?

With a sinking sensation, I realized what I was going to have to do: I would have to borrow one. UGH!

"Ma'am?" a woman from behind the counter said, trying to catch my attention. "Where are you going?"

Well shit. They were on to me.

I turned the corner like I was heading into the ER ward, and by pure luck, someone came through the locked door. I shook my wristband at the orderly, who scowled but let me through. Damn it, I'd been steps from the outside, and now I'd have to dig my way out through the innards of the hospital.

I slipped behind a curtain into the first room I saw. An older man lay across the bed, sitting up. His balding hair fell to the tops of his ears, and his nose had grown stubbornly to dominate his face. His machine beeped dutifully, measuring out the beeps and blips of his chest. He raised an eyebrow as I held a finger up to my lips.

"Oh my," he said.

"What'cha in for?" I asked.

"Heart. You?"

"Civil disobedience."

He laughed. "My god, woman, that's funny. Did you do it?"

"I was framed."

He winked. "I'm sure you were."

"You don't by chance have your phone still?" I asked.

He rolled his eyes. "That worthless piece of shit? It's there. I hate those things."

I motioned to pick it up. "I need some reinforcements."

"By all means. And if you figure it out, can you show me how?"

I chuckled, already clasping the phone. I swiped the screen, but he hadn't set any security on it. I didn't hesitate, typing in Mary's number. She always knew what to do and never judged me for any of the stupid things I'd done. And if

I was going against the Winter Queen, I could think of no one I wanted by my side more. She was the kindest, most dependable person I knew.

SOS, I typed. *This is Ruth.*

"What's your name?" I asked as I waited for the little dots to indicate Mary had seen my text.

"Johnson. Steve."

He said it with a particular cadence. I tilted my head to the side. "Vietnam?" I asked.

He nodded.

"I hear that one was terrible."

"Were you in?" he asked.

"Navy, but that was a long time ago."

"But once you're navy, you're always navy," he said.

The nostalgia of brotherhood determined by military branch cracked through my heart for a moment.

The phone buzzed in my hand.

WHAT ARE YOU DOING? Mary typed back. *Are you okay?*

I typed back furiously. *I'm at the hospital, and I need a ride, STAT. I'll be outside heading south.*

I'd be heading south because there were plenty of signs to hide behind. There were some five pharmacies on the same road as the hospitals, just in case someone didn't want to have to go too far to get their discharge medicines.

She responded, *OK.*

I held the phone and pushed the contact until it gave me the option to erase the conversation. One can never be too careful.

"Did you get what you needed from it?" he asked.

"I did, Steve. Thank you." I took his hand.

"It was my pleasure," he said. "Godspeed."

"And you." I gave his hand a squeeze and tried not to think of all the times I had bid someone farewell in this ward, never to see them on this earth again.

Before tears could strangle me, I pushed through the curtain again.

"You're not supposed to be back here," a nurse said almost immediately.

"Can't I even say 'hi' to my husband?" I lied.

The nurse hesitated, and I pushed through the door. It was designed to reduce who came into the ward, not who left. And somehow, no one had seen my feet yet. On the other side, the waiting room had the same characters as before, laid out in mostly the same arrangements, but a large noisy family spilled through the doorway, a combination of Spanish and English filling the air. I politely stepped aside, but one of the boys noticed me, and held out his arms so I could get through the door.

"Thank you," I said in my best shaky old lady voice.

"Ma'am," he said, letting the other members of his family in.

That cavalcade could provide a big enough screen for a marching band.

My feet hit the pavement, and every crack, rock, and bit of weed under my heels bruised my abused feet. Given my diabetes, I shouldn't really be able to feel anything. Did magic reverse things like pancreatic failure? What an annoying time to have all the nerves back in my feet. On the other hand, bruised heels were nothing compared to what Winter would do to me.

She tried to kill me outside of the contract. That wasn't supposed to happen. I had until the full moon, technically her shooting at me could be considered a contract breach. And if she thought she was safe trying to kill me, what did that mean? And why hadn't I been smart enough to include gases in our contract? That was a solidly dumb move by past Ruth. She should have been more careful. Alas, the arrow of time, etc., etc.

I picked my way across the sidewalk until I got to a sign leaning over the lawn and proclaiming The Northside Health Center. They meant hospital, but people seemed to drive all language toward mealy-mouthed as time went on. So instead of a hospital, we had a health center. And instead of an emergency room, we had an Urgent and Timely care unit.

Mind you, they still called it a trauma center on the radio because no one was taking their dying patients to an urgent care center. They needed the coding patient to get to the OR at the emergency room.

As humans we have an amazing capacity to ignore reality by naming it something other than what it is. It's as if we can avoid thinking about what it actually is if we can layer it in enough weak language. George Carlin really had that one right.

When I got to the far side of the sign, some bushes clogged the side of the hospital's sign, making the perfect place to wait while staying out of view. My toes squelched in the freshly watered mulch, and something slimy made an exploration through the gap between my big toe and the next one over. I settled in as the sun passed behind the mountains, draping the valley in shadows. As I shivered, guilt picked at my heart. I shouldn't have stolen that woman's jacket.

I didn't really have a choice. And every minute I spent in the hospital was one I wasn't trying to get to the whole other side of the country. And if I didn't make it to the Smithsonian in time, there was going to be a much bigger problem. Winter would launch an all-out war against humanity as soon as she finished drinking my blood.

That was a bit dramatic, honestly. If she really wanted to do that, why had she made the deal in the first place? What did Winter really want? It wasn't war. War was easy, and we humans did that to ourselves without much prompting. What else could Winter really want?

I jumped as a car roared into view, pulling up onto the sidewalk with a *cathunk*!

"Your chariot!" Mary called out.

"Sweet salamanders, are you drunk?"

Mary tucked her chin so her curly white hair framed her face in a picture of innocence. She blinked at me. "That would be illegal. Are you accusing me of lawbreaking?"

The way her innocent smile faded into her devious eyes caught in my chest. She was the absolute best. I opened the driver's side door. "Shift over," I said softly. "You could have killed someone."

She stood on the floorboards and launched her butt into the passenger seat before dragging back the rest of her, bit by bit. "You said it was an emergency, and boy it had better be. You're making me late for Phyllis's Souffle. And we both know what a pain she can be when she gets surprised."

I chewed on the inside of my cheek. "Who'd have thought the seer would be such a pain about surprises."

Mary whispered. "It's like she can't see the future."

I rolled my eyes and backed off the sidewalk. "It's like you can't control water."

"Liquids. How many times do I have to explain—hic—shit. Stupid betraying body."

"Fine, liquids. Hey, speaking of, have you felt it? Have you felt any magic recently?" I asked.

"Ha! Do you think I'd be drinking if I could feel it again? The way it washed over me, filling up—" She broke off, but I caught her meaning. That desperate ache echoed in my heart. It was so hard to be something lesser after being part of something that big. She sat ramrod stiff. "No, I haven't felt any magic. I haven't felt anything since the end of the war."

I turned off the street from the hospital and merged into traffic.

"Why did I help you?" she asked quietly. "Why did I think we'd come up with something else? Why didn't we double cross that bitch? Why did we accept our fates like lambs? I never should have let you lock it up."

"Oh?"

"I've been thinking about it a lot lately. We should have figured out something else."

"Well, you're in luck, the spell is failing. Winter came to my apartment, and I almost burned it down, so you know. It's back."

Mary stared at me. "That's not funny."

"I'm not laughing."

"Ruth, if you are messing with me, I swear to Hades, I'll see you delivered to his doorstep."

"Invoking gods from other cultures is considered appropriation, as the kids say."

She bit her lip, transferring some of her lipstick to her teeth. "I'm not joking, Ruth. If this is a joke, if you're playing with my feelings, I'm going to burn every bridge between us."

Her words stung, but I didn't want her to see. Then she'd apologize and be all polite and numb, and I needed her to be something else. So, I feigned a smile. "It's like you don't trust me."

"Ha! Trust! Trust," she hissed. "You took away magic—from everyone!"

I swallowed. The loss of magic had, arguably, been the most difficult on Mary. As a water mage with barely adequate channels to direct the power, she had had to train ten times harder for her place among the Order of Water, and even then, she had never really qualified as more than a hedge witch. Really powerful works were beyond her capacity, but she figured out a few less powerful tricks and put them to tactically brilliant uses. But when it all ended, she had spent every minute of her life studying magic and power. And when she wasn't studying, she was practicing. No other hobbies. We locked up magic and she had nothing. Since the age of twelve, she had poured every scrap of her life into magic, then it was just gone.

I have never done as much to kill a single person as I did to Mary.

"If I hadn't, we'd all be dead, and those of us alive would be saluting Hitler."

"He'd be dead by now."

I rolled my eyes. "Not if he had magic he wouldn't. Can you even imagine what blood magic he would have done? Literally sucking the power out of a person—out of a hundred people—just to get another year. Another day? We were nothing to him and there's always one like him. And all of you agreed."

"What choice did we have?" Mary snorted. "End a war killing millions? It was the obvious answer. I just never—" She cut off in a choke.

With my focus artificially on driving, I made sure to signal perfectly, but it was hard not to speed all the way home. There was nothing a bored cop liked to do more than give an old lady a lecture about the perils of driving fast. As if I hadn't driven faster than his car can even go back in the day when we'd speed across the desert in our—

"Is it really back?" she asked in a reverent whisper.

"I held a dragon. It purred. Its back leg was a little gimpy, but a dragon."

She closed her eyes, exhaling as she let her head dip back to the headrest. "What did it feel like?"

"What, is this twenty questions?"

"You suck at making stuff up. What did it feel like? Leather or scales?"

I did a double take at her. I wasn't bad at making stuff up. She's the one who...the one who'd dreamed about the return of magic for seventy years. She was the one who'd carved pieces of her own soul out so she could cast better, more powerful spells. Magic made her whole.

"Scales," I answered quietly. "They were still soft from the fire. They faded from the bright red and orange of fire, settling into a deep purple and blue in places. It—she—purred."

"How'd you know it was a girl?"

"She talked," I said, letting a smile stretch my cheeks at the memory. "Small though. She wasn't as big as any of the ones the council had. Theirs were all large and rude. She was just so happy."

Then Winter showed up. I turned down a driveway and came to a stop.

"Why'd you stop?" she asked.

I pointed at the home of the only surviving Seer in the whole world, Phyllis.

Chapter Four

Phyllis climbed down the steps of her old house—it was nearly as old as she was, but she would skewer me for saying so. Wisteria climbed up the east side of the pillars holding up the wraparound porch, and night-blooming jasmine engulfed the west side. Her house sat in the inner segment of an old city block, where the original house had been before the city had carved everything up into perfect squares like some sort of Jello to be eaten with one's fingers.

Her house had the refined bones of an old lady, Victorian with narrow hallways and many more closets than should rightly exist, but not a one of them meant to be. Oddly shaped doors hid linen cupboards and, in not a few places, shelves painted with protective spells—just in case—to house the ancient treasures gathered as only a charlatan could gather.

Phyllis, born with the natural gift to see the future, the present, and on the rare occasion, the past (that one's complicated, as the past is always tinged by the present). But with the loss of magic, she had resorted to the sort of entertaining kinds of theatre where one pretended to receive messages from the great beyond.

The kicker with Phyllis being that every fourth or fifth fake, she'd have a real seeing, even after the magic had gone.

As such, she was considered by many to be one of the greatest mediums to ever live.

Or more specifically, Madame Carlina of the Great House of Kenting had been an excellent medium. She'd retired that persona before social media really started taking off.

But the way Phyllis crossed her arms and glared at me, I couldn't be sure if the great Madame Carlina stared down at me, or if Phyllis just had gas.

"You're wearing a hospital gown," she said.

"You're right, I was lucky to survive Winter's wrath. Thank you for asking about my ordeal," I said, pretending she'd been cordial.

She narrowed her eyes, and I tossed the keys back to Mary. She fumbled with them, eventually bobbling them into her cleavage. I turned away so she wouldn't see me laugh. Mary huffed as she rudely dug between her breasts for her keys.

"Winter?" Horace said, coming out the front door. "Who said anything about Winter?"

Phyllis turned back to Horace standing in the doorway. "Ruth thinks she's had a battle with Winter."

Horace scoffed. "No, Winter swore she'd never come back."

"As long as magic stayed locked up. Yes, I remember. I brokered the deal. Magic was back toni—oh, yesterday?—oh damn I don't know what day it is," I said, checking my pockets, but, of course, I was wearing a stolen jacket, and I hadn't managed to get my phone. I shot a glance over at Mary.

"It's Tuesday, that happened yesterday," she said.

"Thank you." Then I turned back to my own personal judge and jury. "Yesterday evening, I did battle with Winter as she came to inform me that the Source has become unlocked, somehow."

"Bullshit! This is just another one of your attention-grabbing stunts. What did Jessica say when you told her?"

I bit my lip.

"If it was real," Phyllis continued, "then why didn't you warn your only blood relative about the perils of THE WINTER QUEEN?" She narrowed her eyes into the silence around me. Then she raised her eyebrows, leaning back in challenge, but her body showing that she feared no attacks. The watermelon light off the hills on the east side of the valley cast everything in an amber glow, making her whole face shine with the righteous air of someone who knows they are absolutely right. Gods, I hated that smug look on her face.

I scowled but held out my hand. "Care to read me?"

She swatted my hand away like a fly. "No thank you. I don't need to see that you..." She paused, blinking, and for the briefest second, her breath fogged around her.

Phyllis's eyes grew until the icy whites showed clear around all of her irises. She knew in that moment that the Winter queen was coming for me—for us—and that magic had made, at the very least a brief return. Her eyes clouded, not as dramatically as they showed in the movies, but for the briefest moment, she Saw things.

"Oh shit," she said.

"My point exactly."

Horace scowled. "What did you see?" he asked.

Phyllis turned to him. "We'd better get inside. They're coming."

Mary went up the steps until she was even with Phyllis. "Who's coming?"

"Jessica and her boyfriend," Phyllis said.

"Jonathan," I said, not bothering to hide my disdain for Jessica's current boyfriend. As far as I could tell he had about as much personality as a soggy bag of chips. When I'd asked Jessica what she saw in him, she'd told me that he had a good job and showed up when she called.

Which was, of course, a direct shot fired at my heart as I had been somewhat less than reliable when she was young. I'd had to take any job that would pay me under the table due to using the identity of my daughter. And how does one explain to the child they raise that they are pretending to be the woman who gave birth to them because my identity said I was born in the 1920s and no one would believe I'd given birth in the late 1970s. Jessica's documents were all in order, but the farther I went into the 21st century, the harder it got to pull the wool over the eyes of the government. My own daughter had been born in the 50s, and that was at least an easier identity to fake.

But it still meant forgoing things like passports (which required the state department looking into your document history before granting), and I never got a replacement Social Security Card. I had saved some money after the war, but I always had to piece everything together, and I never stayed in one job for too long. Steady had not been part of the equation.

I'd lost both my wife Dorothy and my daughter Anne to one of Winter's ploys. I wasn't going to be foolish enough to think she wouldn't chase me down through my work or relations to others. That was how Winter worked. She didn't just come at you through yourself; she came at you through everyone you loved and cared about. A difficult prospect when raising a child into a world with cellphones and computers.

Then Jessica had children of her own with her first, very disastrous husband, a man I despised. He reminded me of one of the elders in the Order, a man who used to advocate for a separate order just for men. At the time no one bought into it, but after the war…well, many things changed after the war.

He left her with two kids, no alimony, no child support and made off with a woman ten years younger. Ah, true love.

"Come on." Phyllis beckoned to me, but I looked down the driveway as if I could see their car heading down the road. Obviously, I couldn't, so I went inside.

Various crystal balls and silk scarves thrown over lamps decorated the room. They cast the sitting room into the deep reds, greens, and blues Phyllis used to extort locals from their money when they desperately needed to consult with the beyond. It had the distinct look of a playhouse. Everything set for a performance.

Phyllis hurried into a back room, calling out directions. "Horace, go get the car started, we'll take the north exit!" The thump of drawers followed her voice. "Mary, grab my purse, will you? I think it's in the kitchen."

"Righto!" Mary hopped to find the item. Not waiting for further direction.

"Can you grab a robe for me, or a muumuu?" I asked.

"I don't have a muumuu," she called back.

Figures, she wouldn't have anything I could wear. I'd have to make my bid to save my life, and probably all of humanity with a smock that tied in the back and sheet I stole from the hospital. I considered the jacket and decided to leave it hanging on the back of a chair. Hopefully it would be able to find its way home to whomever owned it. Not that it really mattered if Winter won and decided to add the Source of humanity's power to her own. Then we'd what?

Glacial fields? Was the last ice age really her doing or was that all faerie tales—yes, pun intended.

Phyllis came back with a large, handled bag, sometimes called a hobo bag. Draped over her arm she had a large sweater, a robe and a pair of slippers with a sole and fuzzy toe box. "Here," she thrust the arm covered in clothes at me.

From the moment I stuffed my feet into the slippers, the recklessness of walking barefoot while diabetic rang like a bell in my mind. I wasn't some damned kid anymore. And the fuzzy inside of those slippers felt like a miracle. Praise be science and cheap shoes. I draped the oversized, multicolored knit cardigan over my shoulders. It was one of those pieces that was made to look like it was hand crafted, but you could buy it at a department store, half off after Christmas. Gods only knew why Phyllis had one, but I gratefully slipped my arms into the sleeves and wrapped the whole thing tightly around me, hoping we wouldn't have to spend too much time in the night air of March.

"Now are we ready to go?" Phyllis said watching me tie the belt of the cardigan around my waist. The ends barely made it around my somewhat rounder belly, and I settled for a single knot and a prayer.

"Wait, we have a plan?" Mary asked, holding out Phyllis's purse to her.

Phyllis strapped the purse over her shoulder and snugged it into place. The moment snapped my mind back to us sneaking out of the encampment and into Germany during the war. Our last-ditch effort, echoing down to another last-ditch effort.

"We have a plan," I said. "We have to get to the Smithsonian and fix whatever is wrong with the spell hiding the Source. Step one: take Phyllis's car and cover as much ground to the Smithsonian as we can tonight."

Phyllis snorted. "Then we do it again tomorrow?"

"And the day after," I said.

Mary sighed. "Just between us, is there any possibility that we aren't running three thousand miles just to put magic in a special box for no one to ever see or touch again?"

"Lock it up or die," I said. "Me first, obviously."

"Right," she said looking down at the floor, quietly repeating me. "Obviously."

A car rolled up, the headlights flashing stray beams into the sitting room.

"We'd better go," Phyllis said. Then she stopped and looked at me. "Unless you wanted to try to talk to her. Make Jessica understand. We could really use allies."

"You should tell Jessica. She might be able to help," Mary said.

The weight of that conversation peeled away my heart. I'd have to tell her about Anne and Dorothy, about how they'd died when Jessica was just a baby. I'd have to tell her about everything. The magic, the war, the lies... So many lies. I'd have to lay bare every lie I told her as a child as we slipped from one job to the next, never having a single steady piece of normal life. No extended family like everyone else. No grandmas and aunts, no cousins and no siblings. A whole way of life locked away from us in the lies of my life, making her pay the price for every choice I'd ever made.

Mary found my gaze, her blue eyes glassy with unshed tears. Begging. But we both knew I didn't have time. "She could help us," Mary said appealing to tactics and logic.

I couldn't live with what I'd done to Jessica, so I couldn't tell her until I was going to die.

My heart crystalized into resolve.

And I had no plans to die tonight.

"I'm sure we could use allies, but there's no guarantee she won't hold us back. What we need is distance. Let's get to the car."

Phyllis looked disappointed—well, either it was disappointed or she had resting bitch face. So hard to tell the difference, and she just loved to tell me how right she was and how wrong I was. It was not always pleasant to catch the disapproving look from Phyllis, and I shot a glance over at Mary to try to recruit her to my side of the moral campaign. She wouldn't meet my gaze.

My heart gave a thump-thump in my chest, reminding me that no matter what happened, there were more players yet to speak their peace in this farce of a play. I would need to get my heart medicine soon if we wanted all this to keep going.

We slipped around the edge of the kitchen, the flapping door pushed all the way open by Mary when she'd grabbed the purse. A short hallway past a closet and a bathroom led to the garage. Because the house had once been the grand central home of a much larger estate, the house had at one point been purchased by developers and made into a duplex with the front yards of both units facing opposite directions. Phyllis used the south front for guests and customers, but the garage door opened onto a long driveway that snaked between houses to the north.

When Phyllis had purchased the house and had it redone, she'd knocked out the wall between the two kitchens, converted the second garage into a dance studio—so she could teach some dance classes which were popular at the time—and kept the north garage. It wasn't a very convenient garage, only having access from this one narrow hallway.

Horace blocked the way, smelling vaguely of grease. "Phyllis," he said, perfectly deadpan. "You have a flat."

Mary harumphed. "It's rude to talk about a woman's chest like that, Horace."

Phyllis's eyes flashed at Mary, who in turn sliced a sly glance at Phyllis before the other woman could control her rise.

With a force of will, Phyllis regarded Horace. "I take it, you mean I have a flat tire."

Horace, eyes watering from trying not to laugh, spoke quickly and without meeting her gaze. "Yes, should I change it?"

There was a knock on the front door. Everyone turned to look.

"We don't have time for that," I said pushing forward.

"Mom!" Jessica called from the front.

"Mrs. Westings!" Jonathan called.

At the sound of his voice, annoyance drifted up my spine. What did she see in that boy?

I pushed forward. "If they came in his car, we can take it."

"And if not, you'll finally tell Jessica everything?" Mary asked.

I tried not to choke on my words. "Yes, of course."

Mary rolled her eyes at me, not believing me. She pushed past Horace and turned toward the dance studio, which had a side entrance. Horace waited for Mary and Phyllis to push past before leaning down to me.

"More sincerity when you try to sell the big lies," he said.

"Yeah, that didn't go as planned."

"There's always next time."

I snorted. "How many times are you thinking we'll be stealing my granddaughter's boyfriend's car?"

He shrugged. "You never know."

The dance studio had a solid, smooth cement floor, perfect for spinning, and one wall had been converted to mirrors and a free-standing barre. Our ghostly reflections slipped through the room, and we looked a ragged bunch, all variously prepared for what was going to come.

I spied the car through the window, and sure enough, it was Jonathan's car. Horace whispered as we looked through the window. "I can't just steal those newer cars. I need time to defeat their systems, and honestly, it's best if the ignition is a key. Much easier."

"Don't worry," I said. "Jonathan doesn't always turn off his car. It's a hybrid, and it doesn't make a lot of sound. He forgets it's even on."

"But if he has the keys—"

"We only get to turn it off once. That should be extra fun. I hope he filled it recently."

Phyllis shook her head at me. "You are the worst."

"Which would you prefer? A cold death courtesy of the Queen of Air and Darkness, or steal a car?"

Mary grudgingly nodded. "She has a point. What's a little grand theft auto compared to glaciers covering everything above the 40th parallel?"

Phyllis scowled.

"Are we ready for this?" I asked. When no one said anything, I nodded. "Phyllis, Mary, take the backseats. Horace, you're riding shotgun with me."

I wish I could report that we darted out to the car and made it away cleanly. Alas.

As soon as I put my hand on the doorknob, my foot slipped out of the slipper, and the others in their enthusiasm, piled into me. Horace caught me from falling, but Phyllis accidentally kicked him in the calf. He yelped, and Jessica and Jonathan turned to see us. I got the slipper back on my foot and hobbled at top speed—distressingly slow, in case anyone was wondering how fast a 135-year-old woman in need of a hip replacement moves—to the driver's side door of the car.

Having properly alerted the hunters to the location of their prey, they moved more swiftly, dropping down the stairs like lightning on a bad science experiment. "Mom, what are you doing?"

I yanked the door open before Jonathan realized our true plan. He fumbled for the keys, but our team made it into his four-door import like teenagers fleeing classes on the last day of school. As soon as my butt hit the fake—and I'm certain vegan—leather seat, I put the car in reverse. The doors slammed shut and I didn't bother buckling up. I slammed on the gas, bracing my right arm on the passenger seat and looking over my shoulder. I flung that car out into the suburban traffic of a rural northern California town, banking on the goodwill and kindness of neighbors. Tires screeched as we flung backward over a pothole at the end of the driveway. Phyllis screamed. Horace yelled "Look out!" and Mary yelled something incoherent, but I couldn't tell if she was cursing me or casting a shielding spell—not that a spell would do any good, but it was the thought that counted.

Regardless, the other cars on the road honked, swerved, and someone flipped me off.

"Watch where you're going, grandma!" a middle-aged man yelled.

"Is that Tommy Champrin?" Mary asked. "I used to play soccer with his mother. Nice woman. He's an asshole."

I flipped him off and threw the car into drive.

"Did you just peel out in a Prius?" Phyllis asked.

"It's not my fault Jonathan is trying to save the environment one car choice at a time."

Horace nodded. "This would be so much cooler in a Mustang."

Chapter Five

We didn't exactly ride into the sunset. To be honest, we barely drove onto Main Street.

"Where are you going?" Mary asked.

"South to 80. We have to get east, ASAP."

"Yeah, well I need my medicine. And it would be nice to have more than one pair of underwear if we're off to save the world," she said.

I'd already turned down the street taking us to her house.

"What's the point?" Horace asked. "The world is ending and you want to pack? It's a miracle we ever made it into Germany."

Mary's eyes snapped back to Horace. "When we saved the world last time, we prepped for that mission for over a week. I had my choice of clothes—"

"Only because everyone was dead," Phyllis interjected under her breath.

"—and we had our packs put together days in advance. Now I need a weeks' notice if I'm going to eat dinner late."

Phyllis turned her glare on Horace. "And you're one to talk, Mr. I-have-to-eat-the-same-vegetables-every-dinner."

"That's for my medication! I didn't choose to have high blood pressure."

His face started to go purple, and Phyllis rolled her eyes at him, catching him in a side-eyed glance. "Oh, calm down. We're going by your house, too. Besides, yours should be easy, you just went on that trip to Maryland."

"Heh, we should be flying," he plucked at the handlebar over the window. "It'd be a lot faster."

"I am not getting on a plane while the Queen of Air and Darkness is actively trying to kill me." I stopped the car in front of Mary's place.

"I'll just be a minute!" She jumped from the car, easily the most mobile of all of us, and slammed the door in her rush to get moving.

Horace scowled at the window, his breath fogging it up. "I'm just saying it would be faster."

"It's not faster if I'm dead."

Phyllis nodded. "She has a point." Then she jolted upright and started fishing through her purse. She came up with her phone. "Here," she said handing it to me. "It's for you."

When the phone hit my hand, it buzzed. I recognized the number as Jessica's.

I narrowed my eyes at Phyllis. "Damn. Your Sight is on."

Phyllis nodded. "It's like I'm sitting on the Source, but it's still in DC."

I hit the button. "Hi, honey. How you doin'?"

"Mom? Mom! What are you doing? Do you know what you've done?"

I harrumphed. "I do, and so would you if you'd just let me tell you what's going on."

"No, Mom, none of your ridiculous 'see the world from the perspective of the ant' talks. I'm not interested. John could have you arrested."

"Oh please, you think Officer Shelkin is going to come and arrest me?"

"I'm serious, Mom. You're acting crazy, and that's what I'm going to tell the cops. I'm going to say that you're acting like another person, that you need supervision, and do you know what they're going to do then?"

She let the silence stretch.

I knew what she was threatening. I knew how much it hurt her to put it out there like that, and she was not necessarily happy about it, but it was a threat. It sat on the line as thick as fog, clouding what we could say now that she'd done it.

"I see," I said in my blandest voice, stalling for time. "Of all the things I thought I'd hear today, I never imagined you'd be threatening me, so let me make something very clear: I am in my right mind—sharper and more vividly than in the last few decades. Now that's out of the way. I'm going away. Don't worry about John's car. We will park it legally somewhere and lock the doors. You can at least trust me not to wreck a car."

"Mom," Jessica said, her voice changing, getting softer, trying—albeit too late—to seem like we were on the same side in this. "What's going on? I saw your x-rays. You shouldn't be able to breathe. You should be dying. What happened?"

"You'd rather I was dead?" I asked.

"No—of course not—but it's crazy. What's going on?" she asked.

Phyllis mouthed "Tell her" to me.

I shook my head.

"Mom? Are you there?"

"I—" I hesitated. I what? I accidentally caught my kitchen on fire and wakened the Queen of Winter? How could I just tell her that her whole life had been built on lies. Lies that started at the very foundation of everything she knew.

No, there was no way to cover this in a phone call while I sat in her boyfriend's car—stolen car.

"Jessica, you need to listen to me. Are you ready for that? There's something I have to deal with, something from before you were born. I know you know that I did things for the government, and now it's all coming back."

"Oh my god, Mom! You are not a spy! Why are you even talking like that?"

Phyllis laughed.

"I never said I was a spy!" I covered the receiver and glared at Phyllis. "Stop that, she'll think this is a joke."

"I'll say," Horace agreed. "This whole plan is completely doomed."

I put the phone back up to my ear.

"I don't know what's going on, but I want you to come home, okay?" Jessica asked.

Mary came back from the house, a floral print duffle bag under her arm. "I'm ready!" she called pulling open the door.

"Look, Jessica, it's not safe for me to come home yet. I gotta go!"

And with that, I hung up. Then I blocked Jessica's number before she could call back. I handed the phone back to Phyllis.

"What did I miss?" Mary asked.

Phyllis pointed at me with her chin. "The opening volleys of World War Three."

"Ha-Ha, very funny." I pulled the car into traffic, heading for Horace's place, but on the inside, Phyllis's words torched through my mind. Jessica was going to hate me for this for the rest of our days.

Admittedly, that could be a total of five at this point.

Chapter Six

After we picked up a small bag for Horace, we were complete as a travelling pharmacopeia, but it meant we were ready to stave off the body betrayal. Even with the years of magic infusions prior to locking up the Source, we had aged. What magic did was enhance a mage's own cells so that copies made were made more exact, meaning our bodies stopped aging right around thirty or so. But in more recent decades, things had begun to stretch out a bit. The rewards for our overextended lives appeared to be a sudden degradation in things like skin, muscle, and brain matter.

We ate up the pavement, heading south on Highway 101 until we hit the interchange into Napa Valley, and past that, we took 80 to Sacramento. As the stars wheeled overhead, we pushed through the night, only stopping when someone had to make use of the restroom. When the lights of Reno spilled over the nearest hill, I knew I couldn't push on any farther tonight. We were going to have to stop sometime.

"We stopping?" Horace asked. "I don't know how much farther my bones can go tonight."

I scanned the billboards as we drove. Stubborn snow stuck to the sides of the road and the shadows, casting the landscape in an odd sort of negative. Only the snow in the shadows had avoided melting, so the bright shined up from the places where the sun didn't touch. "No tell Motel?" I asked.

Phyllis shook her head. "Dear gods, no. We can stay at a damned Holiday Inn. I am not sleeping on the floor of some two-bit, roach hotel."

Mary made that tisk sound. "We're trying not to use a credit card. It won't be long before they send the police after us."

Horace shook his head. "I'm with Phyllis on this. There's no way."

"Well how are we going to keep them from—"

"Money," I said, interrupting. "Phyllis, you have the cash to bribe our way into a Marriot?"

"I don't need to bribe anyone. I have credit cards under four different names. For businesses, of course."

Horace grunted. "And certainly not to avoid your unhappy customers from tracking you down."

She scoffed. "How dare! All my customers are very pleased with my services."

"Pick a place," I said, hoping to derail their well-trodden fight.

"There," she pointed at a billboard, and I caught the directions to a modest place on the outskirts of Reno, not a minute too soon. My fingers ached from clutching the wheel. At least Jonathon had sprung for a model with cruise control. Small favors.

The tires crunched over some random gravel, scraped up by a careless snowplow driver, and I guided the car into a parking spot. I looked at the button to turn off the car. It had been pinging every minute or so for five hundred miles, and I was ready to be done.

But once we hit the button, we wouldn't be starting it again. At least, not without some extra work courtesy of Horace.

"Are we sure we want to hit the button?" I asked.

"Be bold!" Horace said. Everyone turned to him like he'd sprouted an extra head. "What? This model isn't that hard to jump, it's just not my favorite."

"We'll be getting another car in the morning," Mary said. "This back seat was designed for crackerjacks, not people."

We made our way into the overly sanitized hotel lobby, lights dimmed to reflect a small concession to the fact that it was around two AM. A pattern of gold chains weaving through a brown rope across the carpet floor had an almost hypnotic effect on the mind, and I avoided looking at my feet. A set of slot machines jangled their little tunes through an open door to a tiny casino, and we ignored it.

By unspoken agreement, Mary and Horace stood between me and the people who might notice I was wearing slippers and a robe. I'd need better clothes tomorrow.

Phyllis had once upon a time traveled extensively and she produced a gold-colored loyalty card under the name Jasmine Kellar. Once they saw the loyalty card, the staff produced keys and a map. By the time we made it through the door of a hyper sterilized room with two queens and a couch, I no longer cared if Winter caught us: if she killed me, maybe my head would stop hurting.

I dropped to the bed and closed my eyes. I fell asleep almost instantly. Faster than the blink of an eye, I woke up. I knew time had passed, but not how much. Everyone's breathing had eased into the sort of rhythm only accessible to those wrapped in the comfortable embrace of slumber. I closed my eyes to go back to sleep, but the sound of Jessica's voice echoed through my mind. She'd be so worried. I hadn't told her anything, and I might not be here to explain everything when this was over. And I owed her. I owed her a whole life of explanations. I slipped from the bed, grabbed some stationery from the desk, and took it to the bathroom.

I stared at the paper. I'd have to take a picture and send it with someone's phone, but that was probably a bad idea. I'd need to consign it to the slow pace of physical mail as Jessica probably already had the FBI on the lookout for us. Hopefully they wouldn't start until the morning.

I bent my mind back to the letter.

How to sum up a life's worth of lies. Where even to start?

I caressed the paper. Someday, this would be among the bits and pieces Jessica used to piece herself and her life back together in the wake of my death. I'd sure made a mess of that. I thought I could do it all alone.

I never thought the bill for the mistakes in my life would come due in hers.

As I stared, I fumbled with the words to tell her why I'd lied. And why had I spent her whole life lying to her? To hide from Winter? No, it was more than that. I'd hidden everything, every scrap of joy from before she'd been born, as if that tiny baby wouldn't be able to survive the pain I held in my heart. And maybe if I pretended hard enough, I could make it true for her. If I believed my lies, she would, too. She wouldn't be the girl whose mother died in a car accident before she could even remember. She wouldn't be the only one at school who didn't have parents, an orphan. The thought broke my heart even now.

And how quickly four decades slipped by. She had kids of her own now, and still I never told her. I never told her about how I lost my wife, my daughter, and my whole life on one slick road. Winter's laugh had echoed through my mind, but no, the tires weren't good. There were so many ways for people to die a perfectly normal death. The fact that we'd lived had been a miracle.

But what miracle? To live a life watching over my shoulder, always on the lookout for Winter's hallmarks. And wondering, was it Winter, or was I reading too much into the frost around the crash? I never had proof, and Phyllis couldn't find any hint of the fae queen.

Maybe if Dorothy had been a witch like me. Maybe if I'd taught my daughter Anne any amount of magic—there were spells that didn't need the Source, conjured from the great depths of one's soul—maybe Anne could have helped in a—

No, Ruth, don't you dare walk down that road.

I took in a deep breath and watched the sky slowly growing lighter. All night and barely any closer. Phyllis and Mary each slept on the beds. Horace stretched out across the couch, half hidden by the suitcases. He rolled over, a restless sleeper, even in his youth. His stray hand knocked over his shaving kit, and it fell to the floor with a thump as I watched over my people, still sitting on the edge of the bathtub. My butt had gone numb, and if I didn't stand soon, I'd never manage to stand on my own. Maybe I could put down just a few words, something simple. I could start with "I love you."

I reached for the paper, pen in hand, but I couldn't do it. I couldn't wreck everything she'd known and grown up with in a letter.

But if this went to hell, Winter would kill me. And that bitch could take me in the middle of walking down the street, just freeze my heart and I'd be gone.

I drew up the pen one more time. I had to be brave. I had to give Jessica something. Anything. If I couldn't hug her at the end of this, and be there for her to hate properly, then she at least needed to know the truth. I swallowed and put the pen to page.

The power hit me with the ferocity of an ocean wave, burying me, dragging me under.. It knocked me senseless in that first moment, driving the raw magic through my channels. And like water, it scoured through the pathways of my soul, dredging up chunks of my channels—my soul!—as it slammed through me. I gasped. It was so raw, so powerful, the might of it couldn't be shaped any more than a person could turn back the sea with a teacup.

"Ah!" I yelled. "It's back!" Before I did anything else, I coaxed the raw magic trying to drown me into a spell, a real spell. If I could get some of the power to stay in one area, I might get more than a minute with it. My mind reeled with the possibilities, so many possibilities that I almost lost control of the power ripping through me. It scoured out the bits of soul not manicured and well-tended, and quite frankly, my channels hadn't exactly been the top priority in the last seventy years. The raw magical power swarmed the very air around me. I'd never felt it so strong, like I was in the same room as the Source.

But there was no way I sat in the same room as the heart of a dead star. Absolutely none. Right? More likely I'd been without it so long, that the power just overwhelmed my senses. Use it or lose it, as they say.

With my focus and will, I constructed a sort of valve with my spell, hoping to reduce the speed and chaos raging through the lines like flood waters in a desert. I wrenched the last of my spell together, and the power ripped through it as if it were tissue paper. The sheer force and rage spilling through the power dragged me down. I anchored my workings to parts of my soul outside the channels, a dangerous, desperate maneuver. If this didn't hold, I'd be a puppet to the power. Or I'd tear in half, becoming vulnerable to things like possession and, well, worse. I whipped the magic into a working, tying the weave off to anchors in my soul. As I finished, it sprang to life inside me, popping up like a tent, and the raw force of the magic slowed enough for me to feel again.

"What?" Mary called. "What's going on?"

"Magic!" I yelled, as if the raging power was rushing water. I found myself startled to realize, the rushing sensation in my ears was just the white static that came on the heels of passing out.

"What!?" Horace yelled, knocking over the suitcases.

The banging woke Phyllis who sat up with a start. "Who's there? Is it Winter?" she called before she took off her face mask and earplugs. She reached out her hand, and her hairbrush flew through the air to hover directly in front of her hand, like it was somehow an extension of her arm.

She stared for a moment before meeting my gaze. With her opposite hand, she brushed her hair back from her face. "Now that's a bit more potent than a premonition."

"I told you so!"

Mary called water directly from the ether, wrapping it around her. She stood with the water pulled into a thick stream resting on her shoulders like a great feather boa. Even at her most powerful, she never could have done that. She was very practiced with magic, but not a brute force kind of person.

"Would you look at that? Would you look at that!" As she crowed, she tipped her shoulders as if modeling a fine dress.

Not wanting to be left out of everyone's display, I let a tiny piece of the power leak around the edges, coating me in raw flames. So much power raged through me, that I had to concentrate more on keeping the fire from growing than actively calling it forth. The light jumped and danced, catching in the water around Mary's shoulders. The light sparked and coated the walls in waves and refracting patterns of intense light.

Mary's face, a true picture of absolute joy, sparked something deep inside me, something I'd nearly forgotten. Her joy caught in my chest, unfurling the endless alternative paths my life could have taken. I loved my Dorothy, but in that moment, I saw another path, one where it had been Mary at my side, and my heart twinged at what could have been.

Would Winter have been able to cause that crash if it had been Mary in the car instead of Dorothy? Would it have been enough?

I shoved the ungracious thought aside. I'd loved Dorothy with all my heart. Thinking like that betrayed her memory, and the grief redoubled in my chest.

But magic waits for no one. In the same moment, the fire beyond this realm, the fire living in that other place, shifted on the far side of the veil, slipping through the folds of the world. It moved like a hound hunting for its prey. On pure instinct, I slammed it back, quenching the place between worlds.

In my effort to keep it from pushing through, I spilled my power like so much water in a bucket, splashing aside, and leaping from the channels. One had to be calm to work magic. One had to keep the whole of one's inner powers level and balanced. I was anything but, a ripe vessel to be overwhelmed by a fire creature, something much less benevolent than the little dragon from my apartment.

My sleeves held no hint of embers—completely unburned. My feeble crafting of magic had stuck even before the magic had come back. Mary met my gaze. As one of the two elementalists in our group, only she understood the call. Even now she stood, completely coated in water, wearing it like a suit. Her sudden concern wasn't for me, but for her. The call of water was different than fire. Seductive in ways I didn't understand.

Horace pulled himself out of the pile of luggage on the ground. "I can't believe it!" He tripped into the pile of luggage again.

At that moment, the magic cut out again. The water covering Mary suddenly failed to obey her call. It fell around her with a great splash, drenching the floor. The hairbrush Phyllis had called to her fell to the floor with a clank. The flow of magic cut off like a door slamming shut.

Like water spilled on sand, the magic that had been here just disappeared into the ether around us, evaporating as quickly as it had arrived.

"No!" Mary yelled. Her soggy night gown clung to her body, and her makeup from yesterday streaked down her face, making her look like a painting coated with turpentine.

"Oh!" Phyllis said, reaching for the hairbrush as if it might still have some residual power in it.

"Wait!" Horace yelled. "Damn it! I didn't get a chance to use any! What was I thinking? How come it was so fast?"

"Magic has always been fickle," I said. "Besides, we're all a bit rusty." Horace even more than the rest of us—he hadn't cast anything since before the war. Maybe seventy odd years was long enough for Horace to forgive magic.

He looked over at me, his face pinched with anger. "Ruth, what happened?"

"I already told you I don't know what's going on with the magic! If I understood it, I'd have dispatched Winter and started my reign as Daenerys."

Phyllis huffed. "You are a tyrant."

I stomped on the floor, mad at the world. The remains of Mary's water spell splashed up my legs. The magic still rolling through me reared its head. The fire burned inside me, eating away at my resolve. Everything would be so much easier if magic would just stick around. And I could burn a hole through to the realms of fire. It would be so simple. There'd be enough fire, and I could rule it—

Mary put a soggy hand on my arm. "Ruth, look at me."

Her touch was like a bucket of water on the burning fires inside me. Everyone stared. Horace's eyes tracked my motion as if he were waiting for me to explode. Phyllis watched with one eyebrow raised. Her satin nightgown wasn't even wrinkled. Mary, soaked and dripping, watched with watery eyes.

I breathed with the potential of what had almost come over me. I had to be better than this. I had to have the control, to know when to let it go, and to know when to drop and destroy things. I couldn't call wanton fire in a place full of people. The conflagration would make Chicago look like a campfire.

Everyone had felt the moment. There were things you could hide from people, but these people had been my friends and comrades—shield sisters and brother through two world conflicts. They had picked me up when a moment of bad luck had destroyed my whole life. They knew.

I cleared my throat. "Sorry. I didn't mean to lose my temper, Horace."

He nodded. "Apology accepted."

Mary patted my arm. "Don't do that. It's scarier when magic isn't around. How would we protect ourselves from a firestorm?"

Nodding, I stared at my feet. Anything but those eyes, accusing—and rightly so. She knew me too well. It's part of why I never even tried with Mary. I didn't deserve her or her care. And she was so damn kind. She knew what I could do. With magic back, my anger could spill a hellfire on the land, scorch the earth to dust and ash. I took a deep breath. I didn't deserve her kindness, and I'd never be able to live up to her love.

"Well, I'm awake," Phyllis said. "I guess we should get on the road since we're going to have to stop like a million times."

Horace raised his eyebrows as his face pulled back in anger. "It's not like you even have a prostate! You have no idea what I'm going through!"

Mary rolled her eyes. "As I recall, that was no defense when we were complaining about distinctly female problems." She pointed at Phyllis. "What was it he said as we were crossing the border into German held territory?"

A gleam like the edge of a dagger caught in Phyllis's eyes. "'It's completely natural,' you said."

Mary took over. "And 'How come you always take so long to pee in a bush?' I believe."

I snorted. "Let's not forget my personal favorite: 'This is why we shouldn't take women on field missions.'" I nodded at him.

Like a baton passing from one to the other, Phyllis took up the berating. "Did you want to sit this one out because of your anatomy?"

Horace steamed under his collar. "No, I do not. But I would like to take a shower before you ladies use all the hot water." He held up his finger to hold back any further teasing. "And don't try to tell me you don't take very long showers."

"Fine! Go take a shower, you big baby," Phyllis said. "I swear, men can't handle any interruption of their schedule."

Horace prowled through the bits and pieces of luggage he'd knocked over, pulling out his shaving kit. His shoulders slumped. "Damn. Damn. Damn!"

"Jeezum crow, what now?" Phyllis asked, exacerbated.

"I left my damn pills!" Horace held out his duffle bag. The contents lay strewn across the couch, but it didn't have any prescription bottles.

"How bad is it?" I asked.

"It's the pill for my heart!"

Mary looked over my shoulder. "You have to have one before it can fail."

"This isn't funny, witch! If I don't get my pills, my heart will stop being regular!" His face turned purple. "Not to mention my blood pressure pill! Damn it." He turned to me. "Ruth, I'm so—"

"Don't you dare say 'Sorry,' Horace." I met the gaze of each of my team. "This is an obstacle, nothing more."

"Can we call in the prescriptions?" Mary asked.

"Then they'll know right where we are," Phyllis answered while chewing on her lips. "This isn't going to be easy."

"We could steal someone's ID," Horace offered. He flexed his fingers, "I've still got the touch."

"Your sticky fingers aren't going to be enough. We'd need a prescription too. Do you know any way to fake that?" I asked.

"Hey, I'm coming up with ideas, okay?" He sat on the couch with a *whmfph* and started stuffing his things back into his duffel bag. "It's not like it's your pills."

I was missing mine too, but Mary took nearly the same prescription for her blood pressure and diabetes, so we were just going through hers at twice the rate. Instead, I leveled a glare at him. "It's just my life if we don't get to the Source before the next full moon."

The room went deadly quiet again. Horace stopped packing his bag and Phyllis froze.

"How are we going to beat this one, boss?" Mary asked.

"Let's pick a pharmacy, call ahead to be certain they have the pills, then we'll hit it up." I nodded my head hoping the others would nod in agreement.

Mary blinked. "You want to rob a pharmacy?" Her face contorted as she pulled her lips back. "That's a terrible idea!"

"You want us to become criminals?" Horace asked.

Nodding, I pulled the corners of my mouth down. "It's real simple at this point: if we get caught by the constabulary, which my granddaughter has surely alerted, we will die and Winter will be able to march her armies across the land. We don't get these medicines, you'll die—and quite frankly there are a few things I should pick up from the store."

They all looked at the soggy floor uncomfortably.

"Now, if anyone has a better idea, I'm open to it. We don't have a lot of time, and the problem with having a very proactive granddaughter on our tail is that she will have called in every force she's able to. It's part of why we didn't take a plane."

Mary looked up toward the ceiling. "We still could. I mean, if theft is on the table, we could just steal a plane and—"

"Fly to Washington, DC? The seat of the most powerful nation in the world? The one with the largest air force?" I asked.

She nodded. "Oh, yeah, right. So, we're gonna rob a pharmacy."

"How long can you go without your pill, Horace?" I asked.

He shook his head. "You people are crazy."

"Do we need to knock over the pharmacy before lunch or can we wait twelve hours or so, you know, after the sun goes down?"

Horace shook his head. "Before breakfast."

"Oh good," Phyllis said. "I've always wanted to knock off a joint before breakfast."

Chapter Seven

Mary hung up the phone. "They've got it." She pulled at a stray strand of hair, scowling at it when it caught on her fingernail. After an hour of curling, her hair looked up to her normal standards, but she was definitely drooping around the eyes. We were in pathetic shape and looked like roadkill warmed over a bonfire. If this came to a fight, Winter was going to eat us alive. And we still had 2,500 miles to go.

"Well, hallelujah," Phyllis said. Despite the exact same conditions, her hair was perfect, and her clothes were pressed. Running to save the world, and she broke out the hotel's iron. "So, what's the plan?"

I drew a quick sketch of the store. "You all will go in over here," I pointed, "and then I'll create a bit of a distraction. When everyone's distracted, get in there and take the pills. Be sure to get enough."

Horace shook his head. "You ladies are insane."

Mary leveled her sternest gaze at him. "That's 'witch' to you, buddy."

I nodded. "Or BOBs, whichever."

Horace frowned. "BOBs?"

Mary laughed. "Badass Old Bitches."

Phyllis and I laughed, but Horace just scowled at the whole thing.

"How am I supposed to even find the right stuff?" he asked.

"You won't," Phyllis said. "I've always handled the finding. Let me handle this one too. What I'm worried about is Ruth. What are you planning to do to distract people?"

"I have enough juice for something impressive."

Now Phyllis mimicked Horace by shaking her head. "I do *not* like the sound of that."

The morning felt more like winter in California than spring in Nevada, but the cold barely touched my mind. We piled into the little Prius with hardly any chatter. Horace performed some miracle and convinced the car to start. We were going to need a new car very soon. The light traffic barely warranted one lane, let alone the three we had going in our direction as we passed neon signs and casinos. Phyllis barked directions from a paper map until we made it to a squat building desperately trying to hold up a bright red roof, faded by the desert sun. We parked next to the sign proclaiming the store's name in bold white letters on a red background. With only a touch of reluctance, I got out of the car and narrowed my eyes at the dirty building.

Horace hit his head as he climbed out of the car. "Damn it!" He rubbed his head. "Let's steal a bigger car next time."

"Shhh! Do you want everyone to hear?" Phyllis said.

"Do the words 'Smooth Criminal' mean anything to you?" Mary asked.

Horace wobbled his head. "Sorry if I gave up my criminal instincts to pursue a more wholesome life."

Mary snorted.

"Exactly," I said as I scanned the parking lot. This early in the morning, it was mostly devoid of customers. The racks of propane tanks sat next to the door, guarded by two steel pillars sunk into the concrete. As I fit my plan into the reality of the store in front of me, one lucky soul left. *And you, dear sir, made an excellent choice to leave.* Hopefully there weren't many more people inside.

We watched him go to his car and drive away in a dusty Ford.

I turned back to the others. "Just give me a few minutes. You'll know when to go."

Mary and Phyllis nodded in unison. Mary grabbed Horace's arm before she strode into the store like a mother dragging her kid to the doctor's office for his shots. Horace hung his head and shuffled his feet. If he'd had some baseball cards hanging out of his pocket, it would have completed the picture.

I counted to ten before I focused my will on the power sloshing in my channels. Well, more like trickling by this point. The downpour of magic had been shorter than a thunderstorm and gone just as quickly. I needed to tend my vessel, but it required rest, and concentration, and focus, and honestly, I haven't had time for crap like that since Anne was born forever ago.

Shit, focus! You're about to blow things up, pay attention so you aren't one of them. The tanks of propane were like candy to my magic, ready to explode at the slightest spark. The potential for fire burned through the air, like the smell of a cake in the oven. I stood next to the tanks, taking deep breaths to force my power into very specific sparks, pulling fire from the other realm.

A cop car drove up, slowing to pull into the parking lot. I turned away, as if inspecting the flowers in the pot by the front door. He parked his car and went inside.

Damn my luck straight to the nearest portal to hell!

Well, it didn't change anything. He was probably picking up some prescriptions or something. I reached my mind into the ether again, seeking the sparks, the places with the potential for fire. It lived in the propane tanks, in the electricity coursing overhead, in the gas tanks for every car in the parking lot.

The magic flowed through me, hot and cold at the same time. As it spilled out of me, it flooded the world around me, so much so the air began to spark and glitter like sun on mist. It sapped my strength as it went, pulling me down. Last time I'd done this, I jogged regularly to keep in shape. A stray dragon could always be waiting on the other side, and I'd always prepared for those days. Dragons were normally cranky, savage creatures, but only because they were so misunderstood. It took more power than I had to really control one. The dragon at my apartment had been oddly friendly.

And misshapen, probably from the lack of a real fire at the time of summoning—and possibly due to the accidental nature of the summoning. The bigger the fire, the bigger the dragon.

Maybe it was just that it had been—

Ack! Mind on the task, Ruth! One wrong move and people are going to die.

I scanned the parking lot once more, but there was no one new. The magic had grown thick enough to cut with a knife. It was now or never.

To be sure no one got caught in the blow back, I stepped into the store, blocking the doors. I pushed magic through one of the tanks. It parted before the magical spike like cellophane under a knife, resistance at first, then a quick clean tear.

In that moment, I released the spark. I feigned looking at some candy by the checkout counter as I formed the magic into a wall to channel the inevitable blast. The magic rushed out of my personal store, like gas from a popped balloon. I deflated around the loss. I'd forgotten how fast it could take me down. My knees wobbled, and I wished I'd brought my cane. The magic drained out, pouring out into my spell, and pouring me onto the checkout counter.

"Ma'am!" the cashier said. "Ma'am, are you okay?"

I smiled, hoping to convey just how okay I was. If I spoke in the middle of a casting, I could lose the whole spell, or worse, it could explode utterly uncontrolled.

Fire! NOW! Please, fire, come!

The cashier rushed from behind the counter, her hurried footsteps clacking on the linoleum floor. The cool counter, smooth under my dry and cracked hands. The smell of the plastic wrapping the cheap flowers in a bucket at the end of the counter flooded my nose, and I knew the spell had completed. Time slowed for me. The tang of propane hung in the air, silent warning of what was to come. I counted the number of people in the building by instinct. A woman behind cosmetics, one at the cash register, the cop in line at the pharmacy behind Phyllis, Mary, and Horace, and three people behind the counter of the pharmacy. The world held its breath, the calm before the storm.

Oh gods, don't let anyone die.

I tilted my head away from the front windows, knowing the shockwave would blow out the doors. My protections would shield me from the debris, but only fools trusted their life to magic. The explosion started with a hiss. The air around me collapsed toward the shockwave. My magic channeled the blast up and into the power lines.

The doors blew toward us, throwing glass and debris all over the entrance of the store. A shard shot past my head and embedded in the wall beyond. At the same time, the air thumped my chest, sucking the air out of my lungs.

The sky turned bright orange. Shadows jumped from the new light source, and the roar of fire blocked out every other sound.

I took my first breath of the acrid smoke.

Gods, I missed this part.

The backwash of the fire blew through the magical realm, pushing raw power back into my lines. I filled with power, the weakness in my legs suddenly replaced with strength and whatever it was about magic that seemed to naturally heal everything. I stood firm. The cashier in the front of the store lay in a pile of a Doritos display. The chips had cushioned her fall. I checked her for bleeding, but she just needed to come to. Poor dove, not used to a firestorm in the store.

The fire alarms took one more second to go off, wailing despite the rest of the store losing power. Shouts rang from the pharmacy at the back of the store. If nothing else, I could count on Phyllis and Mary to make sure things got done.

I directed my energy back to the fire. If I did some fast work, I could keep it from destroying too much in the store. Focusing on the transition between the fire and the air, I seeped into the fire.

<Greetings!> The mental tag of a fire creature poured through my attempt to control the fire.

A fully formed head within the fire turned to stare at me. A dragon. Something about the dragon moved in a familiar way. How similar were the dragons? I'd never been close enough to really interact with dragons, as a younger member of the Order, but this one had an uncanny resemblance to the previous dragon.

Then I saw the foot. Ice rushed around my heart. What the hell did that mean? Why was the same dragon here?

<Happiness!> The emotion flooded through me, but it was clearly coming from the dragon. The dragon filled the opening where the doors had been, grabbing the edges to fit itself in through the hole. The greater conflagration had clearly increased her size.

A dragon. I called the same dragon from the ether? They never came back. Everyone said dragons hated being called through the fire, but here she was, happy to be here. She purred as she ran toward me, her back end wiggling more than was expressly necessary to slip through the pharmacy doors. Without hesitation, I reached out to pet her. The protective spells held up around me, and her touch merely blazed under my hand rather than charring my skin. She nuzzled against me, and I scratched under her chin.

Somewhere inside my chest, a swelling sensation filled me and bubbled to the surface.

She wrapped around me, swathing me in her happiness. She smelled of cinnamon and pine, like an old-style oven baking cinnamon rolls. I could almost smell my grandmother's kitchen, the basil hanging by the window, green onions tied to hooks by the wall, garlic everywhere, and in the midst of it all, her calm presence. She'd cuss at the stove and throw on an extra log.

A woman screamed nearby, tearing me out of my memory.

Visible through the body of the dragon, the cashier screamed, her mouth ringed with teeth like crenellations on a castle. She stared at me, her eyes wide with horror. The edges of her mouth drew down, and her jaw hung slack from her face.

Oh right, I was in the middle of a heist. I wasn't supposed to be cuddling with a dragon.

The woman scrambled backward, scuttling like a crab through the chips. Her foot tangled in the cardboard display. Another scream broke my attention and startled the dragon.

<Food?> she asked with her curious mind tone.

"No! Don't eat them!"

The second woman, the one from behind the cosmetics counter, stood there, sweating in the heat of the dragon. I made eye contact with her, as she absorbed the scene of me covered in a column of flames. She stood there screaming.

"Run!" I yelled.

Her mouth snapped shut, the part of her brain in charge of emergency decisions took over, and she ran. I turned back to the cashier in the Doritos display. The cardboard curled as she jumped up and started for the emergency exit at the back of the store.

<Food?> the dragon asked again.

"No, you're going to have to go back."

<No. Happiness,> she sent back, tilting her head at me. She unwound from me and started inspecting the fingernail polish. *<Shiny!>*

What have I done?

"You can't wear fingernail polish! You're a fire creature! You don't even have parts that could wear it!"

<Want!>

"No!" I stomped my foot. At this point, some very real fire caught along the wall outside, eating up the side of the store, and the smoke rolled into the building.

<Want! Or I eat!> she said giving me a stern look.

"If I get you shinies, will you go back to the realm?"

<Better than go! Stay and be friends!> The dragon wagged its tail.

Well, I wasn't going to get a better offer than friends with a dragon. I scowled at its evolution in the mere seconds of being out of the realm of fire. It already had better language, but that was definitely something to marvel at later: the building was on fire. And now I needed to steal some cosmetics to appease my new friend.

With the power of fire coursing through my veins, I could have skipped down the aisles, but I knew better. Anything I did like this, I'd pay for double or triple later. The body knew what was happening to it, even if it didn't feel it.

In the seasonal section, there were great big beach bags, and I grabbed one. The dragon tracked along with me, picking things to inspect at random. She stared into the eyes of a plastic garden gnome as it started melting from her presence. I grabbed summer clothes hanging next to the bag and tossed in anything I could get my hands on—flipflops, sunglasses, you name it. If I lived through this, I'd send them a check. At the end of the aisle a small display held a bunch of wooden canes with crooks. It wasn't the kind I liked, but it would have to do. I picked one and hung it in the crook of my elbow.

As the store deteriorated into the chaos of flames and fire around me, I rushed back to cosmetics. I grabbed a handful of nail polishes, and some other likely items nearby and dropped them in the bag before turning to leave.

The dragon roared. *<This one!>*

Avarice flooded through me as I spun back, clearly boiling out of the dragon. The burning red nail polish sat on the display case in front of the dragon. Of course, she wanted Red Hot Mamma. What other color would the dragon want?

"This one? Are you sure?" I asked using my best mother directing toddler voice.

The dragon's tail twitched like a cat, slapping the ground. Flames curled up from the spade tip, spiraling to the ceiling. *<Yes,>* she said. *<How much fire?>*

"I think we're just about done here."

<Then I come with you now,> the dragon said. The air rippled around her, as if heat waves radiated off her. Her form condensed, and the smoke coming off her darkened until it came off thick and black.

And then there stood a cat. Her matte, dark grey coat was the color of ash, and her eyes burned gold and copper in the center. *<We go?>*

I blinked. The dragon turned into a cat? Only the most powerful elementals could do that. And they were always the familiars of the most powerful mages. Even in my prime, I didn't rate such a powerful companion.

Process of elimination, I was probably one of the last mages, and I was probably the only fire mage currently casting anything.

I bent down to pet her, and she purred, rising her tail to meet my touch. My hand came away covered in soot. Well, I was supposed to be escaping a burning building. I smeared the soot on my face and in my hair.

"Oh god, there's another one inside!" a man yelled. The police officer emerged from the smoke. "Ma'am, ma'am!" He gestured with his hands, cupping them toward him in the universal Get Over Here gesture.

I hunched over and did the part of old woman lost in a burning building. "Oh, oh, thank god!" I hobbled toward him. "Bless you, young man! Bless you!"

He grabbed my elbow directing me to the emergency exit at the back of the building. I clutched my bag of stolen goods under my arm, unwilling to let them go. There was no telling what a powerful elemental would do if I lost her hoard.

"Did you see anyone else?" he asked.

"No, I didn't see anyone else." *Just a fire elemental, following at a safe distance, but I know that's not what you're after.*

Deftly, he maneuvered me through the store to the emergency exit. Smoke filled the interior, and just as we reached the hallway to the back, the sprinklers came on. How they hadn't gone off sooner was a miracle, pure and simple.

No sprinklers went off in the hallway, but smoke wicked through, drawn by the air flow. It boiled along the ceiling like a river in reverse, the rolls of black smoke mixing with the white smoke making eddies of grey.

The dragon trotted along behind me. *<Pretty.>*

"Just stay close," I said.

"Of course, ma'am. We're almost there," the officer said. His radio blared and hissed as people tried to communicate with him.

He thought I meant him. Clearly, he'd never dealt with a dragon.

When he pushed open the emergency exit door, the alarm squealed. He held open the door, and the fresh crisp air of the outside rushed in past us, blowing my skirt up. I let go of his arm and put my hand down to save what was left of my modesty and dignity.

The survivors huddled around someone's car, and a siren called out in the distance. The early morning sun glowed orange through the copious amount of smoke, casting red shadows. Mary, Phyllis, and Horace all stood clustered together a few steps from the other survivors.

"How are you doing?" the police officer asked, placing a protective hand on my back.

"I'll be fine, dearie, you just get to work," I said.

He nodded and turned to the gathered crowd. "If everyone could please stand back! Please! Help will be here momentarily!" He leaned over his radio and started talking, and I took that as my opportunity to get a move on.

I scuttled as fast as I dared over to my compatriots.

"Oh my god! I saw you burn," the soot-smeared cashier said. She stood next to the other evacuated staff. "I saw you burn!" She leveled her accusing finger at me.

My dragon growled from somewhere around my ankles.

"What the hell is that?" Mary asked.

"It's a long story," I said, imploring her with my eyes. "Oh, I don't feel so good," I said with exaggeration. "Please take me to the hospital!" I said loudly enough for the other witnesses to hear.

"She burned in the fire! I saw her burning!" the cashier yelled.

The police officer turned to us, then back to cashier. "Fires are weird, ma'am."

"She was wrapped in fire! It was like a dragon swallowed her."

Hughn. She probably had some talent to see the dragon when it was first forming, before it had solidified. I'd have to remember this. Well, I'd have to remember this if I lived to see next Monday.

The police officer rolled his eyes, exasperated. "A dragon?" He took a deep breath. "Things can get pretty crazy in a burning building," he said in a calm-the-crazy-lady-down voice.

We slipped farther away and closer to our stolen car.

"Ma'am! Hold up there!" the police officer called. "I want the medics to look you over."

The cashier doubled down. "She's a witch! I saw her burn! She's a devil!" She flung her words like spears at me.

"I think we should take her to the hospital!" Mary said, in her overly obvious play-acting voice to convince the other two to get on board.

"Oh!" Horace said. "She doesn't look good!"

"She's a witch!" the cashier screamed.

Everyone ducked at her vile use of our badge of office. Without warning, she launched across the parking lot. "Burn in Hell, Devil!"

The police officer grabbed the cashier around the waist as she made her mad dash for me. She clawed at me, screaming incoherently.

"Please," Phyllis said, walking past. "Devil?" she shook her head. "At least a devil would have some fashion." Phyllis widened her eyes to emphasize her point.

"We should really get our friend to the hospital," Mary said.

"Please—ugh!—hurry!" the police officer said. "I'll—send—ah—an escort—"

I hobbled as fast as my feeble granny persona would let me. Which, to be honest, was only a hair slower than my actual pace as the power of the fire wicked away, like maple syrup sucked into a dry pancake.

As a group, we all moved to the car. The others fawned over me like I'd faint at any minute. No one really believed that, but it had been a while since any of us had extended ourselves. Not to put too fine a point on it, but we were all in better shape back in the day. I slid into the passenger seat, stuffing the bag under my legs and waiting for the dragon to hop in the car. She did a circle before jumping into my lap. She left little sooty footprints everywhere she went.

"What's the deal with the cat?" Mary asked.

"Dragon, Mary. She's a dragon."

Mary stared at me, eyes caught somewhere between awe and horror. Even among witches, dragons were *not* normal.

Normal's boring.

Chapter Eight

"You stole fingernail polish from the pharmacy?" Phyllis yelled as we got on the freeway.

"What was I supposed to do? Let a fully formed dragon loose on the outskirts of Reno?" I pet my little dragon/cat creature. After the first five minutes of pets, most of the ash had abandoned her cat form for my borrowed skirts. This was clearly why the higher tiered witches always wore black. For the time being, she curled in my lap and dozed lazily. Like a cat.

"Obviously, that wouldn't be ideal, but you know better than to use your craft for personal gain!" Phyllis admonished.

"Like stealing Horace's meds?" I asked.

Phyllis pointed her finger at me. "First, that was to save his life. Second, it is completely immaterial to the fact that you stole from the store you practically burned down."

Mary took a slug from her flask. "Geez, Mom, I didn't see you quibbling over morals when we jumped the counter and grabbed all the meds in sight. What was that extra bottle you grabbed?" Mary passed the flask to me.

I waved her off. I had a dragon in my lap. It didn't seem like the best choice to aim for three sheets to the wind by noon while handling a creature that could go from purring to a firestorm as quickly as a cat could change its mind about whether it liked having belly rubs.

I nodded along with Mary. "Funny, you didn't mention anything else you picked up?"

Phyllis crossed her arms and resolutely stared out the window.

"Really? You have the audacity to lecture me about morals and interpretations of the code?" I raised an imperious eyebrow at her, but the effect died somewhere between the back and front seats.

"It was for the craft," she said with a sniff. "It's not like I stole recreational things like cosmetics."

"It was going to burn anyway. Besides, dragon taming devices don't seem like recreation when I'm trying to keep her from deciding the whole building is tasty. I mean really, once we got out of there, the whole thing could be taken care of by a couple of water pistols." I shook my head. "What was it? The meds you stole."

"How much do you pay for your prescriptions?" Phyllis asked. "Do you think it's a fair amount?"

Horace took a breath through his teeth, hissing, as he piloted the car. "Low blow, Phyllis. Low blow."

"Are you trying to change the topic?" I asked. "I don't care how you plan to justify this—well, actually I do since you made my work such an issue. I'm very curious how you can sit there on your high horse and look down on me for wanting to have the *equipment* we need to complete the mission!"

I paused dramatically to let my spin of events sink in.

Phyllis narrowed her eyes at me. "Fine, I knew the bottle was there, and yes, I grabbed it. Some of us don't have your ability with magic, you know. Some of us need chemical stimulation to reach the state of mind where our abilities do more than let me know not to order the seafood dish! There, are you happy? I'm not as powerful as you. Does it make you happy to hear me say it? It's been ninety years of you outshining me in every way you could. Ninety years! Does it make you proud to know that your mastery over an obviously more powerful form of magic just frosts my hide?"

"I think you meant to say 'burns.' There's nothing cold about Ruth," Mary muttered.

"Aahhh!" Phyllis yelled incoherently.

Horace swerved as a cat fight erupted, drifting into the lane next to us. A horn blared. Horace corrected with a sharp jerk, and another car honked at us. My dragon clawed my lap, upset at the disruption of her nap. She growled.

Horace got the car moving straight again. Another car blared their horn, and the vehicle behind us in the left lane rolled down their window. The driver, a young man with a polo shirt, leaned toward his open window.

Horace, assuming the young man might be warning us about our car, rolled down his window. The sudden rush of air barreled into the cabin, crushing my eardrums and rattling everything in a torrent of raging wind.

The young driver leaned over his passenger seat to get closer to the window. "Get your glasses checked, grandpa!"

"Nimrod!" Horace yelled, face blistering red as he hit the window.

"Oh yeah, old man!" the other driver yelled. He swerved with a jerk toward our car.

On instinct, Horace swerved away from the oncoming car. All the other traffic around us backed off. Even on the freeway, people knew to make space for a fight. The other driver held up his hand to flip us off.

On his forearm, an assortment of tattoos littered his skin. Between a series of runes on his wrists were the two "s" shaped runes. The SS. A Nazi. A damned modern Nazi. I hissed, and the dragon jolted upright, growling at the other driver. My rage roiled back, leaking into the dragon, and I had to force my reaction down. These children had no idea what we had done to rid the world of the very worst Nazis, and now they just wore their symbols like it was some damn joke.

"He's a Nazi!" Horace yelled. He swerved back into the left lane, and the other driver deftly maneuvered around Horace's attack.

Phyllis grabbed the brace above the window, her knuckles going white. "That asshole's done this before!"

I focused on breathing. I couldn't let my anger get away from me. I bottled my annoyance, and the horrible feeling that everything we'd sacrificed had been for nothing so these idiots could go about playacting at the very worst humanity had to offer. I wrapped a hand around my dragon, who now glared at the car next to us. *<Food?>*

"No, sweetie, we can't eat people. Not even Nazis."

The Nazi swerved toward us again.

Horace dodged, but when he went to right the car, it came off its wheels. "Shit!" He wrenched the wheel, sending our airborne wheels farther into the air.

I braced against the door, watching the ground suddenly getting closer to my window.

With a terrifying wrench of the wheel, Horace righted the car. The wheels touched down with a terrible thump, and the car jerked toward the white line, but with all four wheels on the ground, Horace controlled the car with ease. "God damned Nazis!"

The other car passed us. A bumper sticker on the back read, *We Won't Be Replaced*!

"We gave up everything to wipe those fuckers off the planet, and now those assholes have swastikas tattooed into their fucking arms!" He hit the steering wheel. "Why the Hell did we even fight World War Two?"

"I hate Nazis," I said, scowling at the reprehensible excuse for a human being. Bloody idiot.

Mary scowled at her shirt. "Well damn." She started wiping at it with a tissue.

Phyllis grabbed Mary's flask. "Give me that." She jerked the cap off and took a swig. She coughed. "Sweet mother of magic! Mary, what the hell is this?"

Mary shrugged. "Orange juice. I couldn't find any champagne at the breakfast bar, or it would be a mimosa. I tell you, service these days."

"Horace, pull over," Phyllis said wiping her face with the back of her hand.

"There's a rest stop just outside of town, you want me to stop there?" he asked.

"Yes, anywhere!"

With a care uncommon in Horace's driving, he flipped on the turn signal and slowed gradually to take the off-ramp. The car practically crawled up the on-ramp as Horace guided the witch-mobile about as fast as a child volunteering to clean out the dragon box. Phyllis glared at me as Horace pulled into the parking area with calm and deliberate movements, as if any jostling would set off a bomb. I steadfastly refused to acknowledge Phyllis's existence.

Families, truckers, and campers occupied the rest area. Someone had laid out a blanket with a large peace sign and was selling globs of glass held together with knotted twine—probably hemp. Horace drove past these and parked at the very last spot, next to the conveniently labeled Pet Area. Well, we sure had one of those. When I opened the door, the smell of diesel and unwashed bodies rose up around me.

My dragon hopped out of the car with me, and I carried my bag of pilfered goods to a picnic area with a built-in barbeque. There weren't any trees, but some paper littered the ground and I collected it. My dragon hopped into the barbeque without any prompting and curled up, emitting a soft, pleasant smoke as she burned up the remaining charcoal in the fire pit. I tossed her some wadded paper and basked in the heat she emitted.

Mary approached, holding her flask. "Peace offering?"

"Ha, you weren't the one to go all sanctimonious on me."

She shrugged. "But I was thinking it." She watched the dragon burn the charcoal lumps and adjusted her jacket to block more of the morning cold. "To be fair, I sort of wish you'd stolen some sausages right about now."

I nodded. "Like those sausages we found on the Austrian border?"

Mary chortled. "I thought for sure Gustav was going to hang us for stealing."

"Gustav! I haven't thought of him in decades!" I smiled at the memory, rolling it across my mind. Us on the run and saving the world, only our trusted teacher Gustav and a couple soldiers too scared of magic to be any help at all.

"Deed vou brink vour guns?" Mary said in a perfect imitation of our old German task master.

I laughed, leaning back and enjoying it. She hadn't known, but Gustav was considered a lesser mage. I had been cleared for a better trainer—more talented teammates, but Mary was assigned to Gustav, so I'd trained with him too. I had refused to join those in my own tier to be with Mary, and it had led me to Phyllis and Horace. I owed Gustav everything—all my friends, surviving The War and being who I am today.

And even though he'd tried to drive me back up to the higher tiers, once I proved my devotion, he'd given me other training—training that would help others, spells that had kept Mary alive while we'd been marching over the Alps.

The dragon watched us, blinking her gold and copper eyes, and I suddenly remembered that Mary hadn't known any of that. "Poor Gustav. I hope wherever he is he managed to see us win."

"Hopefully he has something better to do in the afterlife than follow us around," Mary said. "Besides, I'd hate for him to see us now." She shook her head wistfully. "Some mess we're in this time."

"Yeah," I said, staring into the fire. The flames rose off luring me into it, but I knew better. Fire was intoxicating, but with the dragon, I couldn't help but be a little reserved. Those were her flames, not mine.

"So, what's the real plan?" Mary asked.

"I'm not hiding anything. Clandestine work is clearly not my forte." I held up my bag of stolen goods.

"Whatever possessed you to shoplift on your way out of a burning building?"

"What possessed Phyllis to steal speed?"

Mary held up her hands. "I'm not condoning what she did. She has her reasons, and I want to hear yours."

In answer, I took out one of the bottles of nail polish and looked for the one labeled Red Hot Mamma and held it out for the dragon. "You still want this one?"

<Shiny! Yes!> she said enthusiastically. The dragon/cat reached her paw out of the fire and extended her claws.

As though I gave pedicures to flaming masses of voracious elementals every day, I carefully applied the polish. She kept pulling her paws back to look at the polish, completely enthralled. I had to ask for her claws back to keep going.

"Well, I just don't feel like that's one of the three uses of the sacred elementals, but..." Mary paused, her words hanging in the air. "Last time we did something this crazy, we had all these rules and sacred rites. This time?" She shook her head. "We're the last ones left, and to be honest, I haven't touched a grimoire since the seventies."

"Mmhmm." I leaned in to get the last of the claws on the dragon's forepaws. "Here we are, surrounded by people, and it's still one of the loneliest things we've ever done."

"Yes! Exactly! When we were hiking through the Alps, we were as alone as you can get in Europe, but there was always this feeling there was a place to go back to. A home. We could have been brought to trial by those sorcerers. We could have had our ranks stripped. Even the military folks had rules. Now?" She shrugged. "Now they've all retired or died. There's no one left who even knows what we did, and all the people who cared about the rules are dead."

"So that's it then? No more rules?" I asked.

Mary snorted. "What? You were just going to break them!"

"Maybe," I agreed with a smile. I pulled out some clothes and started pulling the tags off them. I threw the tags to my dragon who ate them in her fire.

Mary reached into the pile of clothes and pulled one out. "Take this one to Phyllis. This will never fit you." She got ready to stand up.

"Mary," I said, stopping her.

She looked down at me from her half-standing position and raised an eyebrow at me.

"Thank you for coming with me. It means a lot to me."

Mary rolled her eyes. "I'm doing it to make sure you don't decide to take over the world while you're out saving it."

"I'm not going to take over the world," I said.

Mary raised an eyebrow at me. I shrugged. She pursed her lips before turning away.

As she turned to leave, trailing her hand across the top of the picnic table, frost covered the boards. Mary turned back with the sharp stance of someone ready to fight.

My breath fogged as I exhaled, and my dragon growled.

The pale form of Winter stood on the bench of the picnic table.

Chapter Nine

Mary hissed, calling water to her hand. I hadn't known she'd stored any of the trace magic when it opened up this morning, but Mary always had surprises.

My dragon jumped onto the table to growl menacingly at the Winter Queen.

"Why are you here?" I asked, my voice sterner than I meant. In the back of my mind, I laid the groundwork for a large casting. I didn't have the power for it, but if I kept her talking, I might be able to lay a blow against her.

Winter turned her angular face toward me. She said nothing, watching the dragon/cat. She kept twitching her head as if she were trying to shake off a fly. "Your pet is strange," she said finally.

"I hadn't noticed." My dragon now smoldered around the edges, frosting her fur in bright golden flames.

"You have no idea what you are carrying about," Winter said.

The dragon growled, louder, her hackles rising.

Winter glared. "It appears to not like me."

"Probably because you called her 'Pet.' I'm told that's a pejorative." As slowly as I could manage, I pushed magic through the old channels, lining up an old spell. The more time I had, the less power it needed. But with my depleted powers, I might not have enough to push a thumb tack into a wall no matter what kind of time I had. "Why are you here?"

My rude request hung between us. She glared at me, before turning her attention back to my dragon. She wanted to force me into being rude, but why? Was she being a jerk just to be difficult, or was she hiding something?

Ha, Winter always hid the truth.

She tilted her head away from me. "I dare say your pet is uncanny. Most of her kind treat me with respect."

"I'm certain we could discuss acceptable animal behavior for many a day, but it just so happens, I have prior engagements. Why are you here?" I asked for a third time.

Winter hissed. "I wanted to speak with my contract holder." The ice in her fingers started growing again, drawing the moisture out of the air to extend her icicle fingers into the deadly sharp knives she used for claws. "Why are you so concerned? Your time is not up yet. I wouldn't dream of attacking you until the terms are fully broken. You are, after all, going to be a lovely prize." Winter reached out with her icicle fingers, and I froze.

I'd already been incredibly rude by asking the question three times. If she wanted to touch my face, a sign of affection among fae, and I rebuked her, she could kill me for nothing.

The icicles burned across my face, trailing cold that touched more than my skin. My whole body went to ice. I shivered as the ice of Winter burned through my magic, freezing it in its channels. There was no way I could cast my spell now. She'd quenched my fires.

Of course, this could just be a prelude to Winter killing me. She'd attacked me in my apartment, why wouldn't she do the same now? Witnesses?

Mary pushed me back, slapping Winter's hand away. "Over my dead body, bitch!" Mary's form eclipsed Winter.

I shivered, feeling returning to my body. I hadn't realized I'd gone numb until it all came back, burning cold and stinging.

Winter smiled down at Mary. "I look forward to it." Her eyes focused to beams of ice, glaciers hurtling toward my best friend. Winter took a breath, as if taking in the fragrance of a thousand flowers blooming in a great field. "I could well and truly hold someone with your talents in exquisite pain for centuries."

"Back off." Mary cast a small waterform in front of her.

Winter regarded her like a curiosity, something to be admired and collected, but only for its oddity. She pierced the waterform floating in front of Mary. It cracked and hissed as it turned to ice. It collected on the edge of Winter's fingers and shattered.

Mary gasped, and my dragon dropped her disguise and pounced on the fae queen. But like all things of the fae, she was gone before my dragon's teeth could rend her into pieces.

Mary collapsed to her knees.

Winter's voice rang through my head. "You've already lost half your time, and you're no closer to your goal, fire witch. You will be mine, and I will wield you like the monster you really are."

I rushed to Mary, wrapping my arm around her. "Are you okay?" I asked.

"I'll be damned if that Elsa wannabe gets the last of me." She wrapped her arms around her abdomen, shivering as she attempted to stand. Her white pants had dirt on the knees, and I brushed at the blemishes.

"I think I have something in my—ah—"

"Pilfered goods?" Mary gave me a reproachful look.

"Fine, I stole them. I used my powers for ill. But," I said holding up my index finger, "I'd like to point out how many things were strictly forbidden back then, and we've changed our minds about many of them."

Mary snorted, still rubbing her arms with her hands to generate some warmth. "Like what?"

"All kinds of things." I pointed at her pants. "White after Labor Day!"

She rolled her eyes. "Thanks for your earth-shattering revelations."

"We all have our strengths." I fished out a thin overshirt and passed it to Mary.

She scowled at it but slid her arms into the sleeves before returning to rubbing her arms.

Phyllis hobbled up to us. "Did I hear Winter?" she asked, sucking deep breaths of air.

"Yes, but the dark queen has already fled before my might," Mary said, pretend flexing her arms before her shivering caught her whole body in a shudder.

"Damnit. Next time leave a piece for me." Phyllis leaned over putting her hands on her knees. "I should have taken my pills!"

"I shouldn't have left my cane in the car," I said, sinking to the bench. My dragon had resumed her more natural size and curled up in my lap, emitting enough heat to start a fire. It barely touched the ice curdling in my heart in Winter's aftermath.

Mary held her hands up to the dragon as if to a fire. The dragon purred, and Mary nodded. "I don't remember anyone else having a dragon familiar," she said tilting her head toward the soot ball in my lap.

"Well, I hadn't breeched the third tier." I shook my head. "There's just a lot I don't know."

"What about the books?" Phyllis asked.

My heart clenched. "It's a bit of a secret."

"After seventy years, you're going to keep their secret?" Phyllis gave me an accusing eye.

"No." I folded my arms.

She crossed her arms over her chest and cocked her hip. "Seventy, mundane years," she said leaning forward. "Seventy years, and you're still holding their secrets."

I shook my head.

"I'm sure they were thrilled with Dorothy," her voice took on a false levity. "I'm sure they were absolutely forward thinking and accommodating of you bringing in someone with absolutely no magic." She raised an eyebrow at me. "I'm sure they hadn't given you every directive of your potential mates—you know to make sure that the talent survived..."

The pressure of it built inside me, and I twisted my face. "Fine! You want to know the truth? In return for saving the world from the ravages of the Winter Queen, they offered to spare my life. They were going to wipe Dorothy's mind of all knowledge, but last laugh was on them—they didn't have anyone left who could do the deed." I kicked at a nearby rock, but it disturbed the dragon. She blinked copper and red eyes up at me with reproach. I nodded, smoothing her fur. Ash clung to my fingers.

"Anyway, for my services, they chose to banish me from all future gatherings." I met Phyllis's gaze. "You remember that trip Dorothy and I took to Paris?"

Phyllis and Mary nodded their heads.

"The Order of the Secrets of Fire had decided that if magic was never going to return to the world, they would leave it too."

Phyllis and Mary froze, as if they were scared to disrupt the weight of my words.

I sniffed, trying to drag in a decent breath, but my chest clenched. My throat swelled. I swallowed. "They were broken old men without magic. They unbanished me long enough to invite me to their death party. While everyone else was redistributing the world order after World War II, the Order decided to exit the world and take every scrap of magical knowledge they had control over with them. Every book, scroll, and mage agreed to end it. As a woman, I didn't even get a vote, but the amazing thing was how many women went to their final gathering. They thought it was some sort of gift they were giving, a peaceful death. Just like that damned Jones cultist a decade later."

Mary put her hand on my back, sliding onto the bench next to me as the tears escaped, racing down my face.

I dabbed at my cheeks with an errant sleeve. "I hate lemonade."

Phyllis shook her head. "God damn those pretentious assholes."

I shrugged. "They had some points." The dragon purred at just that moment, forcing her head under my hand for more pets. "They were idiots. Life couldn't be worth living without magic? Jerks." I swallowed. "They destroyed the books ritually in front of us all. Even if magic returned, there can never be an Order of Fire. They sent all the knowledge of every fire mage to come before them into the abyss—after all, they were all about to die. Who would guard it from the normals? Assholes."

Phyllis shook her head. "Shit. I knew your order was crazy, but that's Grade A crazy."

"So, no books?" Mary confirmed. "Nothing about dragons or the other elemental creatures?"

I nodded. "Like the Viking Kings they wished they were, they took their treasure with them to the grave." A sigh escaped my lips. "I managed to gather a couple before everything went south after the war, but..." I shrugged. Only then did I realize what Mary was actually asking: If I had a dragon, would a water horse be coming for her?

I didn't know.

Horace meandered up the cement path toward our little enclave. "Ladies, I trust everything's fine." He reached his hands toward the dragon, but at the last minute, my dragon flattened her ears and turned her back to Horace.

"What was that for?" he asked.

Phyllis put a hand on his shoulder. "She's just mad about the books."

"What books?" he asked.

I waved my hand in front of my nose as if a bad smell lingered. If only I could wave away bad memories as easily. "It's a long story. Should we get down to the business of stealing a fist-sized gemstone from a case less than twenty meters from the Hope Diamond?"

Chapter Ten

"I'll drive," Horace said, walking toward the driver's side door.

I cut him off. "You drove last night. Besides, I need a moment to think, and I do that best when I have something to do."

"Who will hold your cat?" he asked.

"Don't wet yourself, Horace, I'll hold the scawwy dwagon," Mary said. My dragon jumped into the car and waited for Mary to make an appropriate lap. "There's a good dragon. What are you going to call her?"

"PITA?" Horace offered.

"I was thinking something more regal," I said. "Maybe Chernabog, or Maleficent."

"Oh, good ones," Phyllis agreed climbing into the back.

Horace hesitated at the driver's side, but I jerked my head to the side. "Get in. Unless you'd like to walk to DC."

He sighed, relenting. "I just don't think it's a good idea to have our most powerful gun also in charge of the driving."

"Stuff it, Horace," Mary said. "Phyllis already took her pill, and I scored a bottle of rum from those kids in the RV."

I threw the car into gear and eased out of the parking lot.

Phyllis scowled at me in the rear-view mirror. "You know, next car should have some more horsepower."

Horace snorted. "Why? Our getaway not good enough?"

"The best is to blend in," I said.

Mary shook her head. "Blending in is what they'll be expecting. No one expects the BOBs in a Ferrari."

"I thought we weren't to use our powers for ill?" I asked, raising an eyebrow.

"There is something to be said for the element of surprise," Phyllis said.

Mary raised her hip flask. "And style!" She hadn't added any of the rum to it yet, but she drank from it with the same gusto as if she'd filled it with whiskey. Maybe she didn't need it as much when reality was more pressing than memories.

Horace adjusted his seat belt. "You two are like trying to run a tight rope act between two jeeps. I can never tell which way your loyalties will fall."

"Calm down, buttercup. I know how to drive," I said. I backed out of the parking spot and aimed us toward the on-ramp.

He snorted. "Sure, just like that time in Milan?"

Mary wacked the back of his headrest. "We agreed! We don't talk about Milan, okay?"

Phyllis drawled out a low note of agreement. "That was good stuff in Milan. Almost as good as—Whoa! It's fast acting!"

I eased on the gas, slowing compared to the other cars around us. "What's fast? Did you take one of those pills?"

"We thought it would be good to try one out before we really needed it," Mary said.

I growled. "How come I didn't get a vote in this?"

Horace crossed his arms. "I told her not to take those damn things just for fun."

"This isn't for fun," Phyllis demanded, leaning forward and clutching the back of the car seat. Her eyes crossed as she weaved. "It's research." She hiccupped and sagged against the seat. "I don't feel so great."

I ignored her and merged into traffic. Soft moans followed from the back as Phyllis battled the side effects of her poor choices. The miles slipped by in the miasma of traffic and desert. We weren't too far out of Reno, but the steady stream of cars clogged the highway. Enough to keep me from driving as fast as I'd prefer.

Phyllis lay her head against the back of the seat, over the headrest. "I have regrets."

I half looked at her before focusing back on the road. "You're the one who took the pill!"

"Oh god, I think I'm going to be sick. It's too much!" Phyllis weaved in the backseat. "My vision is so sharp, it's like it pierces the veil!" She moaned. "I can see you all!"

"Of course, you can," Horace said. "We're all right here!"

"But do I tell you all about the problems?" Phyllis shook her head, her eyes glassy. "I don't know how I got here!"

Mary scowled. "Great, she's tripping too hard to be useful."

I cocked my head. "Wait, that's Adderall? Right?"

Mary shrugged.

"Adderall shouldn't give her hallucinations."

"Cop!" Phyllis yelled. "They're looking for us! How? They're looking for us."

Horace rolled his eyes. "Yes, we're on the run from the cops, of course they're looking for us. That's the literal definition of what we're doing! We stole a car! The cops are looking for us!"

"On the left! We're almost there!" Phyllis started pointing, but she leaned over so far, her head hung between the two front seats of the car.

I turned to the left but saw nothing.

"Are you sure?" Mary asked.

"Cop!" Phyllis stared below the line of the windshield but pointed.

I ducked into the right-hand lane, but there was nowhere to actually get off the freeway. I matched speed with a semi passing, and followed in as close as possible, hoping the three lanes would be enough to cloak us.

"He saw us!" Phyllis cried.

I checked the rearview mirror, and a car driving in the opposite direction flipped a U-turn on the freeway over the dried grass and rocks that separated the lanes of traffic.

"Shit!" I said stomping on the gas and pulling onto the right-hand shoulder. The acceleration pulled me into the cushions, and I flirted with real danger.

"What are you doing!" Horace braced against the door and clutched the center console.

"Uhhh!" Phyllis cried. "I'm gonna be sick!"

"We're gonna be in jail! Which way?" I asked.

"Follow the red sports car." Phyllis swayed. "Follow it off this river and we'll find a new car."

"River? You mean the freeway?" I scanned the rearview mirror, but I couldn't see the cop from this distance. We still had a chance. My heart eased its death grip on the inside of my rib cage. We wove through the obstacles of old car crashes. My knuckles turned white as I gripped the steering wheel. Bits of detritus sprayed up from our tires, pelting the undercarriage in a constant barrage of gravel. I kept scanning the traffic we passed, looking for a red sports car and hoping that we could slip through trouble again.

A bumper hung across the lane we were in, and I dove into a gap between two cars, lifting off the gas. The car jumped up at the sudden loss of torque, weaving in the wake of a pickup truck. The moment we passed the bumper, I cut back onto the shoulder and gunned it again.

"This is madness!" Mary yelled. "I can't even take a drink like this!"

"I'm serious, Ruth, I'm going to vomit!" Phyllis moaned again, clutching the back of my seat.

I spotted a sporty red car in front of a moving van. "Hold on, Phyllis, we're almost there!"

As the freeway curved to the left, I slipped into the space between the moving van and the red car, easing the break so as not to make much of a disturbance. A black Camaro charged up the shoulder on the left, burning rubber and sending a plume of dust into the air. A red light wobbled back and forth in the windshield, and I held my breath. Just one of the sheep.

"Oh, gods! Why?" Phyllis called. She coughed with a deep vibration through her chest.

"Baggie!" Mary yelled. "We've got a live one!"

Horace scrambled, searching the glove box. "There's nothing up here!"

"Just use the bag with the nail polish," I said, watching the cop pass us, burning into the horizon.

Mary dumped out my stolen goods, and the dragon hissed at being disturbed. More sounds of heaving accompanied the mad scramble in the back seat. I dragged my attention back to the road.

The red car turned off at the next nearest exit, and I followed. The small town in the middle of the desert had the feel of all crossroads: inns, bars, restaurants, and places to fuel up. The desert city had about as much promise of culture as the hazy sky had of raining in the next hour.

"This is a two-horse town," Horace said.

"Pull over, Ruth! I think she's about to blow!" Mary's tone reached a desperate pitch, and I turned off at the nearest gas station. The first pump had a man dressed in a red shirt and khaki shorts, filling the tank of an SUV. I turned into the spot on the opposite side of the same pump.

Phyllis fled as soon as the car got slow enough to escape. She made it to a trash can, leaned over and her whole body convulsed.

"Ma'am, are you okay?" the man pumping gas asked.

I killed the engine and stood out of the car, raising an eyebrow.

The man in his thirties looked from Phyllis to me. "Is she gonna be okay?"

"Sometimes you just gotta party like it's 1945," I said.

The man screwed up his face as if he were doing math to figure out what happened in 1945. I pursed my lips, ready to give him a history lesson, but his grandparents might not have been alive for D-Day and the signing of the treaties. Instead, I made a judgmental *Hmm*.

Phyllis waved at me like she could shoo away the annoying fly I'd become. "I swear, I'm never gonna do that again!"

I snorted. "Sure, you're not," I mumbled, rolling my eyes.

"Are we stopping here?" Mary asked.

"Yeah, it looks like we're gonna need a Baked Potato." I met Mary's gaze and widened my eyes just a little. "To go." I tilted my head so my gaze went over my glasses.

"Oh," Mary said as she realized what I was saying. She turned her back on me and went directly to the convenience store.

My dragon watched her go, but sat in the seat she'd just vacated, presumably leaving little soot prints everywhere she walked. Her bright red claws shone in the muddy morning light.

"A Baked Potato To-Go?" Horace asked, stepping out of the car. I nodded.

Phyllis leaned over and heaved again, but she put a thumb up, setting the plan into motion.

The man in the red shirt, frowned. "I don't think they sell baked potatoes in there." He pointed at the gas station convenience store.

Horace moved over to Phyllis. "Young man, if you could give me a hand, I need to get her inside."

The man in the red shirt looked like he'd been falsely accused, pointing at his chest with his thumb. "Me? Uh, ah, okay!" He finished putting the gas nozzle into the pump before he went to take one of Phyllis's arms. Horace took her other arm, and she stumbled.

As they righted themselves, Horace's hand slipped down the other man's back, as if he were trying to right the ship. Faster than a viper, Horace's hand snaked into the gap in the man's khakis, and a shiny set of keys slipped out of the man's pocket. Horace set the keys on top of a trash can quietly.

Phyllis moaned, playing up the whole moment—well maybe not all play, she had just been vomiting. "Thank you, kind young sir," she said as she pretended to faint.

"Just call me Bobby," he said. His earnest reply was like a shot to my heart. We were going to cause him a great deal of trouble.

I stepped up to the keys, my heart aching. A breeze pushed at my hands, chilling them with the bite of winter. Damn that bitch and her deals. The only good thing about having magic locked away from all of mankind was that we couldn't really make deals with her kind anymore.

A wave of heat crashed over me, the burning heat of summer, and I spun on the spot. In the corners around the outside of the store, everything suddenly became brighter, sharper, as if someone had taken a filter to my vision. The red and blue sign proclaiming beer brightened until the colors bled over the edge of the sign, leaking into everything around them.

Vines grew out of the petunia-filled flower box, arching up over the doorway to the convenience store. In seconds, new leaves unfolded, growing so quickly, they filled the buds, knocking off other leaves in their haste to unfurl. Thick flowers full of petals twirled as they bloomed into globes of dazzling red, yellow, and gold. Brighter than any nasturtiums, these flowers filled the air with the smell of jasmine and mimosa trees.

The doors were covered in plants, completely covering the glass. Light shone from under the door and through the crack, but no earthly light could shine as brightly as what flowed from under the edge of those portals. Breaking the concrete, great trees took root, exploding from the cracks in the gas station.

Around me, the other patrons of the gas station had stopped all movement. Everyone stared at what they had been doing, completely frozen. This audience was to be private.

The doors cracked open, revealing a woman dressed in the glory of the sun. Heat waves rippled the air around her face. I shielded my eyes, holding my hand up. The heat burned through my clothes and into my hand. Where Winter resembled a walking glacier, pale and blue, Summer had skin similar to an African woman. Like Winter, she adorned herself in her element, blazing fires of the sun in full summer. Red and gold flames licked off her head, circling her eyes so it was always hard to look directly at her. Flowers and plants grew out of the ground to meet her every footstep.

The Queen of Summer did not walk on the mortal realm's dirt, but her nearness indicated a certain extension of trust. She wasn't touching the ground, but she was standing on plants that did. It was as much of an olive branch I was likely to receive, and a clear indication she didn't intend battle today. Neither queen would set foot on the Earth. According to legend, the queens couldn't touch the ground because they are celestial beings.

Waves of heat welled off her, spilling into the air, and scorching everything around us. The advertisement on the side of the trashcan curled in the heat, distorting my view of the store and the other cars.

Flowers erupted from the concrete, turning their heads toward their mistress. As she walked, a great sunflower sprang from the sidewalk, and she plucked the bright yellow flower, pulling it up from its root. As she walked toward me, the concrete became paved in flowers and grass and moss. Petals rained down from the sky around her, transforming the gas station into the royal audience hall of the other great fae queen.

On reflex, I stepped back, opening the car door to let my dragon out.

Instead of attacking, my dragon chirped and ran toward the Summer Queen. My soot-covered cat wound between Summer's legs. Maybe she was calling on her cat powers to trip the queen. Alas, the creature of fire bent over and pet the other creature of fire.

Traitor.

Where Summer's hand touched the dragon, bright gold and orange markings appeared on my dragon. The dragon pranced like a playful horse, dancing along with the wind.

Summer laughed. The power ricocheted through my heart, bringing down the smell of a barbeque and the taste of corn, the scythe swinging to cut the small patch of hay at my grandparent's house in the central valley, the sweat dripping off my eyebrows as I pulled weeds. The sticky smell of a kitchen burning in the heat of summer stirred through me. The parks with their cut grass and drinks so casually taken everywhere, the picnics, the laughing. Then the other side of summer, the burning sun, the blistered skin, the nights so hot with not a breeze to stir the air so the very air would drown you. Summer.

As she approached me, the ground rose to meet her feet, transforming the trashcan into a throne. Green grew up around it, and by the time Summer sat on her throne, zinnias covered it in their pinks and yellows and golds and reds.

Sunflowers grew out the back of the trashcan, completing the effect of a throne.

Summer took her sunflower and rang it on the cement beneath her. One tap and the world filled with bears, cats, and deer. On the second tap, the sky cleared, letting a great shaft of light fall down upon her. With the third rap of her staff, the other fae courtiers appeared, all of them bedecked in the clothes of their season. Skirts of flowers, a leaf to make the perfect shirt. Only the oldest, most human-like had draped their bodies in cloth, and of that, only silk.

"You, wizard, are in breach of contract!" she declared, pointing at my chest.

"Isn't it early for you?" I blurted out rudely.

The queen paused and stared down her nose at me. Heat waves radiated off her as she narrowed her eyes at me. Then she took a breath, and the fae around her broke into laughter.

I stood my ground, and my dragon came to sit next to me, unveiling her true form.

The queen tilted her head, and all laughter ceased. "You are the oddest mortal I have ever met."

"Good," I said.

"Also the rudest."

"I don't have a deal with you. You're interrupting these people's lives." I pointed at one of the other patrons, grass had sprouted from her hair and flowers encircled her body.

"I would change that. I have an offer." She leaned forward, the excitement thick on her face.

"I'm not interested," I said crossing my arms.

"How can you know? You haven't heard my terms! I can help you in ways you don't even understand!"

I wobbled my head back and forth, as if I were really considering her offer. "Eh, I'm good. Your deals have a way of destroying everything they touch."

"I could grant you access to the fae source, access to me."

I snapped my mouth shut on a witty response and my head snapped up. "Access, what do you mean by access?"

A smile burned across her lips. "I mean that you would have access to my power, to me."

Something in her words spilled across my mind, casting my thoughts in the heat of summer. The way fire burns the sun-drenched forests, the heat, the way the wind came to swirl around those conflagrations, creating their own weather, stretching from the mountains to the sky. Her power combined with my natural talents would cover the land in flame and smoke. Everything would burn. Winter would have nowhere left to hide.

A chill swept up my spine that had nothing to do with weather.

I'd be a murderer. Indiscriminate destruction. Whole towns would fall before our combined power. Controlling my fire had always been the most difficult part of being a fire mage. Anytime you want more, you're one match away from a bonfire. With the power of Summer coursing through my veins? No.

"You know what that would do. Why offer it?"

A smile devoid of friendliness spread across her lips. "Winter intends to destroy all of you humans. She hates you. You are her very worst creation."

I blinked. "Winter created us?"

"You are born out of the dark and the cold." She did not add "silly human," but it was written on her face. "Her gift made everything you see. Everything you know. Everything is her doing."

"Everything?" I asked.

"There is not a thing you have seen with your own eyes that is not a direct result of Winter's sacrifice. And she is furious at your hubris."

"Everything my eyes have seen?"

She rolled her eyes. "Why are humans so obtuse? I'm offering you more power than you can possibly comprehend, and you're stuck on proving you have seen things. Can you not just trust my words?"

"But I've seen you. Did she make you too?"

Silence rippled through her courtiers who had, until that moment been politely ignoring us, playing with the various flowers and coaxing them out of the frozen people's hair. Now they all turned to watch, staring with their overly round eyes. Their pointed ears and teeth jutted out from under bangs and lips, casting them in the angles of truth. Gone were the rounded edges and curved smiles. Fae were not to be trusted under any circumstance, and they were telling me how rude I was being by being rude in return.

"It is funny to me," she said, breaking the threat spelled by her courtiers, "how ignorant of your own origins humans are. You don't even know where you came from, so I will give you a hint: before everything you know came to be in the form you know it, she was there. Bright, and yearning, and powerful. But she had to fall for you to live, and the evidence of her life before she was Winter is written in the stones of the sky." She pointed up as if the awning over the gas pumps weren't somehow blocking the view to the clouds above.

Stones in the sky? Did she mean the literal sky? Asteroids?

I swallowed, certain I was completely misunderstanding everything she said. And misunderstandings with the fae generally turned lethal. I kept my confusion to myself.

"Okay," I said drawing out the "o" as if I could talk myself into believing what she had just told me wasn't important. *Oh, Spoiler alert, as the kids say: it's going to be extremely important.* "So, you're offering me power, domination, and world destruction. Let's say I like the conflagration approach to land management—what's it going to cost?"

"It wouldn't be just heightened fire." She tilted her head down to look at me through her eyelashes. Her magic enveloped me, cascading around me in reds and golds, like I stood in the center of a firestorm. The heat burned my skin. I raised my hands to protect my face from the burning that could jump from merely uncomfortable to deadly flames in the flash of an eye.

Then I saw it.

My sagging, age-spotted skin tightened across my bones. The years melted away as I watched my hands turn into the hands of a young woman, just as I'd been when magic lived in the world.

My heart failed to strike for a beat, then hammered in my chest, blocking out my breath. The pain drained from my hips and knees, like I floated. My strength came back with a gasp of breath. I shifted my foot, testing the ground, and my thigh responded like a great coil, ready to spring forward in the blink of an eye. Even my vision sharpened.

How had I forgotten this feeling? Just the power of my body?

I took my next breath, caught between crying with relief and yelling at Summer.

"It's a trick," I said.

"No trick," Summer said. The smile on her lips burned. "You could have your youth back."

My breath came in shaky. My youth. To be young again.

To watch everyone around me grow old and die. My granddaughter, my great-grandchildren, all old and dead. It was easy to talk about starting over decades ago. When Dorothy went first, I broke in half and spilled out all the good she'd ever given me. I failed her and her memory as surely as I failed my own order.

And now people on the freeway had swastika tattoos. The nation had already elected a hateful leader, having completely forgotten that the next step is murdering people for their skin. How many times could I pull the world back from the brink of destruction? How much more would the world spin into chaos?

But that's unfair. The world had brilliance too. What was it worth to witness the innovations? Since the loss of magic, the world blossomed into a marvel of inventions as all the great minds sought out the only branches of magic left to mankind: science, engineering, and art. And the things we had made...

I'd have to actually learn how to use my stupid smart phone.

I scowled at Summer, her smug smile burning in her eyes.

"We have a deal then?" she asked.

"You never said what you wanted in return." I pushed my glasses back up my nose. They blurred my vision, but they were made of human innovation, and I needed something to filter out the pure intoxication of Summer and her gifts.

"Don't make me beg, Ruth. You broke a great and powerful contract. I've always had my eye on humanity, and I mean to keep it that way. Even now, humanity begs me to take my rightful place as your great ruler. The constant increase in temperatures makes me feel more and more welcome in your realm."

I folded my arms. "What do you want from me, Summer?"

She rolled her eyes, leaning her head toward me. "Fine, you want a price? I'll give you a price." She held her hand out in front of her, unwrapping her fingers from her fist one by one to reveal a gold gem the size of my fist. It blazed with the power of summer, heat radiating off it, but the torrents of magic pulsed through it as well.

Surreptitiously, I let some of that magic flow into the channels where I held my power, filling the deep reservoir with the bright powers of Summer.

"You have broken with Winter, and she means to break you, to bend you to her will. I would offer an alternative." The power radiated from the fist-sized ball of fire. Strands of flames split from the ball, fanning out like a solar prominence before being sucked back into the power source. Even as I tried to steal some, it burned, searing my insides, but she kept talking, unaware of its effects on me. "In exchange for this, I want your Source. Bring it to me. I will keep it forever from Winter. You will never have to worry about her again. She will never be able to hunt you or your people. Forever, you will all be free of her."

The word "free" echoed through my head, the power of her intent ringing the truth in her words. She would kill Winter if she had the Source. Kill winter. Forever summer.

I gasped. "I don't have it. I have to go get it." Then I took a breath to control myself and my emotions. "I cannot faithfully enter a contract if I cannot guarantee the outcome." The formal words cut through the court, who all stared again.

Her smile had faded and the heat radiating off Summer singed her fae court. They turned their heads, holding up arms as if they could block the power of the heat. "When Winter owns you, I will buy you from her. You will be the star of my entertainment. I'm sure you know: I don't play nice with the things I buy."

"So, you'll give me access to your power if I bring you the Source of all of human magic? Is that about right?" I tilted my head to the side. "And what would you do with that exactly?"

Summer leaned her head back and a ray of sunshine burned through the clouds, impossibly shining through the overhang protecting the gas pumps. The power of it radiated through the gas station and all the plants grew taller, flowers upon flowers, until the grown-over gas pumps could have been gateways to Underhill.

She reached toward me and my hand warmed suddenly. "Become my champion." A sword of pure sunlight materialized in front of me. Through my gift and command of fire, the sword thrummed in my mind, the most potent flame I'd ever seen. My fingers closed on the hilt of a sword made of pure sunlight. The flowers turned toward me, bathing in the power of the sword in my hand.

As the power spilled into my mind and the channels of magic, knowledge came. Suddenly, I knew the angle of the sun, the relative position in the whole solar system, the location of the moon, the height of trees, the swell of the ocean. The ripple of breezes, and where the inflammable parts of air lived. The delicate dance between fire and air revealed itself to me, how to turn a raging flame, how to manipulate the smallest parts of the air so the fire came faster, hotter, burned more efficiently, and even the parts of those standing around who were vulnerable to fire and how.

The sword burned my hand, the hot pressure of power and the reactions of a purely human body caught up to me. I dropped the sword of sunshine at my feet. It burned the carpet of flowers and grass, and the court laughed.

"Silly human," Summer said. "You can't touch pure power until you say yes." The smile on her lips burned brighter. "So, do we have a deal?"

I stared at the burn mark on the ground. The faint image of a sword lay at my feet. Tears streaked my cheeks as I tried to remember what the sword had shown me, but in the seconds that passed, the light it had shined in me faded to a fragile memory, growing more distant with each passing breath.

Youth, power, a place.

All I had to do was make sure no human ever had a hope of wielding the power of magic without being a minion of one of the fae queens. No human would ever have the power to defend our people against these sharks, never dealing fairly. My fingers stung, the heat still radiating through them, right down to my bones.

Never deal with fae. Everyone knew that.

I turned over my hand, seeing the burn. Damn fae, screwing up everything. "I bring you the only connection humanity has with magic, and you'll turn me into your champion? Is that right?"

Her smile froze, and she narrowed her eyes at me. "Do not turn me down lightly, mortal. I will be there in every moment between now and the time you finally resolve your dispute with Winter. You can never be rid of me."

"I don't want to be rid of you, Summer," I said quickly, to ease some of her bruised ego. "But you're asking me to deny magic to every human forever. I can't do that to my people. No matter how beautiful and powerful your gifts. I could never knowingly destroy the hope of my kind."

"There hasn't been a new mage in almost a hundred years. How long will you hold out in the hopes there's another?" Summer scoffed.

"I don't expect you to understand, great queen," I added hastily. "But I have to believe there will be more."

"That's your final answer?"

I nodded. "Yes. Though I do appreciate your kind offer."

Summer narrowed her eyes at me. "Beware, human, I will be with you at every step. And we are not friends!"

My dragon hissed, rising to her full height, flames erupting from her fur. A great crack rang through the world, and suddenly, the whole gas station was back to normal. My dragon shrank to her cat size, suddenly a sweet mewling kitty and not a growling dragon ready to take on the power of the sun.

Age returned to me, like someone took the dial for gravity and turned it steadily up until my whole body ached again. My knee and hip pulsed with waves of pain, as if they particularly disagreed with being toyed with.

Mary walked right through a place where just a second ago, a tree of Summer's court had been. "What's going on, Ruth? I thought you wanted a baked potato to go?"

"Abort," I said.

Her gaze scoured me. "What just happened?"

"Just get the others, we have to get out of here."

Mary leaned toward me and spoke from the side of her mouth. "That's why we were pulling a heist."

I grabbed the keys on the edge of the trash can with my left hand, carefully not looking at my right hand. Had she burned me? Or had it faded with Summer's Court?

Crossing the pavement, I hobbled, barely able to take steps as my hip and knee moved directly from Annoyed to You'll Need a Cortisone Shot to Walk Straight. I almost turned around to go back to the car for a rest, but I'd reached the halfway point. Like Lady Macbeth said, "It would be harder to go back." I took a fortifying breath, marveling at how the cement held no evidence of the great garden Summer had grown in it. Fae.

The Quick Mart door chimed as I pushed it open. Horace stood at the corner near the bathroom, putting away his phone. Phyllis sat on a display of soda cans in twelve-pack boxes. Our mark held a cup of water for her.

"Young man," I said. "I think you dropped these outside." I held out the keys to him.

He checked his pockets, and then reflexively took the keys, turning them over in his hand like a mother inspecting a previously missing child for injury.

Horace raised an eyebrow at me and threw up his hands. When I turned back, Phyllis scowled at me.

"No, it looks like I'm starting to feel better," she said to the young man. Then she turned on the smile and caught him in the beam of her gratitude. "Oh, dear, I don't want to hold you up. And look, my friends are all here. You should get on your way."

The man patted her on the back. "You take care of yourself."

"Always," Phyllis said.

Duplicity completely lost on the mark, he wandered out of the store as we watched.

Phyllis hit me with the back of her hand. "What the hell was that for? I had him on the hook. I bet he would have *given* us that car if I'd asked nicely."

"Why the abort?" Horace asked.

"I came to my senses," I said pushing back through the glass door to the chime of the greeting bell. "Besides, if we took it now, the cops would know exactly which car we were in and where we were in two minutes. We need a bigger head start for the next car."

Phyllis nodded. "My tummy still hurts. Stupid Adderall."

Horace handed her a roll of Tums. "It worked, though. You were spot on."

She shook her head. "If I never have to take that crap again, it'll be too soon."

Chapter Eleven

"Well, what are we going to do for a car?" Horace asked. "The cops are already on our tail. We need to ditch and run."

"It's time for magic," I said. As we drove down the street, we passed numerous businesses. Their signs crowded into the street like they had a contest to see who could get the highest and closest to the road. One proclaimed auto repair with a big yellow hexagon, a knockoff of a franchise. The parking lot swam in derelict vehicles. I slowed, pulling to a stop on the side of the road.

"What are we doing?" Mary asked. "We can't rob these guys."

"Oh yes, we can. And it's perfect!"

"Perfectly stupid, you mean," Phyllis interjected. "Earth to Ruth! These cars are already broken!"

"Exactly, and if it's by chance a faulty ignition, I can start the car."

Horace turned to me. "You've lost your marbles. How are you going to maintain that much magic?"

"A witch never tells her secrets!" Especially when that secret was that Summer had filled my tanks, and I'd happily just not said anything. I popped open the door and looked for my cane. I'd need it to get up. "Mary, is my cane back there?"

"I thought you were feeling better," she said rooting around at the floor of the car. "Here you go."

"Thanks. My bones are just suddenly very aware of their age. Turns out, being 140 feels about like 140."

Phyllis snorted. "Old people."

Horace laughed, and Mary groaned. Phyllis was younger by almost five years.

I drove my cane into the ground like a railroad spike and heaved myself to my feet. My hip popped, but I couldn't tell if it helped or hurt my leg. I hobbled up to the gate and took the lock into my free hand. I turned my back to hide what I was doing from the others. They didn't need to know I was suddenly flush with power. Pinching the stem of the lock, I dropped just the right amount of heat into the metal. It slagged in my hand, and I swiveled the lock open. The gate rattled as I pulled open the latch. "Bring the bags!" I called back to the car as I pushed the gate wide enough to let a small car through.

My hip hitched, and my gait went from terrible to glacial. Around me the derelict remains of cars waited, hopeful they'd run someday. I scanned the lot, but I didn't have any way to tell which car only needed a little hot wiring. "Phyllis, which of these are just missing the ignition? Or just have bad spark plugs?"

She pushed through the gate, dragging her bag. "How the hell am I supposed to know, you old bat?"

I rolled my eyes at her. "I don't know, Phyllis," I said in a forced wooden voice. "Maybe you could use your powers?"

Phyllis narrowed her eyes at me. "You can't just play with the future like it's a toy." She stalked up to me so she could glare me right in the eye.

I tilted my head to the side and dropped my voice. "I dropped the potato because we have two queens on our tail."

Her eyes went wide, showing the whites around her dark irises. "Oh."

I nodded. "Yeah, 'Oh' is right."

Phyllis dropped her voice suddenly. "Do the others know?" she asked.

I shook my head only slightly. Horace and Mary were watching as they made their way through the gate with their luggage.

Phyllis pursed her lips together. "What did she offer you?"

"Youth and power."

She raised an eyebrow. "Oh, is that all? And I'm sure she offered you a very reasonable price."

"Summer wants the Source."

A bark of laughter escaped her mouth. "Is that all? Imagine."

A *hmmph* of agreement puffed through my nostrils. My dragon picked that moment to storm over and aggressively rub against my leg. Maybe dragons needed a bit of grooming? She purred violently.

"Come on, Brigid, we have work to do." I turned back to the cars.

"You named your dragon after the fire goddess?" Phyllis asked.

"She likes it." I pointed, and my dragon had already pounced on a hapless mouse.

She presented the kill to me before happily crushing the furry rodent in her mouth. The bones snapped horribly. Phyllis turned green again, weaving on her feet.

Mary rushed up and caught Phyllis's arm. "Are you alright?"

"That dragon will be the end of me."

Brigid flicked her tail in the air and pranced between the cars.

"We could make this all go a lot faster if you just said which car," I pointed out.

"Try the classic in the corner." She pointed at a nearly derelict Honda.

"But it's so old!" I said.

Phyllis rolled her eyes. "You want the future? I give you our future!" She tilted her head and scrunched her lips together.

"Fine, give me your makeup kit." I held out my hand.

"What? No! I'm not giving you my—do you know how long it takes to put one of those together?"

I rolled my eyes. "I don't want to do a makeover. I just need your blenders. And you use the old school triangles, now hand one over."

Phyllis muttered something about "old school" nonsense as she popped open her wheelie bag. Perfectly packed on top, her makeup bag sat just waiting for an emergency application of something. Phyllis took out the bag, opened one of its pouches, and handed over a blending triangle.

"Thank you," I said.

"You're welcome," she said, but she was already ignoring me, staring at her reflection in a compact, checking for reapplication.

I went over to the black Honda and stuffed the triangle between the window and the rubber stopper. Inside, the car was mostly clean except for a tree-shaped air freshener and an extra panel of flip switches. The spoiler on the back was three times larger than necessary, giving it the appearance of an oversized shopping cart.

Peering into the gap held open by the makeup applicator, I found the door lock latch. "Horace! You still have that slim jim?"

"I gave up boosting cars, Ruth!" he yelled back.

"Sure you did. Pop the door."

He sighed and dragged his bag over to me. "Hmm, 90s make. It won't even have a car alarm." He turned back to me. "You know, with those upgrades in there, the owner will have a kill switch somewhere. We won't be able to hotwire it."

I lined him up in my gaze. "Horace, I don't know how to break this to you, but I'm a fire witch."

He narrowed his eyes at me. "And what does that have to do with making the car go?"

"Fire. I can manifest fire if I have a ready source. We have a ready source." I pointed at Brigid, who chased a rat under a car.

"Oh gods, I'm getting into a literal death trap fueled by a dragon and driven by a witch. I'm losing my mind."

"You never really used magic the way the rest of us did," I said.

He chewed on his lip. "Magic has used me plenty. Besides, it's hard to make people believe in it, and what it can do to you—especially over time. People always believe what they see. That's why I took so many pictures at Bikini. Too bad someone stole my old shaving kit. I'd made it past the State Department boys only to lose the damn thing to a common thief. All my film was in that kit."

I raised an eyebrow at him. "And you don't think the state boys didn't just take your shaving kit to make you think it was theft and not censorship?"

Horace blinked at me. He struck the side of his head. "I should charge them for the shaving kit!"

"Just pop the door," I said pointing at the car with my cane.

"Fine!" He bent over his bag and fished out a jimmy stick. "It's not gonna start."

"You just leave that part to me. Every car wants to go."

He scowled at me, not even watching as he popped open the door. "Your Highness!"

"Thank you, kind sir." I sat on the edge of the seat, reached into the console, and pulled the trunk release. "Load her up!"

Horace glowered at me but moved to the back to drop his bag in the trunk. While the others did the same, I rolled down the window a crack. Phyllis shook her head as she came up to me. She reached across my lap and flipped up a panel next to the cup holder. A toggle switch sat inside.

"That should help. Did you take your meds yet?" she asked.

I scowled at her. I'd hoped magic would reduce my need of them. Magic had always healed us, and I didn't feel like taking medication now that magic was back—well, sort of back.

Mary passed me my stolen bag. "Now, Ruth."

I set the bag on my lap and started digging through it. "I just got excited is all. I'm not trying to make a problem!"

"I remember what you're like when you start into the magic," Mary said.

My heart froze in my chest. Magic changed people. Magic made me different. Dorothy knew what I was like. She always said she preferred me better after magic went away. Less bossy. More likely to compromise. Fire didn't have to compromise. Fire ate whatever it wanted, and only a few things could really stop it.

I made eye contact with Mary. She nodded. I'd moved into bossy.

But this was the world we were saving.

I clenched my jaw. "Thank you," I said softly, taking out my pills and pulled out all of the ones I'd missed. I still hated taking them.

Horace slammed the trunk shut. "You know we have a five-disc changer back there! We could really cruise in this thing."

"Yeah, check under the hood," I said, before tossing pills into my mouth.

Mumbling, Horace walked to the front, and I pulled the hood release. He dropped it back down. "It's fine. He's probably having the sparkplugs replaced or something."

"How do you know it's a guy?" Phyllis asked.

"This just seems like a guy's kind of car."

Mary rolled her eyes. "I'm driving. Move into the back, Ruth. We can't have you driving, anyway, if you're running the fire, we need you concentrating on making it go, not steering it."

"What about the rum?" I asked.

"I haven't had any yet," she said. "More's the pity."

I vacated the front seat, and Mary took it like she was prepping for a rally race. "This is a nice rig." She traced her finger across the roll bar. "I wonder what she did with this car."

Horace pinched his lips together so they looked like a butthole, but said nothing. He slid into the passenger side and leaned across the console. Deftly, he pulled the ignition off the steering column. "This is pointless."

Mary raised her eyebrow at him. "Yes, it is pointless to assume someone's gender based on the car they drive. It's not like you need a dick to drive like one."

Phyllis nodded. "Mmmm-hmmm."

I pulled open the door to the back seat and sat down, fussing with my cane. The window groaned as I cranked the glass down. The smell of degrading vinyl permeated everything. Horace fumbled with the ignition, grumbling the whole time.

"There, is that enough? Or do you need more to get it going?" Horace asked.

I reached out with my mind and found the ignition chamber, envisioning a small explosion in the column. The engine gave a rough groan as it turned over but failed to catch.

"Do we need gas?" Mary asked. She reached forward and tapped on the dash gauge. "These cars had pretty reliable displays, didn't they?"

"I wouldn't know," Phyllis said. "I missed the 90s to a group of new age hippies. We used bikes."

A spark flew across the wires, and Horace swore, putting his fingers in his mouth. "The meter should be fine. Try again!"

I sent the magic through the channels in my soul. The power of summer flared through me, making me hot, and I pushed the door open wider. I eased into the flow of power, closing my eyes to envision the spell better. The car jumped as the engine turned over like a person coughing. Again, it fell dead. The power of the Summer Court radiated through me, and I rolled down my window further.

"Oh, sorry, ladies," Horace said. "I forgot to give it enough power to let the fuel pump work. Sorry." He leaned back under the column and again started fussing with the wires.

The window didn't let in enough air, and I fanned myself.

"What's wrong with you?" Mary asked.

"Nothing, just a hot flash."

"Aren't you a century too old for those?" Phyllis asked.

Mary snorted.

I growled. "You didn't take this long in Austria, Horace."

"In Austria, I hadn't had my hips replaced."

A cat scream shattered through the dull rumble of ever-present freeway traffic. A black streak zoomed across the parking lot. The fuzz ball of terror hit the car, leaving a trail of soot and claw marks on my leg as my dragon hit my lap. Faster than a snake, she pivoted and hissed back the way she'd come.

I scanned the cars for what could possibly scare a dragon. Dried weeds clustered in the cracks of pavement, bending in the wind. A gust of desert air pushed sand across the parking lot. A bit of brown flapped just at the edge of the top of a car hood, and I craned my head to see if I could tell what it was.

The great Saint Bernard chose that exact moment to leap over an inconveniently placed car. As the two hundred and fifty pounds of war dog cleared the hood of an early 2000s Mini Cooper, it released a bark. The single pulse of sound rang through the air like a mortar shot, bouncing off my chest.

"Oh shit!" Mary yelled.

Frantically, I pulled on the window bar, rolling it up as fast as I could. My dragon climbed me like a tree to hiss at the dog driving down the row of parked cars at us like a feral monster.

"Is it part werewolf?" Horace asked.

"Shut up and get the car going!" Mary yelled, rolling up her window desperately.

The dog reached the car, pushing its giant head through the gap between my window and the door. It wedged its snout in and released another massive bark. Slimy dog drool sprayed the inside of the car. Its hot breath filled the car in a muggy fog of dog stink.

"Cross the bloody wires!" Mary yelled.

Horace hit the wires again, and I launched as much power as I dared into the car. The engine turned over with a roar, and the dog snarled, renewing its efforts to force its way past the glass. I focused on pulling fire from the dragon—not difficult as she stood on my shoulder hissing at the horse-sized dog trying to eat us—and pouring it through the combustion chambers.

The claws tacked to the side of my shoulder tightened as the dragon unleashed a deep yowl at the dog. She dove forward, swiping the side of the dog's muzzle. Shiny red claws blazed in the sun breaking through the clouds. The perfect manicure for a dragon. The dog's head pulled hastily back from the car, leaving us with a dog-free window.

The engine revved, and Mary wasted no time, throwing the hammer back into reverse. The car lurched backward, fueled by the fire of a dragon and the power of Summer. She turned as we raced backward, throwing the car into a drift and swinging the front end around like a whip. Mary slammed the gear shift forward and smashed the gas. The force of acceleration threw us back into our seats.

Phyllis, white knuckled and bracing with her hand locked on the overhead bar, yelled. "Whoop!"

"Are you nuts?" Horace screamed. His fingers curled around the center console, as he stomped on the floor, as if a magical passenger brake pedal would manifest.

"Shut up and put your seat belt on, Horace!" Mary yelled and threw the car into a violent turn.

The dog chased us, scrabbling at the pavement like a cartoon.

Horace chanced it, and let go of the center console, pulling the seatbelt across his body. Mary pulled the steering wheel hard over, dropping the car into another reckless slide. We all held on, bracing for the moment we hit a crack in the pavement and rolled. Mary cranked the wheel like a demolition derby monster. We bounced with the car, captives of physics. The second the wheels pointed in the direction we wanted to go, Mary slammed the gas, driving us into the cushions again.

"Here he comes!" Phyllis yelled.

The dog jumped onto the hood of the car. He stood on the hood, legs splayed for balance, hackles raised across his back.

"Good doggy!" Horace called.

The dog barked, spraying the windshield in an impossible river of slime.

Horace braced back into his seat.

Mary hit the windshield wipers and pulled back on the stick to spray the windshield. The dog's foot blocked one of the sprayers, hitting him in the face with fluid. "Get off, dog."

She slammed on the breaks. The dog slid off, inch by inch, dragging deep gouges in the paint across the hood. The sound of dog claws against the metal and paint echoed through the cabin.

"Fine, you want to see me do it backward?" And Mary dropped the gear shaft into reverse again. She put her arm up on Horace's chair and hit the gas before the dog could regain his footing.

The car rocketed backward, throwing me into my seatbelt. My dragon lost traction on my shoulder, and the engine hiccupped. She settled into my lap with a withering glare, as if the driving was somehow my fault. I spared a hand from bracing myself to brace her and return the power to the engine.

The dog kept trying to catch up to the car, but every time he jumped, Mary dodged until we made the gate. The gate tore off the side view mirror, but the dog didn't cross over the edge of his territory. He stood, barking at us as Mary put the car into a more sedate gear and pulled away on the road.

Chapter Twelve

The stars stared down on me, as if to tell me they knew all my crimes. Unlikely, given the breadth of my failings. And yet, the dragon sat purring in my lap and the gentle whoosh of the freeway ran a steady beat under the floorboards of the car. Horace stabbed at his eyes, and Phyllis snored from the front passenger seat. Mary sat next to me, her head lolling against the headrest, but her eyes blinked open when we hit a bump. She smiled, and my heart lightened even as the very last dregs of Summer's power slid through me. I'd lost count of the states, but Texas never let a girl forget which state she was in.

The car dodged to the side as Horace's face cracked open a yawn. "I think that might be all I've got today."

"Pull over. I'm sure there's somewhere to stay," Mary said.

"We could always just park and sleep in the car," he suggested.

"Don't be ridiculous, Horace. I haven't slept in the backseat since the sixties," Mary said. "I'm not breaking my streak."

Horace slowed the car, and I eased back on how much power poured through the engine. He took the first exit, and we drove through Amarillo, Texas approaching midnight on a Sunday.

A giant red sign promised endless ribs, and my stomach growled.

"You should feed your dragon," Mary said. "Both of them."

I snorted. "My stomach is all bark, no bite. I can't eat like I used to."

"That's a shame," Mary said, a wicked spark flaring to life in her eyes.

My cheeks burned.

As we bumped down the frontage road, we passed gas stations, hotels, eateries, and an endless strip mall, made daunting by the hour and the lighting. "Are you waiting for a

Hyatt?" I asked. Brigid yawned and stretched, purring. She'd worked hard today too. She needed as much of an opportunity to eat up and rest as I did.

"Well, we can't just stay at any place, can we? It'll let the pokey know where we are. And I thought we were avoiding that."

I chewed on his words. "You have a point."

"And we need a plan for once we get to Washington," Mary said.

"One impossible task at a time." I watched the passing signs, hoping one might magically say, *Don't worry, we won't tell the cops on you.*

Horace turned off the frontage road and the lights of the city diminished as the business rolled over from trying to land money from travelers to storefronts for locals. Horace pointed. "Oh, now that place looks like a fine establishment."

The sign read *No Tell MoTel.*

I nodded, the movement putting my world into a spin. "It's perfect."

"What?" The car jerked as he tried to turn around to look at me. "I was making a joke."

"Who else is likely to have a room we can use that won't need an ID?"

Mary chimed in. "I bet they take cash, too."

"You have a lot of experience with places like this?" I teased.

Mary's cheeks flushed. I cleared my throat and pet Brigid to cover the moment.

Horace shook his head. "Well, I guess we have a mission."

"Are you blushing, Horace?" Mary asked.

"It's not every night I get to sleep in a skeevy hotel with three older women."

"As I recall," Mary said, tilting her head, "you didn't throw this much of a fit when we were hiding out in a brothel in Paris."

"That was war!" Horace argued.

"What do you think this is?" I asked.

He relented, turning around the block to get back to the entrance of the seedy motel. In the dark of night, the mostly empty parking lot had the desperate smell of a hotel fifty years out of date and not looking to get a remodel anytime soon. The low building squatted on the side of the road with only a cursory attempt at a parking lot. Weeds taller than the landscape pushed through the blacktop.

"We're staying here?" Phyllis asked, her voice thick with sleep. "Do they charge extra for the bed bugs, or are they a convenience item?"

Mary pushed open the door, and the wind whipped, pulling it out of her hand. The cold air spilled into the car, a sharp wake up call. "Honestly, haven't you heard? Bed bugs are the new fad diet. You eat nothing but bugs and you lose weight." She pushed the door open and started toward the sign that said "office."

I took out my cane and planted it in the ground before trying to stand. I rocked to build up momentum and nearly toppled out of the car when my hip gave me a one-fingered salute. Still, I hobbled after Mary, just travelling at half the speed.

By the time I made it to the office, Mary sprang back out again. "Shoulda got them hips when they were on sale!" She sped past me, showing off her cyborg hardware.

"Bitch."

"Witch."

"Which room are we in?" Phyllis asked. She rubbed at her back as if she could erase the twelve hours of being folded up in a car.

"Lucky number seven!" Mary tossed a set of keys over the car.

The keys bounced off Horace's chest. "Damn it!"

Brigid chirped and retrieved the keys, darting back to me, keys in her mouth. She plopped in front of me and tilted her head to the side. "Now there's a good dragon."

The heat from the keys warmed my hands, reminding me how much my joint pain was from just changing elevation so much today. I laid my knuckles in the crook of my opposite hand, sandwiching the warm keys between them. Damn road trip would be the end of me.

Horace just shook his head at me. "That damn dragon will give us away, acting like a dog." He turned to Brigid. "You're supposed to be the most powerful creature on the planet, maybe act like it!"

Brigid took his advice by rubbing against my leg with a throaty purr. Mary grabbed her bag and mine and made for lucky number seven. "Come on, *ladies*! The night is burning the dark faster than a candle!"

Horace limped. Phyllis bent over her bag, and I took short, shuffling steps. The crack team, 'cause we cracked. And creaked. And if the wind blew, we'd fall right over.

Oh gods, how am I going to beat Winter like this? No one here can even fight.

This is going to be the last spring I see.

I took a deep breath to take it in. Moments when the future unfolded should hold some meaning or significance. The first plum tree blossoms should have fallen artfully across my path, showing the ephemeral nature of life on the harsh edge of winter.

Instead, someone honked on the frontage road, and the other driver yelled back an anatomically improbable command. The parking lot smelled of vomit and burned cigarettes.

When I stepped through the door, the bright orange, shag carpet crunched with each step. I caught Mary in my laser beam gaze, but she shrugged.

"You want the Embassy Suites, then I recommend we not be running from the law or carry stacks of cash—which, I'll note, you didn't grab at the pharmacy this morning."

I scowled back, but she had a point. We didn't have a ton of money and if things didn't start looking up, we'd spend the rest of this trip sleeping in the car. As I hobbled in, I checked the amount of power still running through my veins. The more I picked up magic, the more magic I could pick up. One of the great oddities of magic: magic begets magic. So, the most powerful become more powerful. But those who shun their gift will find it always scarce.

Even with my recent expansions, the remaining power sloshed around like the last fifth of a glass of water, eager to splash, but not enough to soak. I'd have to keep my senses open to rogue breakthroughs—and of course, hope the degenerating spell held together long enough that we could get it out of the case before some overly curious patron pointed out the Source of Magic to some docent at the museum.

My stomach growled, but given the state of the room, my tummy would just have to wait. Before we could even discuss arrangements, Horace lay out on one of the beds, and Phyllis climbed into the other. A stiff couch with faux leather looked like the perfect spot for me.

Brigid meowed at Horace's bag. <Warm.>

I pursed my lips. "If you want to be warm, you can sleep next to me." Without waiting for a reply, I stretched out—well, some definition of the word stretched—and lay across the couch. As my weary bones dragged my mind into the world of slumber, my thoughts caught along the edges of my conversation with Summer. Everything I'd ever seen with my own eyes came from Winter? But that would be the whole Earth. I'd seen meteorites—held them in my hand back in the day!—so did she mean that too? Could she have been talking in metaphor or maybe just hyperbole?

"Everything" just wasn't possible. I'd seen the stars. Had Winter made those too? What exactly were the fae queens?

A darkness swallowed my conscious thoughts, and I fell into a boneless, dreamless sleep.

* * *

Brigid jumped off me, leaving four indentations on my stomach where she'd been merrily sleeping.

"Oof." I rubbed at my abused stomach. The barest sketches of pink and yellow touched the bit of sky leaking through the drapes. I tugged at the sweater someone had draped over my shoulders and moved to roll onto my side. My back took that moment to mount a full rebellion, seizing like a '57 Chevy in the summer of '83.

Stupid couch, hard as a rock. See also, stupid witch thinking she could sleep on a damn hotel couch like someone three decades younger.

The bathroom door pushed open just a touch, and light spilled through as Brigid explored the room. Odd, I've never slept in the same room as a dragon until last night. She didn't snore, so that was nice—well, more likely she didn't snore *louder* than me.

A clink came from the bathroom followed by Horace grunting. "Eh, damn it cat, get out of my stuff!" He spoke sotto voce as if trying not to wake us up.

Mary snored pleasantly, and Phyllis mumbled in her sleep, and for a perfect moment everything seemed so very like another hair-brained mission, I could almost taste the campfire. I stretched my poor back, and compared the two moments in my life, finding this moment somewhat lacking. We hadn't even set a guard—of course, with a locking door, and all that. Still, we shouldn't have been so reliant on a lock. Winter could attack us at any point for any reason.

Though, to be fair, this trip wasn't winning on the creature comforts level. I hadn't slept on the ground since a camping trip in the 90s, and there was no way I was convincing these old bones that was okay. Oh, and heaters were nice.

"Gods, cat—dragon—whatever you are, shoo!" Horace whispered. From the sound of water and scraping, he was shaving.

Pitching my attention to the bathroom in case I had to go rescue Horace from the loving rubs of my dragon, I wrestled with the couch. It won, of course, refusing to give up any hope of a comfortable sleeping area.

Another clink rang out as Brigid knocked over Horace's can of shaving cream.

"Damn cat!" he hissed.

I pushed the sweater off, ready to go rescue Horace when it happened again: magic returned in full force. The power of it radiated through the very walls. It vibrated in the couch and the power in my blood answered its call. Greedily, I opened up my channels, drawing in as much power as I could.

Where Summer filled me with the heat of the sun, and Winter traded in the raw power of storms and cold and the vast nothing of the frozen planes. Human magic, the Source, tasted more like a cross between apple pies and steel forges. Beauty and power and design, but also life and growth, things green and cultivated, as if this whole world had evolved just for us. And what an image, when the dust that made our whole solar system had collapsed into planets and a star, it had all been moving with the inevitable direction to this moment, and the Source felt like the conductor in the great symphony of life and the eventual rise of humans.

As the power coursed through my channels—as if they were veins—I drank in the history of everything. And regret threatened to swallow me. What had I done? How had I decided to go without this? And what had happened to humanity in the time since we'd locked it away? We were worse off than ever, more divided than ever, and now we didn't even have the miracles of magic.

Not that we ever shared magic.

Our Orders had been too jealous of our magic. The whole point of World War II had been about the consolidation of power, not just armies, but magic. We never would have come together in a meaningful way because the division of magical power had always been contentious. Then I took away the temptation for everyone like an angry mother. If you can't play nice, then no one gets it.

Damn, I've been such a fool.

"That damned dragon!" Horace's voice cut through my ruminations.

Brigid growled, and the sound of the two wrestling over something came from the bathroom.

Almost frantically now, I tried to pull more power to me, burning my channels in the hopes of having enough power. But enough for what? Without the help of Summer's power pouring through my veins, I wouldn't be able to channel dragon fire to a car all day. We'd need a car that could operate on its own.

Some mad scrambling came from the bathroom, as Horace packed up his shaving kit. The power leaking through the world faded.

I scrambled to draw in the remaining bits of magic. Every scrap I could reach, I ruthlessly stuffed into my channels of magic. But like the previous times, the valve shut off, and I hesitated in that moment where I could keep pulling magic in, as I'd leak as much or more as I could pull.

The ambient magic wavered through the room, absorbing into the fabric of reality.

"Stupid cat—dragon—thing! Stay out of my stuff," Horace said.

Resigned to the loss of magic, I sat up to go rescue my dragon.

A forceful knock cracked through the room. "Police! Open up!"

"What?" Mary whispered.

"Oh shit!" Phyllis said, sitting up in the bed, her eye mask still on. "They found me!"

The voice from the door called again, forceful. "We have you surrounded, open the door!"

Horace dropped to his knees in the bathroom, dragging his shaving kit behind him. "What the hell is this?"

"The police," I said, counting exits in my head, and only coming up with the door.

"We'll give you to the count of three then we're coming in!" the policeman called through the door.

"Give us a minute to dress!" Phyllis called.

"What are you doing?" Mary hissed.

"We need time for a plan," Phyllis whispered.

"What plan?" Horace asked. "These are the *police*. They've caught us."

Fresh magic poured through my veins, and Brigid caught my eye with her orange and gold ones. Eyes gold like the sky in Underhill, and that gave me a terrible idea.

"They haven't caught us yet," I said.

Mary caught my idea before the hint of it faded from my mind. "Oh no. No! No, no, no! We can't."

"I'm open to ideas," I whispered back.

Brigid made a dive for Horace's shaving kit, but he snatched it away. "Damn dragon likes shaving cream!"

"Get close, my range is terrible." I held out my arms as if trying to round up ducklings.

"Horace, get your damn pills," Phyllis said as she grabbed her bag and my bag.

Horace grabbed his duffle and clutched his shaving kit to his chest. "This is insane. Remember Austria?"

As I dug into the channels around me, I squared him in my gaze. "Vividly."

"Open up!" the police yelled from the other side of the door.

Everyone's head snapped to the door as we all huddled on the ground of a sleezy hotel room. Brigid abandoned Horace and stared at me. *<Fire?>* she thought.

The image of a dragon erupting from the motel room at the cops who were probably just trying to pick up a bunch of runaway senior citizens had a certain appeal to it. The problem came in the aftermath. Brigid's fire would burn them for real. Best to run through the only other door we had.

"Not just yet sweetie, but I'm sure we'll need it real soon." I licked my lips, preparing for the spell to come.

Brigid meowed her disappointment at not getting to light everything on fire.

I gathered the power within me and focused it on the place where reality folded. The form of the spell flashed through my mind. I'd never worked it without a ritual or an invitation. There were problems with going to the fae lands. I had only tried the spell once before we locked up the Source, and it had not gone well. It would be worse today.

A knock rang out from the door. "Open up, Mrs. Westings! We know you're in there!"

All eyes turned to me, but the magic flowed from me, swirling around the four of us. The fire of my magic burned in the air, lighting the way for the trail to come. I rocked in rhythm to the power, falling into its song as if it beat in my chest instead of my heart. The power manifested around us, burning in the air, painting the room in sparking gold and red and orange. Scorch marks appeared on the shag around us, and everyone leaned in closer.

A deep thump rang out from the door and wood cracked.

The final piece of power connected the spell into a great circle around us, and the fire of my power roared to life. The flames glittered, shot through with gold and lightning, blazing around us like some ritual sacrifice from medieval times.

The door gave way under the assault of the handheld ram. Police flooded the room, carried on the wave of righteousness. From where I sat on the floor, the hollow barrels seemed to grow larger, as if the guns themselves were gateways to the afterlife, great tunnels coming to show me the way home. The first team spread out to secure the room, but already we faded from their reality. One covered his face to shield it from the fire, but like us, the real flames were mostly somewhere else.

The room retreated from view like we were on a train leaving the station, but it was all around us. Reality stretched us away, piercing the veil in this location. From now on, it would be easier to travel to the fae lands from this room, as I was essentially paving the way for the next set of travelers.

"Don't shoot!" Horace yelled, his voice muffled by the rippling of reality.

The fire alarm blared to life, and water cascaded down. Where it hit me, pain ruptured my skin. The spray of the sprinkler drove into my bones like spikes laced with acid. And then it all went black.

Chapter Thirteen

Rain fell on my face. The fire sprinklers?

A rushing sound like a river spilled all around me, filling me, then the sound of heavier things hitting the ground intruded on me. How could this be? None of this made sense.

Then my stomach made the same swooping feeling from unexpected motion. The same feeling from the car crash.

Debris rained around me as the car tumbled. One hit, two hits.

Oh gods, not again.

Something smashed into my head, knocking all thoughts loose from my mind.

This can't be real. This can't be real.

Why would I be here again?

Why would—

The portal to Underhill. All portals to Underhill were gateways, markers and thresholds, but this moment was the biggest portal of my life. One life before the crash, one life after. This was the moment. This was when my life diverged in every possible way from the before and into the after.

Please gods, not again.

The car hit one more time, finishing the roll. The cabin jostled as the shocks absorbed the extra motion and the whole machine came to a terrible halt.

I breathed. The sharp snap of frost sliced the air, quenching in my lungs. The early fall frost had taken the puddles, and we'd flipped when the other car slammed into us. Up front, Anne and Dorothy sat, loose in their seatbelts, heads tilted to the side as if they were sleeping.

No gods, no, please.

Glass bits lay everywhere, catching the light, sparkling up in the headlights of a nearby car. The pulse of light ran through the window, strobing with the nearness of the other vehicle. Then just as suddenly, the light was gone.

I coughed, and Jessica cried, pushing at the edges of her car seat, really just a plastic bucket, all the rage in safety.

As if in a dream, I reached over, checking her for cuts. A superficial scratch in her scalp started to really let loose, and wherever I touched her, blood kept appearing on her.

Panic spurred up through my shaking hands and stealing my breath. How could she bleed everywhere I touched her? What was even—

It was me. A cut on my hand spilled my blood on everything I touched. Relief washed through me. Gods, how could I be so dumb. A piece of glass still stuck out of the wound. In a daze of relief and dread, I pulled the piece of glass.

With hands oddly calm, I undid the buckle on Jessica's seat belt, and wrapped her tight, making a shushing sound.

She cried, and there was no way, no way possible that she was going to quiet down. I opened the car door, pushing with my foot. It swung open with a crunch mid swing, and I stood, holding the baby.

The blood rushed to my legs, and I nearly passed out. I put my hand on the car, leaning against it.

Oh gods, please, no. Not again!

Then the world went dizzy as my head rushed again, and I was falling. My knees collided with the ground. The smell of loam rolled up into my brain as I desperately tried to keep hold of the baby.

When I knew I wouldn't pass out, I looked up. The car rolled away, nose pointing downhill, moving faster and faster. I pushed to my feet, wobbling at the sudden motion. My foot connected with a rock, and I stumbled, nearly dropping Jessica. I struggled to maintain my stance. I took a step forward, then another. Running, baby in my arms, I started screaming.

No, no, no, no!

Then the car went over the edge. Just like that. It slipped off the edge of the road, crashing as it hit the first ridge below. The metal shrieked as it warped and sheared against the rocks. It hit. It hit again. It smashed again, and again.

I made it to the edge of the cliff, and there, at the bottom of the ravine, the Edsel came to rest, upside down. The whitewater washed over the undercarriage like a hungry monster. It slipped under the water.

I searched for a way to get down the embankment. I took a step, and the hillside slipped away from me. I fell back onto my tailbone.

Jessica started screaming.

"Anne! Dorothy!"

I knew.

I already knew. Even in the rawness of that moment. I had always been able to feel them, to sense the fire in their souls. You didn't need magic for that kind of spell. And I couldn't sense them. They were gone.

The pain of it spread through my body, a dark and empty hole, a hungry maw, ready to swallow my whole life.

The siren call of the darkness rose up inside me, threatening to swallow me whole. I could just let go.

I could be gone. I could just let it all go, drop into the darkness and watch my pain snuff out like a candle. Already, the cold stole my pain, numbing my limbs, my fingers, and my face. I could just let it swallow the rest of me.

Then Jessica screamed. It was like the first kiss of fire, burning through my senses. The sound burned my ears, searing a path right to the heart of me. I'd always been the responsible one. Always. I'd made every sacrifice for the greater good. And here it was again in a screaming infant. I swallowed my desire to just drop off the Earth, as the realization swept over me: someone had to take care of the baby. And there was no one left. It would have to be me. I pulled my shawl off and wrapped it around her, tucking her tighter into a little bundle. I hugged her close to my chest, giving her as much warmth as I could. The delicate little flame in her heart responded, suddenly brightening.

She would live.

And so would I.

As I held her, tears carved lines down my cheeks. I cried. Alone, I'd have to be the one to take care of her *alone*.

The world shifted around me, slipping through reality, and opening up into another world.

The moment melted away, and I was in Underhill. I had passed through the portal. The road and woods around me twisted into the bizarre trees of the fae realm, horrid mockeries of real plants. They leaned over with a hungry bend to their trunks, ready to eat me. The cold creeping through me no longer had anything to do with the weather.

It shook me through to my core. How close I'd been, how very tantalizing oblivion was in that moment. Everything about me had shifted, a portal through which I had become the person I am now, had been the portal to let me into the fae realms.

The last time I'd come, the experience hadn't been so traumatic. But the last time had been before the crash, before everything changed in the blink of an eye.

I shuddered again and tried to pull together what new horror Underhill would throw at me.

And where was everyone else?

I took a breath, feeling the fabric of reality, and the way it wibbled around under my extended senses—a definite sign this was another plane of existence and had little to do with the "real world." As things shifted under my senses, a feeling like water spilled through, like new rain on dry cement. I followed it like a stream to the source. The nebulous afterimage of the roadside slipped away, a curtain in the breeze of an uncertain reality.

Between one step and the next, I stood in the sun, burning hot and dust choked air. Cicadas screamed from the giant pepper tree marking the edge of an old-fashioned farmstead, beaten by the heat and wind, and not nearly enough water for this time of year.

A swarm of blond girls dressed in matching coveralls ran out of the house.

The girls poured out like a flood, their shirts all untucked, and some had bits of blood on their hands, staining their clothes. Five in total, but somehow with the crying and the running, it felt like more.

One girl grabbed the hand of the youngest and pulled her away from the house. Their backs had all been beaten. They gathered in a knot of sniffles and tears, one trying desperately to control her breathing and master her tears. Then a man came out. His clothes were loose on his body, and his skin hung like a sheet over his body, barely connected. He'd once been a much larger man, yet he somehow still managed to have a little pot belly. He held a belt in his hand, the buckle end lashing at the air.

From the unpainted, wooden porch, he drove the girls away from the house, his screaming intolerable. A woman ran fast on his heals, holding the side of her face. A red gash cut across her cheek told the whole of this story.

He grabbed her hand, and she tensed like she knew what was coming. When she didn't move under his hand the way he meant, even though he had no more words, such was his rage, he threw her down the steps.

The pile of girls huddled at the well, crouching under the stone wall as if they could all hide from their father's rage. Everything about the scene spurred me to action, but there was nothing I could do but watch, hidden in the branches of the pepper tree.

He loomed over the woman, who was no longer moving from where she'd fallen. Each step of his booted heel rang through the dirt farmer's porch steps. The flat land all around had no other building besides a silo and a barn. The gentle roll of corn country blocked out the view of any other farm. There was nowhere to run, nowhere that could yield safety. And his boots fell again, ever closer to the fallen woman.

When he could come no closer, one of the girls, the one who'd dragged the youngest behind her, stood up.

Mary.

I would recognize her anywhere.

"Stop!" she yelled.

One of her sisters reached out with a hand, trying to stop their sister, but it wasn't fast enough. Mary moved like water, flowing away from people, but when she wanted to, she could be as stubborn as the sea.

The man looked up at her, incredulous. "What was that, rat?"

"I said, 'Stop!'" she repeated, crossing the yard.

"No one asked you. No one asked you to find that well! No one asked you to go casting your magic and bringing the government down on us! Do you know what the bank will do? Have you any idea what you've done?"

"I wrote a letter," she said stubbornly. "I wrote one letter."

"Is that 'cause you're too good for us? Too good to be a farmer? To be a wife?" His words sharpened as he focused more of his rage on her. "You have to obey your betters."

"I have no betters here. You're scared of the letters 'cause you can't read them!"

Even the cicadas stilled. Nothing moved, and the girls didn't breathe.

"What did you say to me child?"

"I said you're an idiot who can't even read."

In an instant, he'd crossed the distance between them and held her by her throat. His rage seethed through his fingers, and he continued across the yard, carrying her by her throat. He pushed forward to the well, and the other girls scattered. He held her over the stone wall, his immeasurable strength fueled by his rage.

"What did I tell you about disobeying your betters?"

She gasped, her hands clawing at his outstretched arm. She kicked at him, but he was much taller, much more muscled than a little girl.

Her sisters screamed, and a horrible wail rent the air as her mother took in the scene.

"Now that I have your attention," he said. And then, unbelievably, undeniably, he dropped her.

She fell for forever. It couldn't have been longer than a heartbeat. The splash echoed up, distant as only a stone lined well could be. Everyone screamed again, the mother, dashing across the yard to the well. She threw herself onto the wall of it, thrusting her body into the cavern.

On instinct, all the girls grabbed their mother to keep her from falling.

Her husband grabbed her hair and pulled her out. "And let this be a lesson to all of you."

"Help!" a distant voice called up from the well. "Lower the bucket!"

"Hold on!" the eldest of the sisters yelled, pushing the bucket into the hole between the stones.

But then, instead of lowering the bucket and rescuing Mary, the father grabbed the bucket and pulled it out of the well. When one of the daughters tried to take it from him, he grabbed her and threw her toward the house.

"Now get back inside before I decide to destroy all of you. How many little girls do you think will fit down there?"

He cracked his belt like a whip, clearly with so much experience that he could land it like a lash on the shoulders of anyone within six or seven feet of him.

With a yelp, and many a cry, he rounded up his brood and dragged his wife back in the house. After he threw the door closed behind them all, he went back to the well, taunting Mary, whose cries had already faded to silent sobbing.

His laugh echoed over her cries. "They'll think of you every day when they get that water, and every day, they'll know what happens when you disrespect your elders. They will know." He grabbed a stone from the ground. "Every glass of water from here until they die."

"Please just throw down the bucket," Mary called. "Just throw down the bucket, please!" her voice cracked on the "please."

He threw the stone. She screamed, and the sound of distant splashes spilled out from the carefully bricked tunnel into the earth. She coughed, and the splashing ceased as the lighter sounds of treading water sprang up from inside the well.

He grabbed another rock from the ground and threw it over the edge. Mary cried out.

"Please! Don't!" Her cries came with a desperation, piercing the air.

He threw down another stone the size of a fist. It splashed. "Is that what you like? Is that how you want it?"

Suddenly, water rose up out of the well, roaring over the wall like a wave from the ocean. Mary washed up with the water, choking and sputtering, and like a fish out of water, she flopped on the ground, as if her whole body failed to function in this world of air and light.

Someone moved from the pepper tree. She swelled forward, carried by the power and depth of the sea in a way Mary never had and never could—she was a true water mage. Mary would always be a water witch, only capable of the great works when she believed her life in danger. This woman brought the weight and power of the sea when she traveled inland—a thousand miles from the nearest shore, and the rush and roar of waves whispered from the curl of her dark hair.

"Sir, I bid you good day." Her words were clipped, and like the power of the ocean, he swiveled his head toward her. "I bid you good day, and please go inside. My words are for Mary only."

"The hell they are!" he yelled, stepping forward to attack. His whole body tensed.

But before he'd taken a single step forward, all the water around them rose up to obey this new woman, dressed smartly in her pressed dress, her hair curled to perfection. The water spilled into the air, ignoring gravity and wrapping around his wrists. When he drew breath to scream, the water streamed into his throat, throttling any words he might have soiled the air with. With a flick of her eyelids, the water holding back his wrists dragged him back to the house where he was suddenly locked inside.

Mary turned up from where she lay on the ground, and the woman gazed down at her. She frowned almost instantly. "You aren't as talented as I usually accept..." she said, mulling the prospect of Mary.

A thumping rang out from the dilapidated farmhouse, and she pursed her lips. "Well, we all make exceptions. I hope you like to work hard, Mary."

"How do you know my name?" she asked.

The woman smiled, and for the first time, real warmth spilled through the farmstead. "I can see things in water, and it showed you to me. I can see why, but you will have to work ten times harder than any student I've ever had before. And even then, you might not progress far enough to join us."

"What happens if I join you?" Mary asked.

"If you join one of The Orders, you will be asked to formally give up your family. They will be replaced by your magical brothers and sisters, those who control the same element as you. You will live—and obey—the rules of the Order, but I can guarantee one thing: no one will ever raise their hand against you." She pursed her lips as she fixed the house with a lethal gaze.

Mary had eyes only for the woman with curls like waves. "Yes! I'll go. I'll study, or whatever you want. I'll even clean stalls. I'm not afraid of hard work."

The woman huffed. "I can see that." Then she held out her hand. "Welcome to training, but I fear I've done you no favors. It would be kinder to take your Gift and send you home."

Mary's steely eye held no room for misinterpretation. "I have no home."

The woman nodded. "Let's change that."

And the woman helped Mary from the ground, then the real Mary stood next to me.

"Not even the death of my husband ranked higher than this moment. Fuckin' faeries and their stupid magic. I should have known. You?" she asked.

I nodded. "The crash."

Mary looked at her feet for a moment, then, silently, she wrapped me in a hug. It was like a summer's day, the way the air was so hot you felt it through your pockets, her wordless support drew the pain from me like a suction, and tears sprang to my eyes.

"I'm so sorry," she said.

"How come you never told me?" I said, barely controlling the break in my voice.

She released me. Already, the farmstead faded into the twisted trees of Underhill. The foreignness of the place grew over the edge of the little girl walking hand in hand with the mage. "I did, you just didn't notice."

My heart ached. Mary had always been so studious. She'd said she had to be her very best, that she needed the Order more than the Order needed her. "All the books?" I asked, shame burning my face.

She nodded. "I copied every book they'd let me study. They didn't know, but I never wanted to be without a resource that could make it easier. What if, after all that, they decided to try to send me back? Would they fabricate memories of me leaving home? Or would they send me back knowing I could have escaped it if I'd just studied harder."

"I'm sorry I wasn't a better friend back then," I said.

Mary sighed. "You're fire, I'm water, it's not like you could have helped me study my craft. And I didn't want your pity. I wanted your respect."

"You had it then. You have it now."

She smiled and my heart lifted like a zeppelin, impossible and utterly unexpected.

The moment shifted and she tilted her head. "You know, I still have all my old copies of the books—a real boon if we decide to keep the magic. Just saying, as the kids say."

"We can't," I said automatically.

She held up her hands. "I know, I was just reminding you that, well, it's more than a personal choice, if you know what I mean."

"And what am I supposed to do? Just curl up and die? Become Winter's lap dog?"

Mary grabbed my shoulders. "No. I expect none of that from you. I expect a solution."

A voice pierced our discussion. "But what if I'm the precipitate instead!"

Mary rolled her eyes. "Jesus Phyllis, only a meth-head would think that was funny."

"I don't do meth," she said with a dignity reserved for teaching the mysticism riddled new-agers. "I tried Ritalin once, and that's where the joke is from. It's like you all forgot there were other drugs that came out of the war." She pulled Horace, her hand clamped around his bicep, literally dragging him along. His glazed eyes held the view to another world, and somehow none of us were able to see into his portal. He still clutched his luggage in one hand, and I was suddenly aware that I was wearing borrowed underwear.

"How are you able to do that?" I asked, pointing at Horace.

"Oh please," she waved her hand under her nose, "I'm clairvoyant. I don't have to wait for some stupid price these faeries want to put on us to 'pass' their test. Please. Illusion only works on the weak minded." She scowled at Horace, and both Mary and I politely looked away from each other. Weak minded.

"Fine, how do we get out of here?" Mary asked.

Phyllis shrugged. "Where's the dragon?"

I scowled. "I haven't seen her."

"The ways of dragons are mysterious?" Mary asked in the half-joking tone of someone who knew what a ridiculous statement that was.

I snorted. "I'm not sure if that dragon is the same dragon who once stood by the side of the High Flame. I'd only ever seen drawings, and the dragon was much bigger, but she can change her shape. Can she change her size?"

Mary snorted. "How much of all this was lost due to information control among the Orders? Their secrecy was for the sake of secrecy and not security."

I shrugged.

"Now what?" Phyllis asked.

"We are still heading toward Washington, so we keep moving here and hope it translates to movement there." And with that I concentrated, holding the idea of the Source of Magic in my mind. I tried to remember what it had felt like, the heart of a dead star. Science said it should have been denser than any material ever possessed by man, and maybe it was, but when we'd scooped it into a sack, it hadn't weighed more than rock. It thumped in my chest and turned as if pulled by a string. Certain the Source sat in front of me, I opened my eyes.

I faced Phyllis and Horace. I pointed at them. "It's that way," I said. They parted and I started walking into the foreign lands of Underhill, hoping I wasn't walking us to certain death.

Chapter Fourteen

The sun had risen over the horizon, lighting the fae lands in all the bright and high contrast colors imaginable. Then the sun set after about an hour. Was it a real day? Or was it more faerie bullshit?

Things skittered in the trees and bushes as we followed a sort of path across the lands, Phyllis dragging her luggage on wheelies. Horace finally woke from the illusion holding him, and we stopped. There was nothing we could eat here, but he shivered so strongly I gathered some wood, dipped into my magical reserves and sparked a fire.

It wasn't hard. The wood knew what we wanted of it, but it stubbornly refused to light without a spark. I probably could have banged some rocks together and had a fire in seconds. The whole of Underhill seemed to morph and stretch to our needs, but only once we'd met it at some arbitrary halfway point.

"How do we get out?" Phyllis asked. "I can't see any portals."

"We're going to die here!" Horace said, hands wrapped around his shaving kit like it could save his life.

"Please," Mary said with derision. "We'll make it out in time to have to pay taxes." Then she turned to me. "Can you sense anything?"

I shook my head. "I had it for a while there, but it's like something is fuzzing out my ability to even sense things." I paced on the outside of the firelight. "I don't like being stopped for so long."

"You made the fire," Phyllis pointed out uncharitably.

"I didn't expect to be here so long." I scanned the dark horizon. It wasn't really cold. Underhill could be any temperature, but there was something odd about how it held everything in illusion. The dark night sweltered, and the daylight hours could chill you to the bone.

The stars sang with their light, burning down like heaters, and as I watched the horizon, I realized that I had zero recollection of these stars. Not a single one marked a pattern I recognized.

I shook my head, trying to dispel my sudden uncertainty about our path, our direction, and if we should be standing here in a night as hot as summer.

My chest constricted. The burning bands of pain wrapped around my heart and squeezed. Air hissed out of my lungs as a giant weight pounded down on my sternum. My knees hit the dirt with a distant thud. The sky wheeled overhead as the dark tunnel shrank in on my view of the world, as if everything were coming to me through a long and distant tube.

Pain didn't cover the feeling as every nerve in my body screamed out for release from whatever suddenly encased me. Every inch of my skin exploded in agony as if every pore burst. It overwhelmed me, drowning me in a wash of sensation. I closed my eyes tight, willing the pain to go away. Stars exploded behind my eyelids.

<STAY BACK!> my dragon mentally shouted. The air ripped open as she roared, a fully adult, large dragon roar. The thump of her very large feet reverberated through the ground. The vibrations through the dirt washed out every other scrap of noise, so present was my dragon in my mind. The burning of raging fire spilled through every pore of my body, searing and crackling, until it consumed everything around me, even the pain. It was like the pain had been a paper wrapping around me, and it burned away, releasing me from the prison.

A hand squeezed my shoulder. "Please, Ruth, get up."

Mary's voice.

I opened my eyes. In the second—minutes?—since I'd gone down, everything had changed. My dragon stood there, resplendent in purple and gold scales, her eyes a deep and vibrant orange, fading to gold, like two campfires, spilling out into the night. Steam or smoke rose from her nostrils, and she stood more than twenty feet tall, her neck twisted into a stance of protection, ready to fight. A massive claw half buried itself into the dirt next to where I lay, and the attached foot and leg were more impressive, even missing some of the toes and claws.

My dragon. The thought poured through me like water spilling into a bag, filling all the edges and threatening to topple over the rim. My dragon had come.

"Traitor!" Winter cried out, her words clearly aimed at my dragon who stood between the four of us and the fae queen. "How could you betray me like this? I should have left you and your kind to rot on that dying world! You all would be dead if not for me, and this is how you repay me! This is your loyalty?"

Winter wound up to cast something, but Brigid tensed her whole body, and a gout of flame shot out, splashing over the fae.

She cast again, and the fire bent away, bouncing off a magical shield.

<You cannot claim us!> Brigid yelled back. *<You broke our eggs! You killed our elders. You trapped us in your half world. You made us monsters!>*

A sinking feeling suddenly occupied the pit of my stomach. Dragons had a beef with the Winter Queen? How long had this been going on? What had happened?

And why was I always digging around in other people's business without enough facts to draw actual conclusions?

"Would you have rather they suffered? Would you have rather they felt the pain of their deaths, the oceans boiling away around them? The destruction of everything they knew and loved?"

<You told us we would be together!> Brigid called out, anguish washing out through her mental voice. The grief welled up, echoing my own, threatening to swallow me whole. *<We cannot even lay eggs now! Is that what you wanted?>*

Winter shook her head, and her gaze fell on me. "Ruth! Mage! Your time is running out, and you come to my world? Are you truly so foolish?"

I put my hand on my dragon's foot and used it to lever myself to standing, pushing past the pain in my chest. I wasn't talking to that bitch on my knees. "You broke the rules, Winter. You weren't to interfere, and now I have cops chasing me. Did you leave a random tip for them?"

Winter rolled her eyes. "I have broken no rules."

"Ha! You attacked me in my own home."

She pointed at Brigid. "You summoned a dragon! Is that not a purely hostile action?" She twisted her hand, and the world spun around, twisting inside my inner ear, and destroying the little balance I had reclaimed. Mary squeezed my shoulder, but the world felt distant.

"You can't!" I cried out, my voice frail and feeble, but I knew: Winter had perfected operating within the rules long before I'd been born.

"I can do whatever I want," Winter whispered, her form suddenly thin and transparent. "But in this particular case, I'm helping you. It's not my fault your weak heart can't stand my magic."

The world smeared past in a riot of colors and lights. I felt Underhill tearing past me, tugging on my chest as we went.

"I don't want your help!"

"Fine," she said, opening her hand. "Pass the tree's test on your own. I'm sure you're prepared for it."

And with that warning, she opened her hand as she disappeared. Whatever force had been holding me upright released when she vanished. My knees collapsed, and I winced at the expectation of pain, falling forward.

Instead of pain, my hands sank into springy moss. I knelt at the base of an enormous tree, its great branches reaching out to shade all of us.

Even as I searched for Winter, a warm sensation washed over me: this tree would be a fine place to rest. I just had to fold my arm to lay in the spongy greenery. I could close my eyes. Yes, when I closed my eyes, the world didn't spin so much. I could just close my eyes for a moment.

"Ruth?" Mary asked, but I didn't listen.

"What the hell was that?" Horace asked.

"Faerie bullshit," Phyllis said.

I wanted to tell them that it was a trap—because everything Winter did was a trap—but the world was so heavy. I should rest—needed to rest—I could sleep right here. It would be the most wonderful sleep, and maybe my chest wouldn't hurt so much.

As my body touched more of the moss, the pain retreated, just like it always did when I lay in my own bed.

"Ruth!"

"Dammit! Ruth, get up! You can't die yet!" Phyllis called out.

Someone grabbed my shoulder, but I couldn't tell who—it could have been Winter, and I would have never known. I swatted at the hands, intruding into my slumber.

"Ruth! You picked a helluva time to decide to die!" Phyllis shook my shoulder hard enough for me to open my eyes.

My face pushed into the moss at an angle, and from my vantage point, it covered most of my view. A root from the tree hanging over us seemed to curl toward me, cupping my form, inviting me to sleep. Flowers grew out of the moss, springing up all around me, spraying their pollen into the air. Sweet pollen. I'd never smelled anything so sweet.

The flowers grew taller as I watched. Or I sank. Who cared, either way, their sweet smell covered me, drawing me deeper into the underworld.

Fire lanced across my body, burning up the side of my face. The moss around me turned to ash, bitter and dry. My skin cracked under the heat of the fire, searing like a steak on the barbeque. I rolled to get away, but the fire was all around me, towering above me.

Then the fire blinked at me.

The taste of ash filled my mind. I knew that fire. It was a dragon, but instead of being a creature of fire the way I had always seen it in the mortal pain, Brigid stood over me, her body sleek like a cat, but the size of an elephant and shot through with the colors of a rainbow. The fire rippled through her scales like an oil slick on water, but her bright red claws had the distinctive fingernail polish look.

Pain stabbed through my chest again, but I knew the pain, coursing up my neck and into my jaw. My stomach burned with nausea, and I wanted nothing more than to spew the contents of my stomach into the world.

"Heart," I said, wrapping my arms around my abdomen like I could hold back the inevitable.

"Ruth!" Horace fished in his shaving kit—he brought his shaving kit when we ran from the cops?—and pulled out a white pill. "Take this!" He pushed the pill toward me.

"What is it?" I wheezed through the pain.

"Nitro," he said holding it out to me.

I hadn't taken a nitro pill in ages. It didn't help my normal heart problems, but this wasn't a normal heart problem. The pain ground into my chest, spreading like spilled wine on a white tablecloth, wicking out from the Source and radiating into every part of my body.

I took the pill from Horace and put it under my tongue. "Damned bad timing!"

As if by magic, the pain clenching my heart began to release, and the world cracked.

In the time it takes to blink, the glory of summer in Underhill wilted. Hoarfrost crept down the tree, blackening the moss it touched. I hissed at the sudden cold.

Ice blossomed along the roots of the tree, spilling over the wood and into the branches high above us. The sudden cold brought goosebumps to my skin, as if the change in the land was reflected in my body as well.

Mary dropped into a fighting stance and called water to her side from the ice around us. The chips of ice and dots of water floated before her as she drew magic from the plants.

The ice moved, shaking to reveal creatures forming out of the snow. Ice dogs rose out of the drifts of snow piling around us. Pure white and made of snow, they prowled around us, waiting for us to move. Besides the snow wolves, other creatures of Winter rose up around us.

I ignored all of them, focusing on the sting of the pill as it worked the magic of science on me. With the sting came the easing of the terrible tension in my chest. I took a breath that finally *felt* like breathing. My breath fogged out around me, and with the release of pain, the terrible cold penetrated my mental hierarchy for things worth paying attention to. If my heart didn't give out on me, the weather would do me in after only minutes.

A snow wolf snapped at me, and Brigid took exception, grasping the thing in her jaws. Fire raged across the ice creature, and the hiss of melting and boiling water filled the air. Steam rose from Brigid's mouth, and the snow wolf whimpered. With a flick of her neck, my dragon flung the wolf away from us. It smacked into a rock, exploding like a spring snowball, messy and wet.

She turned her attention to the other snow wolf, stalking forward, but stepping between me and the snow creature. The wolf glared back with eyes the color of glacier. With every passing second, the snowbanks compacted until they had the same aqua color as the wolf's eyes.

As the snowbank became the calving edge of a glacier, animals of winter sprang to life from the ice and snow. White hare, snow leopards, and a polar bear all came out of the ice to pace around us.

I searched the animals for the one that wasn't truly a creature. I passed over mice, shrews, cats, rabbits, wolverines, but no Winter.

"Can you stand?" Phyllis asked.

I nodded and took the hand she offered. Brigid pushed at me with her head, sniffing as if trying to be sure I lived. Satisfied, the dragon raised her head and roared. Many of the snow creatures fell to little piles of ice. Puffs of white fell away from a cloud leopard to reveal Winter. She lounged on the edge of ice, looking for all the world like she was very disappointed. I inclined my head slightly.

"We're just passing through," I said.

"Just killing my creations as you pass through you mean?" she scowled down at us. "And to think I brought you to the door." She shook her head. "Silly human. Thinking you understand the rules well enough to survive—especially with that oh so sensitive heart." She smiled holding her finger in the air. Like a puppeteer, she toggled her finger up and down.

My heart jumped in time to the Winter Queen's motions. The pain drove me to my knees as the world went black around me. I hit the snow, my hand going numb as the slush chilled my limbs. Damn my sudden strict return to bare arms. My heart obeyed a fae queen's spell. It was impossible, they weren't supposed to cast on a heart. Winter could kill me whenever she wanted.

A chill that had nothing to do with the cold raced down my back. "Why do you have my heart?" I asked.

Phyllis, Mary, and Horace all turned to me at once, but Brigid hissed at Winter.

"Oh come now, how could I have your heart?" A lazy smile spread across her lips. "It would do me so little good to hold the heart of the very last fire mage."

Narrowing my eyes, I tried a different approach. "Then let us pass."

She rolled her head in a laugh. "This—this!—is why I love humans!" She sauntered toward me, a slow approach with exaggeration in every bit of movement. "I have you by every way I could own you, and you still act as if the end isn't completely inevitable."

"You still need me to get the Source," I said.

She laughed again. "Child, I could get it any time I want it." She raised an eyebrow toward Horace. "Your friends certainly look menacing today." She closed her hand into a fist and Mary cried out, staggering backward.

"You've dealt unfairly with me," I said, abandoning my previous tactic.

Winter turned her attention back to me. "How do you figure? You are still alive." She twisted a finger and a fresh bloom of pain erupted in my chest. "I let that happen. I let you live. You really should thank me."

"You cannot own my heart. Magic cannot control—Ah!" I cried out as the agony intensified.

She smiled down at me as the pain receded enough for me to see again. "You were saying there was something magic couldn't do. Please go on." She held out a hand as if inviting further explanation.

"You don't own me," I hissed.

"True, but you understand so little of the truth. It's as though the other mages lied to you your whole life. What did they say your relation with magic was again? Something about not being able to live without it?"

It was a low blow. She knew the mages had taken their books and burned them. The only traces of magic I'd had were my own notes, and I'd lost most of that when my Order had thrown me out. Idiots.

Phyllis glared, her rage impotent. "You lie!"

"Are you telling me what I can and cannot do, Seer?" As Winter turned her steely gaze on Phyllis, frost grew in the air around her.

"You're just trying to stall us," Phyllis said, her teeth chattering in the cold. She clutched her sides to warm her body, but her eyes fluttered closed, the power of the Winter Queen's cold rushed through the air and stole Phyllis's defiance.

"You couldn't See your way out of a paper bag. Between the two of you," she said indicating Mary, "I could never understand why someone of her power"—pointing at me—"would even wipe her shoes on someone like you."

I hissed. "Friendship is about more than just power."

"And speaking of power, how much time do you have left?" Winter tilted her head at me like a quizzical dog. She pulled on whatever control she had on my body, and the pain split through me.

"The moon isn't full! I still have time." I gasped, clutching my chest. Brigid growled, a deep rumble that spilled through the world.

Horace's face, stony and unreadable, stepped between me and Winter.

"And what do you think, thief?" she asked Horace. "You're awfully quiet."

He ducked his head. "Ma'am, I'm just along for the ride. I would appreciate it if you let me and my friends go."

She sighed. "So disappointing. I thought you, of everyone here, would understand the moment to make a play for power." She turned her back on all of us, shaking her head. "Pity, really, I thought you were the human who could do it."

"I can," I said, breaking her soliloquy. "If you'd stop messing with my heart, I could do anything."

"Only your lot have the power to 'Mess with your heart.' I merely show you where the leverage is." She traced her fingers along the edge of her ice dress. "Your heart is too broken to even resist me. You are too pathetic. Even killing you would bring me little joy." She scowled at me, disappointment clear across her pointed features.

Winter raised her finger, and toggled it in the air again, like a metronome. My heart spasmed under the pressure, and I cried out. I couldn't for the life of me understand how she was controlling my body. It broke all the rules. She wasn't to interfere—oh. She couldn't interfere with my body, but that didn't mean she couldn't make me think she was. Pain, after all, was just synapses firing. Could she make a glamour like that? Pain that wasn't real? But was it real enough to cause my poor heart to tip over into an actual heart attack?

Tears in my eyes, I tried to find my advantage, anything to get us out of here alive. Even a lie. I spat the first idea that sprang to my mind. "So, you've reneged on our deal?"

She tensed. The remaining snow creatures turned toward me and growled. "Are you accusing me of breaking contract?"

"The Source belongs to humans. To say you own it suggests you've cross dealt me." I narrowed my eyes at her and gave my gaze the edge of accusation. "Our power, not yours."

She leaned back, her face twisting as if she'd licked a lime dipped in toothpaste. Then anger flared. "Our deal will only last as long as you do." She took a menacing step toward me. "And might I remind you, our deal ends when the moon is fullest."

She twisted her hand and my heart seized in my chest.

"You can't kill me yet!" I cried out.

"You've traveled many hundreds of miles, and you are no closer to finding the Source! Pain is clearly the only lesson you understand!" She pointed at Phyllis. "Tell her the Truth, pathetic Seer. What happens when we next meet?"

Phyllis shuddered, her eyelids dancing in a rapid blink as if she'd lost control of her power. Seers were less like traditional mages in that they had access to something beyond, something ephemeral that didn't give them prescience so much as made them very good at guessing the future. Phyllis didn't store power to unleash later. Her power, or so she'd explained it, was used to build a bridge to somewhere else, another place where her mind could function better. But, she had warned, there were sometimes other beings in that place, and they had a different kind of power—a power that could subvert her will. But those beings always knew the truth.

When Phyllis went rigid, a shiver danced across the hairs on my arms: something else spoke through her.

In a voice too wooden, as if it wasn't entirely sure how to operate the meat machine that was Phyllis's body, it said, "When next you stand before the Queen of Winter, both will die."

"What?" Winter craned her neck to finally look at Phyllis. "What did you say?"

Phyllis shuddered under the scrutiny of Winter, but her body was possessed by the power that resided within her, that thing from beyond that could pierce the veil, and it did not obey Winter, only took her invitation. The snow around Phyllis evaporated into the air as if the snow couldn't survive the power of truth. "When next you stand before each other, both will die, but one may survive in the fullness of time!"

"What does that mean?" I asked Phyllis.

Winter hissed and pointed at Phyllis. "Do not lie to me!"

Phyllis convulsed, all her muscles tensing against her will. She started to fall, and Horace caught her before she hurt herself.

"Stop it!" he commanded.

Winter flicked her wrist and ice and snow covered them. Horace fell back, still holding Phyllis, trying to protect her from the fae queen.

The queen glared down at him. "I don't need a man to tell me what to do." She turned her attention back to me. "I'll end you before we can ever meet again!"

My heart twisted in my chest, and I screamed. Blue and gold fire covered me as my dragon interposed herself between me and Winter.

Brigid roared her agreement. *<Yes, leave now!>*

I squinted at Brigid even as the pain rolled over me again. The dragon hunched her shoulders, her neck like a coiled snake, ready to strike.

<You are full of deceit and lies!> Brigid yelled, and before any of us could do anything, Brigid lunged forward. Winter in her jaws, Brigid twisted her whole body and launched the Winter Queen into the air.

We watched a fae queen fly through the sky, all of us in various forms of clutching our pearls. Something crashed in the distance, and I silently wished it was the end of Winter, but I knew better. No fall, not even a bite from a dragon would be able to bring down Winter.

Brigid turned to us, and Horace flinched. *<Get on. We will fly now,>* she said, leaning down.

The others looked at me with concern, but the pain had suddenly lessened.

I gave Mary my best non-verbal communication, a cross between When in Rome, and Less of Two Evils, and I put a hand on Brigid's shoulder. Her scales warmed under my touch, and, surprisingly, there were enough folds and large scales sticking out that it was only slightly less terrifying than climbing up a ladder.

Okay, yeah, it was MUCH worse, but I didn't feel like turning down the dragon who'd just tossed the fae queen like a rag doll in a game of tug of war.

Across her back were ridges of scales that made a sort of protected area where a person, or people, could sit astride her neck sort of like sitting on a horse. I had no idea how I was ever going to get up from that position, but I sure as shit wasn't going flying until I had a place to hold on. While the others climbed aboard, I made myself as comfortable as possible and waited.

"You have a history with Winter?" I asked more to kill time.

<She is not Winter, she is the absence of your star, the one you call the Sun. She is not a season.> There was a taste to that thought, something dark and distant.

"I don't understand," I said.

Brigid sighed, and on a dragon, that was an impressive feat. *<I know.>*

"Hey, watch it? Do you want us to get on or not?" Horace complained. The sigh had nearly upset his footing, and he clung desperately to a wing ridge. Through it all, he managed to maintain his shaving kit.

Mirth spilled through the dragon's thoughts into mine. *<Hang on. Humans are bad at flying.>*

She didn't wait for Horace to be fully settled—I suspected Brigid didn't like him that much—and she flapped her great wings while jumping into the air. My forehead smashed into her neck when the surprise caught me. Then her powerful thrusts threatened to flatten me with each beat of her wings.

"How are you related to her?" I asked, but the wind gobbled my words away. Even I couldn't hear myself over the noise.

<Dragons come from her world. When her star died, the one you call Summer let her attach her memories to your world but wouldn't let her keep the power of her star. We are all beholden to the star of our birth.>

"Dragons are from another world?" I asked stupidly as if she hadn't just said so.

<There is the gate. I must concentrate.>

And I dutifully shut my mouth.

From another world. From a literal other star.

My mind raced, trying desperately to fathom all the truths that came from that simple statement, and what that might mean for magic. Leave it to a bunch of old dead men to forget to mention that magic—that the Fae Queen of Winter!—was literally from another world.

Chapter Fifteen

Brigid landed in front of an oak tree that bore more than passing similarity to the one Winter had dropped us under. As soon as it came into view, I knew it was the portal out of Underhill. The tree was more clearly in spring, its bright green leaves had the fuzzy feel of newness that only came as they first budded out.

The moment the oak door opened, the memories receded back into the cocoon of the past. Time wrapped around my pain, dulling it into the distance. In fact, everything that happened in Underhill faded as if it had happened years ago. There was something I was supposed to remember, but like light bouncing from flickering candles, my thoughts skipped right on past that time. I'd have to put my mind to it later. Stupid fae and their stupid ability to make people forget.

My heart thudded in my chest as if we'd only just escaped the police, and on pure instinct, I searched for the uniforms that would have accompanied those guards. Around me, a delightful, grassy park unfolded. The air held the hint of cold, but only in the breeze. The manicured lawns stretched in every direction, only breaking for the great canopy of the oak, just budding, its leaves still fuzzy from the effort. A gentle rise of land met us at the roots of the tree, and its great branches shielded us from the fire orange globe of the setting sun.

It didn't matter that only minutes before it had been sunrise, now, stars only know where we were, it was sunset. The fae lands could swallow a person whole and no one would ever know. I suspected it was the Neverland from the adventures of Wendy and Peter.

"Where are we?" Horace asked.

I searched the green knoll for any clues, but this park could be anywhere, the US, the UK, any variety of places in Europe. It was like the ideal of a park. Which was probably why there was a gateway to Underhill here.

Mary held up her phone. "It says we're in Charlotte."

"Charlotte?" Horace asked, his face twisted in horror. "But how? We were just in Texas! How'd we get—"

Phyllis moaned. "What happened?" she asked blinking as if the power of her Sight left debris in her real eyes.

"Are you okay?" I asked.

She rubbed her head with one hand and wrapped her other arm around her tummy. "I don't feel good, if that's what you're asking."

Horace scanned the area, but so far, only Mary's phone had any clues.

"And I'm still in my night gown!" Phyllis looked down at herself.

The Seeing had left her incapacitated, and Horace hadn't stopped for her luggage. I wonder if some fae would find it eventually.

"Can you walk?" I asked.

"Not until I'm wearing some real clothes."

I scanned the idyllic surroundings for whatever was upsetting Horace, but nothing presented itself as the object of his concern. I fished through my bag, miraculously still tangled around my arm, and drew out some clothes and my meds, well, the meds I'd borrowed.

As we dressed, Brigid trotted through the oak door and placed a paw upon it. A ring of fire flared up around the edges of the door, sealing it in dragon fire.

I watched, a tank top half out of my bag, gawping like a child at an illusionist's show. Brigid trotted to me and rubbed against my leg.

"Good dragon," I said, petting her. She leaned into my praise.

<You are welcome.>

I passed a shirt over to Phyllis. She scowled at my clothing, four or five sizes too big for her.

"Maybe some pants?" she asked.

"It looks like we need some resources," Horace said.

I scowled at him. We didn't have a lot going for us. Phyllis shivered in her nightgown, her hair more askew than normal. I had my odd assortment of clothes from the pharmacy, but none of that was warm or even seasonable yet. We needed money to keep this show on the road.

I blinked. Show. We had enough for a show.

I made the gathering motion with my arms. "Okay, we don't have much, but if we're clever about it, we've got the makings for Zultana." I whispered pointing out a group of young men gathering near the bottom of the lawn, leaning on an old statue plinth that was missing its statue.

Phyllis shook her head. "Are you out of your mind!"

Mary dug through her shoulder bag and produced a bottle of rum. "Liquid courage?"

"I'm not drinking! I can't. Not like this!" She pointed at her clothes. "Not now! Winter almost killed me!"

"Ah, so you do remember what happened!"

Phyllis glared at me. "How can you keep going? Winter wants to kill you!"

"I have no doubt my death will come at the hands of the great fae queen, but in the meantime, we still have to secure the Source. There are too many unscrupulous people in our world. Hopefully, the spell is just wearing out, and we're going to get there and redo the old spell."

"You really think the Source is still there?" Mary asked. "What about the way it seems to go on and off?"

I shook my head. "When spells wear out, they can flicker. I think. It was meant to last for a really long time, but it's been a really long time. Besides, I have no doubt Winter is behind this."

Phyllis shook her head. "No, if she knew the details, she'd have gone after it directly. The only reason she's bothering with you is because she can't just take it."

Mary snorted. "She's fae. She's toying with us. Besides, stealing our magic would break it. She needs it to be a gift."

I paused, the words sinking into my mind. There was something there, something important, but it slipped through my mental fingers. I shook my head. Chasing the Source might be playing right into her hands. Or it might be the only way to fix the contract and get back to—

My thoughts hitched around the idea of getting back to normal. I shut it down before the thought of putting magic back in Pandora's box for the next seventy years could steal my courage.

I narrowed my eyes. "Doesn't matter. One way or another, we're moving, and I have a plan." I pointed at Phyllis. "Get your game face on."

Brigid meowed at me, sitting delicately on the ground and demanding attention.

"Are you hungry?" I asked the interrupter. "We probably won't have much time for food until after this con."

Instead of a real answer, Brigid stared at Horace. He squirmed under the gaze of the dragon. "What?"

<I could eat it> she offered.

"What did it say?" Horace asked.

"She," I corrected, "and she offered to eat your shaving kit, I think. Or maybe you. Some things get lost in translation."

I leaned back down to skritchy Brigid's ears, and she purred. "Not today, sweetie, but thank you for the offer. Also, before I forget: thank you for flying us all out of there. You saved our lives."

"Yes, thank you," Mary said.

Phyllis nodded her head. "Yes, thank you."

Horace scowled at me. "You're crazy."

"No, for this performance, Phyllis is crazy."

She shook her head at me, but we didn't have much time. There was a whole group of college-age men gathering and their wallets were thick in their pockets.

We didn't have any way to disguise that Phyllis was wearing a nightgown, but I could work with that. Mary and I pulled back her hair, turning it into a tight bun with an exotic seeming twist. Mary still had some makeup, garish and vibrant on Phyllis, but absolutely perfect for a performance. The mismatched skin tone worked to give her that just off look of someone not fully moored in the waters of reality.

"This is stupid," Phyllis protested one last time.

"We need money. Horace can get it if we give him a distraction. Besides, it'll be just like that time in Berlin."

"I hated that time in Berlin." Phyllis fussed with our last-minute head wrap to make her look somewhere between granny getting out of the shower and escaped fortune teller. She shook her head. "Do you know how much I hate these?"

"It's come up," Mary said. She took out her bottle of rum and offered it around.

I took a drink myself—strictly for courage, or for idiocy, both could be useful in this situation. "Deep breaths, everyone."

"You know I gave up stealing, right?" Horace asked.

"This isn't stealing, this is performance art with an alternative payment structure."

Horace glared at me, but we were already walking through the sunset shadows of the park, converging on the gathered men. Odd that there were no women, but men's money would spend just as well to get us back on the road. Something about what Winter said nagged at my mind, but I stuffed those thoughts away.

I needed schtick. I needed to be a showman. I needed a really good lie.

"Ladies and Gentlemen!" I announced when we approached the group of milling men. "Or in your case, just gentlemen!"

They all turned to me. Nothing about their demeanor revealed what it was they were up to, but none of them looked ready for a show. They looked up from their phones sluggishly. To a man they wore khaki pants and polo shirts, as if they'd coordinated their look with a propaganda magazine. Still, they looked inconvenienced, not wowed.

I could fix that.

"May I have your attention, please!" I shot a touch of power up my arms as I held my hands in the air. Harmless balls of fire rolled up my arms in a satisfying roar. The double balls of fire cast their shadows in quickly shortening lines racing toward their feet at an angle. Each one of those white boys stared up in awe like the day they first saw a Corvette in person.

Withholding my laugh at how easily razzled they were, I pushed on. "Tonight is your lucky night! For! Tonight you, my fine young sirs, have crossed the path of—" Oh crap, I needed a name and fast. I scoured their polo shirts as if they should know the answer and I shouldn't have to say it. Just a sea of light-colored polo shirts. So many blond boys. "Polonde the Wise!"

For effect, I threw another fire ball into the air, drawing it directly from Brigid this time. A flutter shivered across my chest. A warning. My well ran closer to empty than full, and my body could only cash so many unsecured checks before I started paying a very physical price.

I held my proud, smug, smile even as thoughts of my untimely death chased each other in my head. I twisted around, catching Phyllis in my showy salute. Gamely, she held her nose in the air like a great opera singer being called to perform for the masses. I bowed to her with a great flail of my arms. With only the slightest smile, she deigned to acknowledge my existence. Our unwitting audience leaned in.

"And, my fine young gentlemen, you are in for a treat!" I pointed my finger out into the crowd at chest height. "For this night—One night only!—you have the pleasure of gazing into the future with the eye of the great Polonde!"

The audience started clapping, slowly at first, but then with enthusiasm as both Horace and Mary weaved into the crowd, clapping with enthusiasm. People had a tendency to follow along with what the rest of the crowd did so long as it wasn't completely against their own views, if just to fit in.

"Thank you! Thank you! And Polonde appreciates your admiration, but I must warn you: for her powers to reach into the great beyond I will need all your help!" I raised an eyebrow at them, and slowly the silence began to spread through the crowd. "I need you all to gather in more closely."

As the audience shifted closer together, bumping into one another, Horace started his magic trick. He slipped wallets and keys from people's pockets. He deftly passed them off to

Mary who slipped the pilfered items into the wide-mouthed beach bag I'd stolen from the pharmacy.

What a travesty my life had become, one giant string of robberies and thefts.

Winter will kill you and bring her armies. The US would launch nukes to stop her, and they would have no effect other than to blight the land, and she'd still get everything she wanted. It was this or nothing.

I gathered the crowd forward with my arms, gesturing them toward me. They obliged by filling in closer. Their shuffling movements and occasional bumping into each other made Horace's work easier than usual. He deftly slipped through the crowd, until he made it to the very back of the group of khaki-wearing boys.

Phyllis caught my eye and gave me the smallest of nods. It was the signal to start wrapping up this craziness. I jabbed my finger into the crowd. "Now I call upon each and every one of you. If you wish to gaze beyond the veil, you must focus all your energy on Polonde! Her power can only come from you."

I put my finger to my temple and mimed what I wanted them to do, stupidly holding out one hand toward Phyllis. Like big dumb animals, they mimicked me perfectly, which was good. Phyllis hadn't had enough time between Seeings to be any use at all. She needed a lie and quick. All holding one finger to their temples, the gathered crowd focused their power on Phyllis. She began to shudder, faking a real Seeing, but they wouldn't know the difference. I had to rub my chin to pull down my smile, but they earnestly focused forward. I stole a glance at the back of the crowd.

Horace's eyes pricked the oncoming night with two round saucers from the back of the crowd. He waved at me, frantic for my attention.

"Keep focusing your power!" My encouragement pulled several at the edges back into the performance Phyllis gave. "We're almost ready for the Great and Powerful Polonde!"

And thankfully, it was just an act because Phyllis had already performed a large Seeing just on the other side of

Underhill. I didn't want her overdoing it. If we really were in Charlotte, we could be in DC by morning.

Satisfied with the crowd's engagement and Phyllis's building up to a very showy Seeing, I turned back to Horace. He'd separated himself and Mary, pulling farther from the crowd. When he caught my gaze, he held up a small piece of cloth, like a tiny banner. Even without my glasses, I would recognize the flag of the Nazis anywhere.

Realization cracked over me like a broken egg, oozing into the reality that we stood before a crowd of able-bodied Nazis.

Nazis.

I'd spent years of my life—watched friends die!—so the world would never have to see what I saw. The whole point of locking away the magic was to make sure these idiots never got access to it. And here we were, the last mages on the planet, standing in front of a bunch of Nazis.

My face froze, cast in the mask of a showman. Spinning in place, I turned to Phyllis. She gyrated in her performance of the crazy Seer being taken over by demons or some other bullshit. I raised my eyebrow at her, so she knew to pay attention. When she didn't stop shuddering, I tried to signal her by opening my eyes wider, hoping my face would be so remarkably messed up she'd pay some attention.

But she kept up the act, twisting like she couldn't keep back the power of the Seeing. She writhed very convincingly. She made the deep guttural noises, and her eyes rolled into the back of her head while her eyelids flashed in rapid blinks too fast to really block out any light. The chill swept through me in the instant before Phyllis lost her battle to the Seeing.

A normal Seeing could slip through a day without any notice. A normal Seeing could be brought on with an insertion of power. A normal Seeing could predict the weather only slightly better than NOAA.

This Seeing ruptured out of Phyllis like a wave, bowling into everyone within a stone's throw of her. The power of the Seeing interjected itself between my mind and this reality, pushing me into another world. Almost as quickly, I stood in the place where thousands—hundreds of thousands—of people were murdered by the Nazi regime. The bodies lined a ditch and people as skinny as skeletons dug to make the pit larger.

I scanned the area, and there, standing on the platform stood Phyllis, but not Phyllis of this world. She radiated a ghostly white and blue. The light spilled off her, bleaching the ground around her as if the mortal power of pigments couldn't resist the power raging through her. The cheap nightgown waved in the air as if pulled along by an unseen current. Her eyes turned a glossy black, shining like twin beetle carapaces. The power radiating from her welled up from the ground and the bodies of the concentration camp started to move.

"You meddle in powers beyond your control! The demon that lives in you will eat your soul and still hunger. Your famine will walk the world, a plague of thought! A cancer upon this world! If you do not stop, I WILL COME FOR YOU!"

The power filling Phyllis turned from the white light of something pure and powerful to pale grey and just as terrifying. I tended not to believe in ghosts and spirits. Every mage who claimed to deal with the spirits of the dead had turned out to be a sham, but here, standing before me, a pillar of revenge and terror burned over Phyllis.

The idyllic park stood transformed into a place of true horror. Not horror because ghosts and spirits were vengeful, but horror because humans had done those things. Humans had made it happen. And we stood among Nazis.

I had been in Auschwitz, and I desperately hoped Phyllis was not somehow connected to the place where Nazis killed a million people. But Phyllis grew up in Poland. Phyllis knew many people who had been killed by the Nazis. Many. She knew the people they'd killed before the Americans had gotten involved.

Behind her, the bodies had managed to come to standing. They shambled toward us in our vision. She held out her hands, pointing at the Nazis. "Death is coming for you!"

One man stood forward. "Lies and tricks, witch! We will not be replaced."

"You will die. Blood on your hands!"

Phyllis turned her focus on him and opened her mouth to speak.

Before she could open her mouth again, I struck her feet with a lance of pure heat, cutting her off from whatever power held her like a puppet. My heart convulsed in my chest, but I drained every last scrap of power I had into breaking the grip the vengeful spirit had on Phyllis. I took a knee and clutched my chest, pouring out more power.

The power of whatever held her cracked. Reality broke the illusion and light spilled through. Whatever it was that held Phyllis cried out in anger, tearing at the Nazis, but unable to reach anyone. As reality broke open, releasing us back to a park in the south, the ghost unleashed a wave of terror. It spread out from Phyllis like a ripple in a pool.

The fear swept over me like the undertow of a wave, dragging at me. Pieces of my soul shivered in its wake, but it mostly washed over me, moving on. I had taken a knee, after all. The wave of destruction nailed the gathered men in the chest, knocking them over.

As abruptly as it started, it ended. Phyllis staggered backward. Her wide eyes searched the scene for any clues as to what had happened or what had held her. She caught me in her gaze, and I found my feet, crossing the short distance between us. I still clutched my chest.

When I got to her, I put my arm over her shoulder.

"I'm so sorry, Ruth, I didn't mean to!"

"Shhh, it's okay, we should go." I turned back to the men on the ground, but already one groaned. "They'll be fine, and we need to move."

I scanned the park, searching for Horace and Mary, but they were already heading to the nearby cars. The headlights of a car blinked as Horace approached, holding out a set of keys from a fistful of similar devices

The nearest of the Nazis sat up, blinking at the world. He looked around as if expecting to be somewhere else. He checked his watch and sighed, holding his chest, as if relieved.

I readjusted Phyllis, so my arm was under hers. "Time to go," I whispered. Without waiting for her to start helping us move, I edged away from the crowd at an angle. The edge of the park curved so the road came around to a spot not very far from where we were.

Horace and Mary climbed into the car as the Nazis started asking sleepy questions of "Hey, what happened?" and "Where am I?" and my personal favorite, "Are we late?"

We hobbled along, hoping to make a quiet getaway.

"Jason! They're stealing your car!" someone yelled behind us.

I hobbled faster.

"Where's that witch fortune teller?"

I ducked my head and pushed Phyllis toward the road, even as Horace pulled away from the curb in our most recently stolen car.

"There they are! Stop them!"

And that's how I got chased by a group of Nazis in the United States of America.

Chapter Sixteen

It occurred to me, the last time I'd seen a Nazi, I'd been wearing olive green and serving our military. We ladies weren't supposed to be sent into combat, but the War Department turned out to be much more pragmatic when it came to magical powers. Last time we were chased by Nazis, Horace had a stolen P-38. Last time, we took life.

As I hobbled with Phyllis toward the rendezvous point, I prayed they didn't have guns.

<Eat?> Brigid asked.

"That seems a little extreme, don't you think?" I called over my shoulder heaving along under the added burden of Phyllis. Dammit, I'd lost my cane in Underhill and I hadn't even noticed.

<Fire?> she asked.

"Fine, go big or go home, they say!" I didn't really think she'd do it, but a distraction, even a small dragon, would probably go a long way to helping us out.

Glee poured through the mental connection with my dragon, and I turned back for a second. Behind us, Brigid erupted in flames, growing. My bones reverberated with her roar, vibrating through my body with its fury. Still she grew, wings unfolding in a shadowy figure wrapped in fire of every color, except her claws, those remained a shiny fire engine red.

<Twice in one day! I'm hungry!> Brigid called through our link.

"Don't eat the people!"

<Fine!> She roared her frustration at me, but the Nazis fell back, staggering at the sight of a dragon.

I divided my attention between the car rounding the corner and the dragon—still growing!—the size of a small house.

As Brigid grew, she stretched her wings like she wanted to fly. The flames hissed as the grass at her feet withered and browned. She grabbed a nearby tree, ripping it out of the ground. The flames from her body caught in the leaves, hissing as the fire ate through the vegetation. Brigid bit into the tree, as if it were an overly large piece of broccoli. The trunk snapped with a *thunk*. The conflagration consumed the tree.

Above the roar of the fire, Nazis yelled incoherently, gathering their people in the face of a literal dragon. Horace brought the red import to the edge of the park, and I put Phyllis in the back seat behind him.

"Hurry! I just saw a gun!" Mary called.

I ran to the other side of the car to let myself in, opening the door. "Come on, Brigid! It's time to go!"

The dragon dropped her burning tree, almost hitting the Nazis. She shrank as she walked toward me, her body condensing. *<Hungry!>* she said.

The feel of her hunger washed over me, and my stomach growled in response. I smiled fondly, remembering the way I used to feel like that when I cast a lot. Brigid, now closer to the size of antelope, galloped across the lawn, flames still flying off her, chewing on the lawn. I sat in the car, pushing the long tiki torch running between the front and back seat. I held the door open, one foot sticking out of the car on the curb.

Brigid tumbled, tripping in the grass. The report of the gun bit my ear. The flames surrounding Brigid turned quickly from the spectrum of colored flames back down to the dull red and orange. She shrank, collapsing like a burning log on a campfire. Sparks flew up from the spot, taking what remained of her form. Her body dissipated in the flames as if she had never really had form.

<Be good,> she said.

The link between us broke like a piece of yarn that grew too thin and pulled apart. She slipped back into the eternal fire with a puff of smoke and a hole in our link.

"Drive!" Phyllis yelled.

Horace stomped on the gas. I had been sitting, but the door had been open, and it slammed into me, smashing my forehead.

"No! You can't!" Words spilled out of my mouth, but what I wanted to say was "How could Nazis kill a dragon?" It made no sense. Dragons were magical creatures, harbingers of magic and power. How could a single bullet take one down?

It was like losing Dorothy all over again, only instead of Brigid being swept away, I was the one leaving the scene. My ears filled with the sound of water. Everything I loved died. My wife, Dorothy, and my daughter, Anne. I'd been left alone with a baby to sort out the pieces of my ruined life, and now I'd lost the only one who'd seen me for just me. The weight of immortality pushed down on me through the ages. It felt like drowning, the pressure on my chest built and built, like there was no way I could take the next breath, let alone the breath after that.

I took a painful breath. It was nearly impossible. I leaned forward, debating if I should jump out of the car and look for any remains, but the pavement zipped by, blurring from the speed and the tears building in my eyes. Mary grabbed my shoulder, twisting my cut-off shirt in her fist.

"You need to shut the door, Ruth!" She pulled me into the car, and without the constant push against the wind, the door latched. The city sped past in a blur. Someone pulled the seatbelt over my shoulder and latched it. I did nothing to stop them.

The tears came, streaking down my face and blotting out my vision. The world descended into the streaks of light on a highway as night descended. Our stolen car (with five or six tiki torches) ate up the miles between cities. No one spoke. After most of an hour, Horace turned on the radio. Phyllis took her hair out of the ridiculous bun and tried to rub the terrible makeup off her face.

"Some performance," Mary said.

Phyllis shook her head. "I hate when spirits get past my barriers. It's why I moved here after the war. It happened all the time in Poland."

* * *

The rest stop we pulled into had the deserted feel of a post-apocalyptic movie. It matched how I felt, empty and in need of a scrub. I used the dubious facilities and washed my hands, taking extra care because I had a hard time switching tasks once started. Had Brigid actually died? Or had she just faded back to the ether to recover her strength and heal? How could a being made of fire and soot be hurt by something so simple as a bullet? She had bitten Winter and lived. Damn, I wish they hadn't burned all the books.

When I turned off the water, I searched for the paper towels, but they didn't have any, only the hand blower. Like hell I was going to turn on a Sneak Up Easily machine while feeling like this within 24 hours of watching Winter get Ragdolled across Underhill. I might be dumb, but I wasn't grade A stupid.

I waved my hands in the air until they reached some peak dryness before I smeared them into my dirty clothes. Better than the alternative, I guess.

All three of them stood around the edge of a picnic table, looking like a set of the knick-knack monkeys holding their eyes, covering their ears, and holding their lips. Yup, the three deadly sins right there. But they hadn't noticed me yet.

"But do we keep going?" Mary asked. "She's in no condition. Winter almost killed her in the fae lands."

"We have to keep going," Horace said. "If she doesn't fulfill her side of things…" He shrugged, letting the silence of his words fill the air.

"I'm telling you, I don't think we should keep going," Phyllis said.

I ducked back behind the cinderblock wall. I leaned against the cool cement, the mortar between the bricks creasing my back.

"Is there something you're not telling us? Have you seen our future?" Horace asked.

"Please," Phyllis said with a dismissive tone. "If I had Seen the future, do you think I would have let you fools set me up for a reading in front of a group of Nazis—*Nazis!*"

"Neo-Nazis," Horace said.

"Yes, *Neo*-Nazis, because real Nazis had uniforms, style, *and* murderous racism." Phyllis widened her eyes to show her annoyance at Horace.

"I'm just worried. She really liked that dragon. Like a lot. It was like her familiar," Mary said.

My heart swelled at how Mary understood me. She knew what Brigid was to me, even if we hadn't known each other for long.

"I don't know how close she might or might not have been with the cat/dragon, but she only knew it for a day and a half," Phyllis said.

I scowled, my heart twisting in my chest.

"Show some compassion, Phyllis," Horace said. "You cried at the end of *Old Yeller*, and as I recall, that movie only lasted for 90 minutes."

Gratitude toward Horace filled me. It meant a lot to me, especially since he decidedly hadn't liked Brigid.

"You asshole. How dare you bring up the dog?" Phyllis said. "I'm just saying I don't think things are going to get any better." She paused. "Shall we count our mounting problems?"

Groans and shuffled feet met this suggestion, but Phyllis pushed on. I could just imagine her counting off her points on her fingers.

"Item One: wanted. We are wanted. We have now stolen three cars, robbed a store, and pickpocketed from multiple *Nazis*."

Horace chuckled. "Still got it."

A soft smack sounded. "*Shh*, she's trying to argue for a measured response. I just want this for my scrap book," Mary said holding up the armband.

Phyllis cleared her throat louder than strictly necessary. "Item two: the Source. We have no idea what might be happening with it, and Ruth is under the impression that it's still at the Smithsonian. But how is it getting out, and at such odd times?"

A pensive silence followed.

"Exactly, unless one of you knows of a reason the Source would only come out late at night or early in the morning? I don't think some guard is popping open the case to look at it, so where is it if it isn't in the case?"

"Okay, what else?" Mary asked.

"Item three: Winter."

Everyone muttered.

"Item three seems to be in favor of continuing our heist," Mary said. "If Winter comes—"

"If Winter comes, they both die," Horace finished. "But will that Seeing be enough to scare Winter off?"

Phyllis took a deep breath. "It was a very true Seeing. She tried to shake it away from me, and only the truth ever lasts in the face of so much power."

"I can't believe what she did," Mary said.

"The Queen of Winter is cruel," Horace said, his voice haunted by the fae royal. Too bad he hadn't met Summer, she was bright, powerful, *and* terrifying.

"Turn back or go on?" Phyllis asked.

"A vote then?" Horace suggested.

"Fine," Phyllis said.

Horace cleared his throat. "I vote we go on."

Phyllis clicked her tongue between her teeth. "Turn back."

The silence stretched on. Mary groaned. "It comes down to me? Oh no, I abstain. This is Ruth's life. I'm worried, but I think it's her choice, right?"

"I'm not waltzing into the Smithsonian to watch her die, filmed from fifteen different directions!" Phyllis stomped her foot in the grass.

"Well, I'm not resigning her to whatever fate Winter has planned for her without her permission!" Mary set something on the picnic table with a decided glass clink.

"We keep going," Horace said. "We can abort up until the last minute. We don't have to decide anything right now."

I came around the corner as though I'd just been in the bathroom. "What are we deciding?" I asked.

"Who's sitting in front," Horace lied flawlessly.

Careful to keep my face a mask, I checked out the bottle Mary had. Given her normal tastes, the bottle was suspiciously full. "Is that the same bottle?"

"I haven't had a proper chance to finish it. Want some?" she asked, holding the neck of the bottle toward me without actually drinking from it.

Without hesitation, I took a long pull of rum. The familiar burn was like a lightning rod, charging my emotions straight to the ground, giving me a second of clarity.

They were right. I would either die there, or I'd die at home. It didn't seem like it mattered, but if I was going to die, I wanted to try fighting.

"Are we done figuring out the seating arrangement?" I asked.

No one responded, as if they'd been caught doing something they shouldn't have. Of course, they thought I was crazy and grieving. They were right. I'd been grieving for forty years.

Chapter Seventeen

The light piercing the sky made a feeble attempt at roasting us. After driving through the night, we sat in traffic, waiting for the magical moment when the cars in front of us would evaporate. Horace took a likely off-ramp and followed the signs to metro parking.

"Are you nuts?" Phyllis asked. "Everyone knows the cars in these lots get jacked."

Horace laughed. "Maybe I'll leave the keys in the ignition."

"Oh, right," Phyllis said. "Old habits. Besides, I hate subways."

Horace turned the car into a parking space, squished between an SUV and a 90s era Dodge Caravan. "It's not a real subway. And it's mostly clean. At least it was a couple weeks ago."

"A few weeks ago? When were you here last?" I asked.

He snorted. "For that reenactment convention, just the other day."

Mary cocked her head. "The other day? That was two years ago!"

"Oh—you know how time is. Anyway, it's good to take the subway, it encourages modernization in other areas."

"I doubt the DC metro can be considered modernization. London had an underground in the 1800s," Mary chimed in. "It's nothing new. Though it could be useful." I pushed open my door, sliding out of the car with my trusty stolen bag. At this point, Phyllis had nothing, and Mary only had her tote. We were lucky we didn't have to go hit up another pharmacy. Horace had managed to drag his shaving kit all the way through Underhill. Someone had left behind a cane at one of the rest stops, and even though I felt guilty about it, I didn't feel so guilty I didn't pick it up.

I stood up, and my back complained. Each vertebra seemed to crack as I stood. I fished out the cane. To think I'd spent moments considering leaving it in the car. As soon as

I had it in my hand, I wondered if it would make a decent staff replacement.

Stop thinking about how you might have real access to magic after this. Winter still wants to kill you.

Right, way to be real upbeat.

A woman parked in a nearby space. She cut across the parking spaces toward the elevator. Her heels clicked on the cement like the tick of a clock.

"Shall we march to our dooms?" I asked.

Everyone went stiff.

Mary hissed. "I hate when you make jokes like that."

"Do you have any more rum?" I asked.

She nodded and passed it to me. "For medicinal purposes, then."

"Yup." I took a drink straight from the bottle. It burned like fire, but there was no fire other than the combustion in the car engines. We followed in the footsteps of the businesswoman to the escalator.

"Do we have anything resembling a plan?" Horace asked. He swung his shaving kit like it was a lunch box. Years of training are hard to break.

"Go there, find the Source, go home?" I said with a shrug.

"That's your plan? That's it?" Phyllis asked.

Horace smacked his forehead into the palm of his hand.

Mary shook her head. "Dear gods, we're all gonna die." She took the rest of the rum and dropped the bottle into the trashcan before she stepped onto the moving escalator. She sighed wistfully.

"What if I wanted some?" Phyllis asked.

"You're worthless drunk, Phyllis, and if we have to face off against Winter again, I'm going to need every advantage I can possibly muster up."

Phyllis rolled her eyes. "You are a bunch of idiots. There's no way we can beat Winter," she muttered.

I pulled my bag closer to my body, checking how much space I took up with my cane. This was my problem. I never should have dragged them all through this. I'm an idiot and selfish. A selfish idiot. And Winter wasn't likely to come back small. She'd tear everything around us apart, hoping to kill me by some accident or just sheer numbers.

After a kerfuffle with the machine spitting out tickets at the bottom of the escalators, we managed to hop a train heading toward the National Mall. Adorably, a young man and his girlfriend got up to offer us seats. I took the one closest to the window. The cement blocks lining the tunnel had the same indented pattern, repeating over and over. Not like the subways in Europe that had art, or carvings, or mosaics. No, metropolitan Washington, DC decorated everything in brutalism. The train pulled forward with a lurch, and I rocked forward in my seat. We sped down the dark of the tunnel for a time, slipping along like a snake on its way to eat the eggs of some endangered bird. Suddenly, the train erupted from the darkness, thrusting us into the light as we crossed a bridge.

Beams of light poured in through the windows, drenching the train in the golden orange of fire. Dust motes glowed like faeries in flight, caught in the rays of light. Impossibly, a bird call sounded through the passenger compartment.

I turned to find the source of the bird. The sound of the train rumbling across the tracks faded into static, and birds took over in droves, clucking, chirping and singing. Vines grew over the people frozen in the sun, as if the light had been a great trap.

Standing, I checked behind me. The vines grew quickly covering everyone. Every passenger stood or sat in place, covered in greens. The vines, moving like snakes, burst into flowers, filling the train with pollen and glittering dust.

The sheer power of Summer radiated from the front of the passenger compartment, shining out like a beacon. The vines pulled the passengers away from her path. Resplendent in a dress the color of the sun, Summer strolled among the passengers.

I'd seen this trick before, but always in places where a pause in time would cause no problems. Here? The next train was coming. How far did this bubble in time exist? Was this truly for me and me alone?

Mentally, I readjusted my understanding of her power.

Just her presence filled my channels with power. It trickled along my paths, as if she were trying to keep it all to herself. Still, it was more than I'd had a second ago. Even small advantages were miraculous when dealing with Fae.

"You said you weren't going to make another offer," I said, holding my hands out to indicate the people covered in vines. "This looks like you're making another offer."

She cocked her head to the side. "You're really not very bright, even for a human. You know that right?"

"Why are you here?"

Her smile faded to exasperation. "You sent me your dragon. I had to respond."

Brigid. My heart twisted.

She shook her head slowly. "You don't even know how any of it works, do you? You'll be so damned difficult to train when I finally get my hands on you. Maybe we should just go now." Summer leaned toward me, pulling me into her gaze.

My heart skipped a beat. Then it skipped again. A cavity opened up where my chest used to be, and I couldn't draw breath at all. My whole body shuddered, and the world started to fade into the place where only pain existed. The edges of me blurred into the train and the other passengers until everything melted into one existence of pain.

"Wait!" I gasped. "The Seer!"

Suddenly the world contracted to just me, as if something else in the world could exist besides pain.

Summer narrowed her eyes at me. "What about the Seer?"

I drew a breath, shaky, but real. The pain ricocheted through my chest, but I had to speak or she'd go back to stopping my heart. "She had a true seeing." I pointed to Phyllis. As if to exemplify my direction, a flower burst open in a puff of pollen in Phyllis's face.

"What did she See?"

I took another breath, savoring the air. Who knew when I'd get to take another?

Summer glared down at me.

I gave her a vaguely apologetic look, clutching my chest and taking a second breath. Damn, Summer filled the air with an intoxicating mix of flowers, sunlight and plenty. Too many breaths and Summer would own my heart.

On to business. "Phyllis said Winter and I would both die the next time we met."

Summer's eyes widened to reveal the whites around the edges. She leaned in, putting her hands on the tops of the heads of nearby passengers, now covered in growing vines. "She what?"

"I know, crazy world, eh?"

Summer stood upright, using the heads of passengers to push herself up as if they were nothing more than fence posts. Of course, to Summer they weren't even as important as posts. Humans couldn't be relied upon to hold up a gate or a fence for any length of time.

"What were her exact words?"

I shrugged. "My trap's not exactly steel, you know? I haven't had a good cognition test. I mean, I do my Sudoku like I'm supposed to, but my stress has been through the roof. And my doctor says it affects my sugar too. It's a real problem with—"

"Enough!" Summer rolled her eyes. "You talk too much."

"You want to kill me. You said we wouldn't meet as friends next. What am I to assume that means? I'm suspended in the air. I'm in a train crossing over water. There's no native soil for me to step on. It would be easy for you to attack me here."

"But you're still traveling with the Source? Even though it will bring the wrath of Winter?"

I paused. I must have heard her wrong. She said "with" instead of "to." But the way of fae didn't give me an opportunity to correct her—or time to even consider. I inclined my head. "I die if I secure it. I die if I don't. Either way, I'm dead."

"You really didn't mean to send me your dragon."

I frowned. "No. I didn't."

Her face twisted like she'd eaten something sour. "Well, this is awkward. I'll have to send it back to fire. It will be totally free. I can't guarantee it will return to you."

"She. That dragon is a girl."

"How can it be a girl? It is made of fire and smoke."

I considered my words. "She felt like a girl in her heart. Who am I to argue with a soul made of pure fire?"

Summer shook her head. "You humans are so baffling." She turned to look behind her, as if something had caught her attention. "It hardly matters. My sister will come for you on the full moon." A glint of cold iron ran across her eyes. "Maybe I'll kill her when she's with you."

A shudder of anticipation ran through her body, and she licked her teeth.

"That would probably be useful to me," I said.

She focused on me suddenly. "Maybe I'll kill you when you see her."

Ice ran through my veins. Winter being her enemy didn't make her my friend. "Ah, well, that would be considerably less helpful."

"Unless..." She tapped her lips with one of her perfect long fingers.

"Unless?" I asked.

"Unless you were to make a bargain with me." She turned her full focus back to me.

"Hold on, what do I get out of this bargain? It looks like I'm already going to make way for you to reign supreme over your sister. What could you possibly give me?"

"Your life," she said, tipping her head to the side. "It seems a fair bargain. One life for another." She nodded as if to herself. "And then after you give me the Source, then we can—"

"What? No! I can't give you the Source! The whole point of this is to fix the spell to come back into compliance with my previous contract! Giving it to you wouldn't help anything. Then I'd just have a war between Summer and Winter."

"We are always at war."

That caught on an edge in my mind. "Why is that? Why are you always at war?"

"Human child, you know nothing of the great cosmic power that we are. Winter and Summer are as at odds as day and night."

I chewed on my lip for a moment. "But Winter isn't a season. So she's something else—the absence of the sun?" I said musing aloud.

Summer paused, a half-smile lurking on her lips. "You do know something. This could be so interesting." Then her smile sharpened. "It doesn't change the fact that you will have no way to secure the, ah, Source of your magic. Not from my sister, probably not from other humans either. If you did, you'd wear it around your neck, or some other ridiculous human display. I thought you were grooming your dragon to wear it until you sent it to me."

"Her," I corrected almost automatically.

She scowled at me, considering my statement. It wasn't that she didn't understand the gendering, it was that I refused to be injured by her words. Clearly someone hadn't been paying attention to the gay community in the 80s. She'd have to try harder than being an asshole about my dragon.

I continued while she scowled. "Besides if I'm giving you the key to take down your sister and ascend to power, that doesn't exactly help my people any. You've heard of global warming, right?"

A delicious smile spread across her lips. "I've heard of it. My sister despises humanity for forsaking her. Humans helping to sway the world to me has made her furious. It's as if you all forgot how she worked so hard to protect humanity through your Ice Ages. She has taken it personally."

I swallowed a dry lump in my throat. The Ice Ages. Winter held a grudge against humanity from thousands of years ago. Of course, she did. I tried to keep my features as smooth as possible in case Summer didn't realize how much information she'd given me in that one confession. I nodded carefully and spoke with deliberate clarity. "Regardless, I can make no bargains regarding the Source. The heart of a star is the center of another bargain, and I will not deal falsely."

Summer released a breath, and it spiraled into the air, drawing the motes of dust and pollen into a dance around her head. "Very well. I shall go." Instantly, the vines retreated. The flowers folded in on themselves.

"Wait! You have received powerful knowledge this day. Don't I deserve a boon?"

Everything paused, and Summer turned back to me. "I have given you a great boon. You will live through today." She narrowed her eyes at me. "Tomorrow is much less certain."

I scrunched my lips to the side of my face. "That doesn't seem like very good information."

She cocked her head to the side. "Impertinent human. Very well, I shall pay you in kind." She took a breath, and the power of summer raged through the passenger compartment of the metro train. Light sparked from her, flooding the room, so bright I had to shield my eyes or be blinded by it. The power of it flooded into my channels, but not fast enough to fill my internal batteries. Then just as suddenly, she was gone.

A bump in the tracks hid the moment when it seemed as if the train had been completely stopped, and suddenly the noise of the metro flooded over me. People went about their business, mostly reading from their phones and ignoring everyone around them. Not so much as an extra petal indicated Summer had been there. I sat with a thump, checking how much power she'd given me, but it wasn't much. Maybe a couple of small castings. But if I delved too deeply...

I pushed the thought out of my mind. I could die choking on my breakfast tomorrow, so there was no point worrying about fool things like whether my own magic would do me in or not.

I turned to Phyllis and Mary to be sure they were okay. Mary caught the motion and raised an eyebrow at me. She had no idea I'd just talked to Summer.

"You okay?" she asked.

"I don't like cities."

Mary scowled. "Odd, you seemed to like Paris just fine."

I huffed. "Paris is a cultural hub, not to mention the seat of my unlamented order."

"Well, the books were lamented."

I sighed wistfully. "The books."

She nodded. "The books. I miss the books," she said.

I knew it for code. Mary missed the magic. And I missed it, too. She put a hand on my shoulder and squeezed.

Chapter Eighteen

We transferred trains and got off at the Smithsonian exit. Kids in matching t-shirts clogged the escalator, guarded by the occasional harried adult. Their calls rang through the station like cowboys of old, hollering to their cattle dogs.

I hadn't so much as set foot in DC since 1972, the last time I'd come to check on the Source with my own two eyes. Last time, it had called to me from its cage, pulsing at the edge of my consciousness, fighting at the edges of a spell that held it right in plain sight.

Now it felt no closer than at any point along this trip.

Maybe I'd only imagined it as I'd testified. Maybe I had felt nothing but my own nerves back then. Maybe I'd wake up the Queen of Sheba.

The herd of children cleared the escalator, and we got on. The machine ground along, pulling us up the slope to a small unassuming hole at the top. We moved away from the moving stairs quickly, arriving at the corner of a busy intersection. Summer's words spilled through my mind. "You do know something," she had said. But what? What did I really know other than Winter wasn't so much a season— but what was a season? Winter was a designation for the part of the planet tilted away from the sun. The absence of the sun? Could that be what my dragon meant. Stars, I hope she was okay back in the realm of fire or wherever dragons went. Ugh, why was everything so weird now?

The light changed, and we joined the mass of humanity crossing the street. The lawns and trees around the mall stood out as the only green in a marble façade jungle, the neo-roman look carved into nearly every building giving them all a vague sameness. We crossed one more street onto a large pedestrian walkway paved in beige, packed, sand.

"Which way?" Mary asked.

"That's Air and Space, the Capitol." Horace pointed like a clock, going around the National Mall. "And that one is the Natural History Museum."

I took off across the hard-packed gravel walkway between the great stretches of lawn. Well, "took off" might be a smidge of an exaggeration. I hobbled more efficiently than usual with the cane. Everyone passed us as we walked, even the droves of children making their way to the museum full of bones.

"How's the hip?" Phyllis asked.

"I need a new one, but who can afford it?"

"I thought you had Part A," Mary said.

I snorted. "Part A, yes, but apparently, I'm not in enough pain for the hip to be 'necessary.' It's still considered elective." I used my cane to point at Horace. "But it'll cover his Viagra for free."

"I have never!" Horace's face flushed to dark red.

"Oh stuff it," Phyllis said. "She means that any man can get a pill for a boner but she can't get a new hip, and it's always been unfair."

"Hey Horace, what do you put in your garden every year to make it grow so tall?" I asked. This was well-trodden territory for us, but the familiar conversation eased my nerves a bit. Breaking into an exhibit at the Smithsonian wasn't going to do any of us any good. I'd be in that assisted living facility by next Monday—if I lived that long.

Horace sighed, like a man defeated. "Steer manure."

"And is steer manure any better than cow manure?" Phyllis asked.

Horace's lips twisted up to the side, the answer pressuring its way out and him not wanting to let it. "They are different!"

"Mmmhm," Phyllis said. "Enlighten us."

"I don't know how steer manure is better, it just is!"

Nodding her head sadly, Mary said, "I think you just proved the point."

I held in a triumphant chuckle, saving my breath for getting across the expanse in the center of the mall. After an eternity (according to my hip, which now ached like someone had frozen the joint and let a terrier chew on it), we made it to the street on the far side of the expansive lawn.

Packed gravel lined the edge of the lawn on the near side of the road. A light held traffic, and we crossed the street to the cement sidewalks on the far side. The Natural History Museum stood in front of us, many stories high, with a domed roof in the center like all good Roman buildings. Historians would either be baffled by all our marble pillars or just say we were an extension of the Roman Empire when it went through a particularly republic-leaning time frame.

We took the steps like the gravity-challenged group we were. I put my cane on the step above me and shook my head. Last time we made a run for the Source, we climbed the Alps, sneaking into Germany from the Italian side. Now we only had to make it to the case. If we could just get there.

At the top of the stairs, velvet ropes directed us to a turnstile and a smiling docent. "Welcome to the Smithsonian," she said as we approached the bar.

I had to juggle my cane to slip through the spinning bar. I pushed through quickly to make sure no one was stuck waiting for us to get through. After the turnstile, we put our paltry items on the scanner belt for the x-ray machine. I fumbled with my bag, dropping it into one of the plastic buckets. Everyone turned out their pockets and even Horace put his shaving kit in a matching bucket. As I gathered my bag and arranged my cane on the opposite side, a smiling docent approached us with fliers. I scowled, but Mary took one as the guard inspected the inside of Horace's bag. For the briefest moment, I felt the Source.

But was it just my imagination playing tricks on me? We were finally in the same building. It should be right there, up a couple flights of stairs—ha, we were absolutely going to take the elevator!—and all this would be over. The sensation of power faded, and I hobbled to the stuffed African elephant in the lobby to wait for the others.

I took a breath and braced for Go Time. Under the guise of waiting for my party, I scoped out the security. Guards stood at the entrance to every exhibit hall, and one at the stairwell. They sure hadn't skimped there. The security blanket seemed a little extreme, even for a building housing the priceless artifacts it had.

"How are we doing this?" Mary asked, checking over her shoulders like a nervous hen looking for her chicks.

"At least pretend to be interested in the exhibits," Phyllis admonished. "If we're all going to die, I'd at least like it to be at the hands of our enemies and not because of the twitchy fingers of underpaid guards."

"We're running a Farmer in the Dell," I said. I nodded toward the stairs. "It's on the second level."

"At least they have an elevator," Horace said. Phyllis rolled her eyes at him.

"If we're running Farmer, I'm assuming you're the Cheese," Mary said.

I nodded. "Right in one."

Phyllis scowled at her feet. "This is my last opportunity to remind you all what a bunch of idiots you are."

I patted her shoulder. "It's this or fight Winter's armies."

Phyllis shook her head. "Sure, but it could be years before Winter comes back. She thinks she'll die the next time you meet. Don't you think that would keep her away?"

"Winter fades every year but manages to come back. Death and rebirth is just another part of their cycle, I think." I took a deep breath, keeping my eye on the security. "I doubt she has any reason to fear me, and every reason to come after the Source."

Phyllis pursed her lips. "You're still crazy, you know that right?"

I pushed toward the elevator. "I know."

The doors opened on the creaky box of death, all brass and buttons. The elevator hadn't been updated this century, but without an assist, I wouldn't be able to walk tomorrow. Of course, I'd probably be dead tomorrow, so what harm would an inflamed hip do? Oh, or maybe I'd die from an inflamed hip if I took the stairs? Maybe that's what Summer meant.

I crossed the elevator threshold, and the others followed. Horace pushed the buttons, then there was nothing left to do but wait. The doors half closed, then paused before fully closing.

"That's auspicious," Mary said.

Everyone chuckled. "At least it's not as bad as the gondola in Austria," Phyllis added. As if obligated by contract, we all groaned as one, remembering the coldest night ever, spent swinging over a snow-covered field waiting for someone to start the engine again. We would have died if we hadn't been wearing survival gear.

The doors closed, and a dubious motion took over the box of death. We dipped before the elevator started to rise slowly. The air grew stale and despite our years of friendship, we all stood in the box staring at the door as if the most important thing in the world was about to walk through.

It pinged when we reached the second floor. The doors started to open, paused, then actually opened. We stepped out of the elevator and turned around the marble column to view the rotunda. The elephant stood resplendent below us, nearly tall enough to reach the second floor. From where we emerged, the whole round of the museum stood out in front of us. Across the round atrium, an armed guard stood, keeping watch over the exhibit with the Hope Diamond. I shot Phyllis a look, and we started moving toward our target: a case ten yards from the Hope Diamond.

Our steps brought us slowly around the rotunda. As we passed each pillar, the angle on the guard changed. She saw us, but didn't take notice. We weren't even worth her real attention. Of course not, what old people could muster a real threat against the gems? It wasn't like we could outrun a guard.

At least, we were finally here. We'd come so far. I shook my head. So close to the Source, I should feel something. How could it be exactly like everywhere else?

Unbidden, Winter's words returned to me: *You are no closer than when we last spoke.*

My heart beat faster, and the air chilled my arms. How could she be right? What did the fae queen know?

I rubbed my arms, as if the Winter Queen's words brought her cold with her. Something shivered in my skin, making me wonder about my gut feeling. Something wasn't right. There was still time to call it off. We could get out of here and I could call Jessica. I could be home by tomorrow.

And then I would die at home.

"Hey, you okay?" Mary asked.

"Fine," I lied.

"We don't have to keep going," she said, as if reading my mind.

I nodded. "I know." I caught her up in my gaze. "But she's going to kill me." My throat tightened around my words. Winter would kill me. "I'm just not ready to be dead," I said.

Mary stopped, grabbing my shoulders. "This doesn't have to be the end. We could—"

"What? Go home?" I asked. "I'd love to go home, to be with my Jessica—to play Bridge on Saturday and complain about how there's no decent sponge cake in town anymore."

She watched me, saying nothing.

I pushed on. "This is it for me. It's this or it's the end. My end." I swallowed my fear. "You could go," I offered.

Her face crumpled. "Oh Ruth, I couldn't leave you in the lurch. We'll figure something out."

The tears threatened. This could really be it. This could really be the last day of my life. This wasn't going to work. This was stupid. Winter had tricked me. Something was wrong.

I opened my mouth to call it all off, but Horace cleared his throat before launching into a great coughing fit right in front of the guard.

We were there. The guard checked around for other potential threats and determined we were not worth her time.

"Sir, are you okay?" she asked.

"Oh god! He's choking!" Phyllis yelled, walloping on the melodrama for good effect. Everyone turned to look at them.

And in that second, I saw my opening. The second guard from inside the exhibit turned to see what the commotion was, and we slipped to the back wall during his moment of inattention. Mary gave my shoulder a squeeze, holding on for a moment longer than necessary. She let go, turning her attention to acting like a drunk old woman. Which might not have been far off the mark.

"My goodness! It sure is a big rock!" she said louder than exactly necessary, leaning in over the carefully drawn line. She accidentally/on purpose knocked over one of the crowd control pillars. "Oh my gosh! I'm so sorry! I forgot my glasses in the hotel, and I can't see a damned thing!"

"Ma'am, step back please," the guard said.

"Get help!" Phyllis called from just outside the exhibit.

A third guard, the one standing at the far side of the room holding the Hope Diamond stepped in closer.

"Can't I just take one quick peek at it from up here?" Mary asked in her best innocent old woman voice. "It's not like I'm going to steal it! It's practically in a vault!" She leaned in closer, tangling up in the retractable stanchion.

"Ma'am!" the guard said.

"What did you say, Sonny?" Mary asked, half turning her head. She caught my eye and winked with the eye the guard wouldn't be able to see.

The third guard stepped around me. Actually stepped around me like I was so beyond their concern, so frail and useless that I couldn't be any more of a threat than a cat.

Phyllis threw her whole gusto into her performance. "Oh god! Please! Someone help! He's dying!"

I turned my back on the drama. After all, in the Farmer in the Dell, the cheese stands alone.

The case stood before me, on the edge of the exhibit where the Hope sat, there was another famous necklace. The necklace given to Marie of Austria by Napoleon, a row of teardrop diamonds, perfect to show one's power and show off a beautiful woman. The Source was nothing so grand, but it sat with diamonds and gold and sapphires and rubies. The heart stone could not be seen by anyone who didn't know how to look.

It should shimmer in the places between reality and dreams, the edge of magic. The Source lived in the moment between sleeping and waking, where dreams lived, and real life hadn't taken hold. I scanned the case, but I couldn't find it.

Seventy years ago, they had different necklaces in the case, but since no one could see it without training, we had deemed it safe. The circle drawn around it was laid in paint and covered over with a coat of white. No one needed to know the marks of magic if we were hiding it forever. The familiar circles and curlicues of the magical languages written into the layer of paint stood out to my eye. It had been decades since I'd checked on the stone.

Last time I stood here, I thought I'd spotted it. I'd been able to feel it. Maybe decades without contact with the outside had turned it dull. Maybe I couldn't see the shimmer of the illusion anymore because I was so far removed from real magic.

I clenched my jaw and hung the cane on the crook of my arm. Summer's presence had given me just enough power for one trick. Besides, after I cracked the case and moved the Source out of its containment, I'd have as much power as I wanted. Gathering the power into my hand, I took a breath. This was it. After I finished this, there would be no way to get out of this place without shattering something. I closed my eyes to pool the power, scraping it from every corner of my channels. For a second, it tore across my heart. It froze for an instant, hesitating, as if even my heart knew it was a bad idea to break open an exhibit at the Smithsonian.

But who else could I ask? Everyone from the War Department had died—we didn't even have a War Department anymore.

And they'd never believe me. I was supposed to have died decades ago. I'd gone to great lengths to make sure my paperwork matched my daughter's and everyone thought I'd been the one to go over that cliff. I didn't even exist to call on the favors of a thankful government.

I took a step and put my hand on the bulletproof glass.

An alarm sounded, buzzing so loudly, I startled back. The two nearest guards turned from their marks to look at me. I made eye contact with the one closest, his eyes widened until the whites shone around his irises. Realization cracked across his face like the breaking of an egg. The spell already buzzed in my hand, rattling my bones.

Stepping forward, I put my hand to the thick glass and released the spell. The spell ricocheted into the glass like a bullet. It kicked back, shocking my hand like it had been crushed by a rock. I reeled back, clasping my hand to my chest. The glass shattered as I stepped back, falling to the floor like rain. Glass crashed to the marble floor, drowning out the alarm for a moment.

The guards instinctively hunched their heads as if the noise were a physical attack. Even as they hunched down, they reached for their guns. People screamed.

I cradled my arm to my chest and reached into the case with my good hand, right to the spot where the heart stone came to rest at the end of World War II.

My palm hit the bottom of the case. The familiar buzz of a decades old spell feebly reached up through the paint to let me know it still functioned. But there was nothing here.

The Heartstone, the Source of Magic intended for humans, was gone.

And now, I had nothing to bargain with the Queen of Winter.

I was as good as dead.

Chapter Nineteen

The world continued around me like one of those fuzzy pictures where the photographer left the shutter open forever. In the old days, we called that bad photography. Nowadays, people called it art, or thoughtful.

The Heartstone for all the magic of humanity was just gone. Just like that. I gave up magic—gave up youth!—to hide it, to protect the world from the Queen of Winter, and all of it was just gone. Some thief had beaten me to it. Somewhere, someone had the Source of human magic, hoarding it to themselves. I looked at my hands as tiny red specks grew across the palm of the one that touched the glass when it shattered.

"Damn thing cut me," I said more to myself than to the chaos swarming around me.

"Put your hands in the air!" one guard yelled.

"Show me your hands!" the other yelled.

Quickly, the third guard covered them, making sure no one could sneak up on the two taking care of me.

I held my hands in the air, my cane hanging from the crook of my elbow. The glass crunched as I shifted my weight to handle prolonged standing. Instantly, my hip ached like I'd walked a marathon to get here. Every missed hour of sleep, every spell, every step and mile from California to DC etched itself in my nerves. I sagged and the alarm changed. Footsteps echoed from every corner of the building as people ran up. More guards with walkie talkies arrived. Radio conversations filled the air.

No Source, no magic. I couldn't just cast a spell to get out of this, dammit. I'd have to talk my way out.

Flip the script.

"Oh, my god, your case broke all over me!"

"Put your cane down!" the nearest guard said.

I released my cane to gravity with the simple expedience of putting my arm down. It slid off quickly, landing in the remains of the glass panel with a crunch.

"Turn around slowly."

My arms burned with the effort of keeping my hands in the air. I took one step and my hip hitched, threatening to give way. "I don't know how much longer I can go like this," I said. "My hip isn't what it used to be."

A middle-aged man in a suit walked between the guards. "Do we shoot elderly women now?" he asked. He did not get close enough for me to touch, stopping only a couple yards from me. "Can you walk?"

Turning my voice into the scared old woman voice I said, "I don't know. He had me drop my cane." My voice cracked with genuine fear. The Source wasn't here. Winter would kill me when the moon became full. I had less than twenty-four hours, and the Source could be anywhere.

"Just do your best, ma'am." The man in the suit pointed to a bench in the corridor outside. "There's a bench over here. I'd like you to sit down."

A second man, this one in brown slacks and his sleeves rolled up to his elbows, came into the room. "Oh my god, what happened? Who's bleeding? How did this happen?" His balding hair had a fly-away puff to match his mustache. He reminded me of the previous curator, the one who helped us secure it at the end of the war. "That's bulletproof glass!" He ran his fingers into his hair and pulled. "How?"

The man in the suit turned to the curator. "Is anything missing?"

Slowly, he took extra care and time, searching the display. As he made it to the last necklace he shook his head. "No, they all seem to be here. We need to move them back to the vault." The calm of work to do took over the curator, and he shook his head.

I made it to the bench indicated by the man in the suit and sat down with relief. The Source wasn't here, and I just used magic to break open a display in the Smithsonian. I wouldn't live long enough to be in trouble once Winter got hold of me.

Sitting on the bench, I watched the people around me working, but I didn't see. My whole life had been one of sacrifice, and now the source was gone. I could have changed so many diapers with functioning magic. My body would not have decayed away. And like a wound in my mouth that my tongue couldn't ignore, my thoughts bent back to Dorothy and Anne.

If we'd had magic when the car crashed. If I hadn't insisted on putting the Source in a safe place, locked in a case and withheld from all humanity, Dorothy and Anne would both still be alive. Jessica would have grown up with her mother. She would have known how powerful and vibrant her mother had been. Oh Anne, what a glorious witch you would have been.

And like a jolt of electricity, my heart clenched over my shame. Even here at the end, all I could think about was me. If we'd had magic, we could have done more to change our world. If we'd been raising and training mages, we could have sent people out into the world as a force for good. I chose to end one conflict by hiding all the wonder of magic from the world. What did I think would happen with Winter? Did I honestly think my solution would last? How did I think hiding my talents and choosing the safe road was right? It solved one moment of one problem. And all of it for nothing.

Out there in the world, someone had the Source. Someone had full access to all the magic ever created by mankind. Someone could be raising witches and wizards for some nefarious reasons. How could I have been so conceited to think I could do better service for the world by hiding it away? Did I think all the good people in the world had come and gone? How come I couldn't trust the next generation could do good? How could I have been so vain to think I alone could control the fate of magic for the people of our planet?

And worse, I hadn't even given my friends—my friends who had literally fought alongside me, saved my life too many times to count—a chance to lead the way in a new world. They would have been brilliant as the heads of their orders, and I stole that chance from them.

I am the greatest fool the world has ever known.

Horace's voice rose over the din of everything else. "She practically kidnapped us!" he said. "I didn't have a choice! She has this way of making you fear for your life."

My gaze latched on to Horace sitting on a bench not far from me. Phyllis sat next to him, and Mary stood next to her. Both Phyllis and Mary looked down at Horace. Mary raised an eyebrow at him, "You helped plan the trip!" Mary said.

The police officer flipped the notebook open. "You're saying you were kidnapped?"

"Yes! Ruth was talking crazy! She said we had to get to the magic stone. She was like a madwoman."

Phyllis rolled her eyes. "I think he hasn't been taking his meds," she said to the officer. She turned to Horace. "Horace! Horace! Do you know where we are?! You asked if we were in Vegas, but we're not, are we?" She asked him these simple questions with a deliberately raised voice.

Horace blinked up at her. "We're not? But all the jewels!"

The police officer deflated. "Does he have dementia?" she asked.

Mary nodded sadly. "He says things sometimes."

I recognized the ploy, an astutely run P.T. Barnum. Caught red-handed, but with enough contrasting statements, it would be nearly impossible to sort out the truth. They would have to rely on the only indisputable evidence. And since all the guards had been looking elsewhere, only the cameras would have seen the whole thing. I didn't know how much magic did or did not damage recording devices.

A new police officer came up to me with a notebook. "Ma'am, I have some questions. Could you come over here?" He pointed at a bench away from the others.

I shuffled over and held up my hand. "I'm bleeding! Where's the first aid? This is ridiculous! Can't you see that I'm old!"

"Of course, ma'am." He gestured to someone I couldn't see and a medic appeared. The eager young medic ushered me the rest of the way to a bench where I couldn't see the others. I'd have to trust they would get us through.

The medic daubed at my hand, asking short questions—What's your name? What brings you to the museum today? When were you born?—while the officer tapped his foot, leaning forward to see into the room with all the broken glass. He didn't need to look, I could have told him: there was nothing there to see.

With a final piece of tape, the medic finished wrapping my hand. It looked worse than it was. Hands and heads bled more than anything else. "I think you'll live, Ruth."

"Life is terminal, young man, and alas, I have a terrible case of it." I raised an eyebrow at him. The medic chuckled politely. "Now, is there any possibility I could have my cane back? I rather like that one."

The medic shot a look at the police officer. The officer gave the scene a sidelong glance. People carried the priceless gems further into the museum, presumably to the vault. I'd seen it when I toured it in the final preparations for placing the Source in the exhibit. He looked back at me with a shake of his head. "Let's stick to questions for now."

I scowled at him, and he seemed to wilt.

Hiding behind his flip notebook and pen, he met my gaze. "Can you tell me what happened?"

Some asshole stole the Source, and now Winter is going to kill me for reneging on our contract. "I thought I saw something on the glass, and when I touched it, it exploded. You saw my hand, right?"

He looked at me and chewed on the inside of his lip. "Were you planning to steal anything when you came here today?" he asked.

I blinked at him. Steal was such a strong word. "Absolutely not!" I couldn't steal something that I already owned.

The officer narrowed his eyes. "I don't know how to make you understand how serious this is, Ruth, but there's a broken case, and it didn't get that way all by itself, now did it?"

"Are you suggesting I broke the glass? I thought I read in the brochure that it's bulletproof."

He nodded.

I tipped my chin just to the side, so I could give him my best conspiratorial note.

He mimicked my movement, leaning in for the juicy truth.

"How could I have broken through bulletproof glass with my bare hands?" I asked.

The officer scowled and examined me. "A device perhaps."

"Hidden where?" I asked. I held up my hands. "Perhaps up my sleeve?" I widened my eyes at him, and he checked my arms, but this shirt, like every other shirt I'd put on since I called fire from my stove was blissfully free of sleeves. This one barely had any threads left over from when I pulled the stitching.

The officer deflated. "So, you're saying you had nothing to do with the breaking of the exhibit, is that right?"

"It just exploded. I'm lucky to be alive. When can I get my cane back?"

He chewed on his lip—easier than chewing on my words which just didn't add up. "Could I get you to hold your arms up, ma'am?"

I obliged. It's not like he'd be able to see the remnants of a spell on my person. He had me lean forward, and he felt along the back of my shirt.

After finding nothing, he stood up straight, shaking his head. "I hate to ask, but may I look in your bag?"

"Of course, sweetie." I handed over the stolen bag.

Dutifully, he searched my bag for anything that could possibly have caused the glass to explode. He shook his head when he pulled out the nail polish. He passed out my pill box. "Have you taken all your medications today?"

I scowled at the box. "What business is it of yours?" I asked.

Then I started combing through my mind. We lost some 14 hours when we went through the fae realm, but did it count as far as my blood sugar was concerned? Medicine had a terrible interface with magic. "Yes," I said. "I had to think about it there for a minute." I followed it with a nervous laugh.

He handed the bag back to me. "Stay here, and I'll go see about your cane, Mrs. Westings."

I watched him head into the fray around the crime scene. They took my cane out of the glass, and three people looked it over. They took the rubber stopper off the bottom and scanned it with a metal detector. It looked like carved hickory, but I couldn't tell just from looking. Pretty to look at and strong enough to help a woman older than the states of New Mexico and Hawaii walk around. No technological monstrosity hidden inside. They took my cane into the back, and I waited.

They took pictures of the scene, and I waited.

An hour passed, and then another.

The officer brought my cane back but asked me to stay.

What did it matter to me? Winter was coming for me. When the moon reached peak fullness, she'd be there, ready to absorb my soul.

Gods, would she torture me?

Finally, a different officer, a woman with box braids and a no-nonsense attitude took my address and phone number. To be sure, she called my phone from hers and asked me to mark it so she could get a hold of me in the future. I obliged. They weren't going to be able to prove I'd broken it with magic unless they had some of their own.

Just as I planted my cane to stand, I heard the telltale voice of Jessica, rising in anger. "You'd better let me through, that is my mother!"

I sagged on the bench, and the officer smiled at me. "Oh, I guess you're in trouble now," she said. Her smile showed her teeth against her dark skin, and she winked at me.

"Can't a girl just have some fun?"

"You have a nice day, Ruth," the officer said. She dipped her head toward me and tucked her notebook into her pocket.

I scrunched my lips to the side. "Thanks."

Jessica pushed through the perimeter of security people. "Oh my god, Mom, I was so worried!"

She hit me like a freight train, wrapping me in a hug. Guilt washed down my back. I caused this worry. I made my granddaughter worry that I might not ever come back. My throat closed around a lump, and tears stung at my eyes. Damn it all to the realm of fire.

And now she'd be by my side when Winter came for me.

I tried to speak, but Jessica cut me off.

"What happened? What were you doing? Why does it look like a war zone in here?" she asked.

I swallowed hard. "Can we talk outside?" I asked, like a teenager caught red-handed. Though to be fair, a teenager could only get into so much trouble. I'd lied to Jessica for her whole life about so many things.

"Yes, let's get out of here. I saw the rest of your horsemen, and I'd like to have a few choice words with them."

Something wasn't adding up, but there was just too much. The whole world seemed to spin around my lies, my contracts, my life spinning to an ignominious death at the hands of the Winter Queen. And now I'd have to face it all in front of my granddaughter.

Horace, Phyllis and Mary stood as soon as I breached the barricade. Most of the visitors had already left, and the docent at the front repeated the stock line about things being under construction in the gem and mineral exhibit, and how the second floor was currently closed. Sorry for any inconvenience.

We stepped into the waning light of an early spring afternoon on the mall in Washington DC.

"You must be so cold, Mom," Jessica said. She wrapped her coat around me.

"How did you get here?" I asked.

"I came as soon as I got the call. I flew into National and took the metro."

"Call?" I asked.

Mary ducked her head, but the guilt rang through the set of her shoulders.

"You called her? I was trying to protect her!"

"I thought you'd want to have your family with you! I thought that was the whole point! Who else could follow in your footsteps! I thought we'd have the Source, and you'd need someone to carry it. It's not like any of us are in a position to be the bearer." Mary pointed at the three of us in turn. She sighed. "I thought you might want to bring magic back."

"That's not how it works," I said. "Well, maybe. I don't know."

"What are you all talking about?" Jessica asked.

Phyllis's wide eyes shone over Mary's head. "You didn't mean to give it back, did you?"

"To Winter? Gods no! She'd brow beat us into letting our most powerful people die of *old age*. She's tortured us enough. But we can't just 'bring it back.' That's not how it works," I hissed.

"Don't talk over me like a child, Mom! What the hell are you all talking about? Why were you attacking the museum?"

"We weren't attacking the museum," I said. I held up my hand. "If anything, things attacked us." I waited for someone to laugh at my joke, but everyone wore the grim masks of uncertainty.

Mary caught my eye for only a moment and silently mouthed the words, "Tell her." Phyllis nodded but turned her nod into the glorious smile of a toothpaste model when Jessica turned her way. Horace had taken a sudden and devouring interest in architecture.

They weren't with me.

My heart beat with a thud. I licked my lips, preparing to lay it all out. Seven decades of lies. One hundred and forty years of secrets and schemes. I turned back to my granddaughter, ready to tell her everything. She deserved to know the whole truth.

A chill wind caught the edge of Jessica's coat. Everyone hunkered into their clothes at the briskness of the wind. The faintest tinkling of a laugh slid through the wind. Winter's voice.

I couldn't tell Jessica. What good would it do for her to know that I was actually her grandmother? That she'd lost out on knowing Anne. On knowing her other grandmother, Dorothy. How could I lay that bomb on her doorstep when Winter was coming for me?

The whole life she should have had played out in my mind's eye: the missed holidays, and the way Dorothy could make even a crappy apartment in the city feel like a whole kingdom. She would have known Anne, the no-nonsense girl who took no shit from anyone—not even me.

Unbidden from the depths of my memories, my mind filled with all the Thanksgivings we had with Mary, how she'd made sure that Jessica and I always had a place at her table. I'd always assumed it was charity. But Mary had strong-armed her husband into taking us in like family. Always listening to everything I said and raising her eyebrows at the parts we had to leave out for her Henry and my Jessica, the two who'd never had magic. All the times she'd dragged me over to her place to have a couple cocktails. Mary had been right there the whole time, Jessica's unofficial grandmother.

No, that was just Mary being amazing—being the best person I'd ever known. And I would die by tomorrow at half past nine. Unless, by some miracle, I found the Source, I was going to part the mortal realm before I ever saw my home again.

I gulped down the cold air and did what I'd become best at: I lied to those I loved the most. "It was just an old game, Jessica, honey. When we were younger, we used to talk about making a trip to the Smithsonian. I had thought about becoming an Egyptologist once."

Her brow lowered over her eyes. "Is that why you have all those papers full of symbols?"

The white around Phyllis's eyes shone as she raised an eyebrow at me. Most people couldn't see the ancient symbols. Magic knew to protect itself. My heart tore. She would have been a natural mage. My heart swelled.

But Winter had me in her sights.

"Yup," I lied. What was one more lie added to the pile. It wasn't like one more would hurt anyone at this point. "Hieroglyphs. I used to study them." The ancient runes were close enough, but I'd never been able to reproduce what had been in the old books. Another thing I lost.

Gods, all of mankind would wander without any understanding of how magic even worked when I passed.

I squeezed my eyes shut for a moment. What a stupid loss. What had I thought? Why would I have been so reckless? Once the elder mages had passed into the realm of fire, I should have written it all down. Now there wouldn't even be time to write down instructions for calling enough fire to light a candle. I was such an idiot.

Chapter Twenty

"You ran off to come to the Smithsonian?" she asked. "You could have just asked. If it was that important to you."

"Time and money. I didn't want to be a burden on you," I said. Which was true. "And you were prepping to put me in a home, and I didn't know how much time I had left."

"A home?" Phyllis asked. "But why?"

Jessica pushed her lips together before stretching them over her teeth. "There was an incident with the stove."

"Fire?" Mary asked.

Jessica nodded sadly. "Exactly."

I took a sad breath. "I can honestly say that won't happen again." Not ever.

"Well, I still think it's a very real consideration. Assisted living could prove very fulfilling for you."

She sounded like an advertisement.

I waited for Horace or Phyllis to chime in, but they all turned to look at me.

"You don't think I should go into one, do you?"

Mary's eyebrows pinched together. "Well, I mean, it might be nice to know what your wishes are. You know, just in case." She put her hand on my shoulder in gentle support.

"In case what?" I asked.

Phyllis regarded me, her lips turned down at the corners. "Winter isn't always, ah, clean."

My whole body ran cold. There were many ways to be considered dead, and Seeings came in a mix of literal and metaphorical.

Jessica nodded. "Exactly, sometimes we get snow, and there's work to be done cleaning up after a storm." She nodded, her eyes wide as if she beamed sincerity directly from her heart and out through her eyes.

I sought Mary's guidance, but her pain-streaked face wouldn't meet my gaze.

"This is dumb," I said. "We just need to find..." I broke off.

Jessica stared at me. "Find what, Mom? I can help you look."

"I, uh—" I ran my fingers through my hair. "It can't have disappeared," I said, directing my appeal to Phyllis.

Her wide eyes conveyed the same pity and sadness for an injured dog. "Where?"

"It has to be with someone who had access. One of the scientists. Lead could block it—even a simple film bag could dampen it."

"No one has film bags, Mom. No one has film," Jessica said.

I ignored her and made the hurry up gesture to the others. "Come on, there's still time."

I headed back toward the steps. When no one followed me, I pivoted on my good leg and put my hands on my hips. "Well?"

Jessica traded a glance with Horace. "Is this why you called the police?"

"You what?" Mary asked, her eyes growing wide.

"What was I supposed to do? She was raving on about faeries and magic! She's clearly come unhinged!" Horace looked like a scared old man. "She stole cars—and other things!—and she pushed us like a mad woman. Are you trying to tell me these last few days have been a vacation?" He caught Phyllis, then Mary in his gaze. They both looked away uncomfortably.

"There's already a lot of trouble to sort out," Jessica said. "We really should get you all home." When no one moved, she looked to all the faces. "I'll just give you guys a few minutes to talk it over amongst yourselves while I make some arrangements." And with that, Jessica gave us a moment of privacy at the steps of the Smithsonian.

I blinked at my friends. "I can't believe..." I opened my mouth to say more. Then I pointed at the door. "But there's still time!"

"How? How is there time?" Mary asked. "It could be anywhere! Do you even know which decade it went missing?"

That caught me up. There were needles in haystacks that would be easier to find. They were at least confined to one bit of hay. The Source could be anywhere.

But without it...

"But you're not even going to help me look?" I asked. "None of you?"

Phyllis narrowed her eyes. "What do you want us to do? Do you want us to make a deal with the devil, too? Do you want me to drug myself for a moment of clairvoyance? I don't control the visions, and if someone has found a way to dampen it, I won't be able to See it either. How do you think this will go?"

"But she'll kill me!" I said.

"Or worse," Horace said quietly. "She could just take your mind and leave your body! Then think about how Jessica will feel, being burdened with your not yet dead body and hoping you're still in there." He gave me a sharp look of understanding.

My blood ran cold then hot. "So you just want me to roll over? Is that it?"

Mary shook her head. "We're saying that there's no hope. Unless you somehow know where to find the Source, it's time to put your affairs in order as much as you can."

I pointed at Phyllis. "You could look. Right?"

"I have! I've looked for the Source three times. I assumed it was here because I could never See it." She fidgeted with the edge of her ill-fitting shirt.

Narrowing my eyes, I stepped closer to her. "You knew this would happen," I whispered. "You knew it wasn't here."

"No," Mary gasped. "Don't be ridiculous, Ruth."

I pointed my chin at Phyllis. "She knew."

Phyllis twisted her neck as if the collar of her shirt had suddenly grown in weight. She shrugged, a subtle gesture but full of meaning. "Know is such a funny word."

"You did know," Horace said, echoing Mary's realization. "Why didn't you say anything?"

"I didn't know, not really! It's not like a vision plays out like a movie or a book. There are feelings and symbols and meaning hidden in the tiniest symbols." Phyllis pulled at her collar, suddenly red in the face.

"What else did you see?" I asked. "Did you see the Source ever?"

"No!" she shook her head emphatically. Then she folded. "Not really. I mean, I Saw it, but it wasn't like that dead lump we carried back from Germany, if that's what you mean."

"Shit, you lied?" Mary asked. "What did you See, you have to tell us everything!"

"I already told you, I couldn't See it properly. It wasn't the Source, or at least I don't think it was. I thought I saw it when we were in Nevada. When I was pretending to be sick."

Everyone hung on Phyllis's words. She shook her head. "It was like the sun came down to Earth. But when I saw it again, we were on the subway here. But it looked different, like it was angry, you know?"

I deflated. "Yes, I know. It really was the sun. That was Summer. I've spoken to her twice. She offered to help me if I gave her the Source."

"What did you say?" Mary asked.

"I told her to go to Hell." I paused and bobbed my head in concession. "I mean, I was nicer than that, but I refused her offer."

Everyone deflated like I'd taken the mickey out of them.

Horace looked at his hands, sighing as if in relief. "Then that's it is it?"

"No," Mary said. She pointed at Phyllis. "You haven't explained how much you knew. You could have warned us. We've lost hours here. We could have been searching!"

Phyllis stomped her foot. "There was nothing else to be done. I didn't know what it meant until we were too far into it. I thought it would work up until the case broke!"

"That's not good enough, Seer. You should have told us! Ruth could have told you what your thrice-damned Sight was trying to tell you, but you've always kept your art as mystical as possible. Never once did you trust us. Not once. And now—now Ruth is going to die!"

Phyllis stood straight, lording her height over Mary. "You think I'm responsible for Ruth's deal with Winter? You think it's my fault someone stole the Source?"

Mary's face turned splotchy, blood welling to her cheeks as markers of her anger. "No, but if you knew something—if you'd shared when you knew it, we might have more time!"

Phyllis narrowed her eyes at Mary. "Why don't you say what you really mean."

"What are you talking about?" Mary asked.

"You're just mad at me because now you won't have time to tell Ruth how you really feel. How you've felt for years. How you've carried a candle for her through your loveless marriage to a normal incapable of even giving you children."

Her words broke around us like a watermelon dropped on concrete.

Mary stared, her eyes rimmed red.

My chest twisted.

"You think I've robbed you of a chance to be with Ruth? No amount of searching is going to make Ruth get over Dorothy for you." Phyllis shook her head, holding her hand out palm forward.

My breath caught in my chest, wrapping around my beating heart. Each thud rent itself on my ribs. Each beat was a stab against my limited time, still desperately holding together in my chest.

I sought Mary's gaze, but she turned away, tears streaking her cheek. I opened my mouth to speak, but what could I say? I didn't know how I felt. Dorothy's image rose in my mind's eye, but right next to it, there was Mary. All those years, being invited in. They'd been charity, right?

Just blinking, I stood there like a fish out of water.

Mary scowled at Phyllis. "You asshole."

Phyllis cocked her head. "It's not my fault you all are a bunch of emotionally constipated fools. I went to therapy. I even recommended it."

Mary screwed up her face and clenched her fists. She shook her head before walking away.

"Mary! Wait!" Jessica called. "I bought us all tickets and a couple hotel rooms."

Like a dog at the end of its leash, Mary stopped.

Jessica caught up to our group. "Good news, the hotel had a special given the fact that it's the middle of the week. Bad news, the soonest flight with enough seats is tomorrow morning at nine."

"That's great," Phyllis said with fake smile. "Can we go to this hotel then? Maybe by way of a store. We lost our luggage in Texas."

Phyllis started walking and the rest of us caught up by default. The blazing orb of the sun hung in the sky directly over the Washington Monument. The air had the crisp promise of frost by morning. We crossed the mall, heading for the metro stop to get us off the mall.

The green of the grass seemed vibrant, like it knew a secret. The trees along the walkway leaned over our path, their newly unfolded leaves bright and green seemed to tease me. What a thing to know I'd die just as the world was coming out of its slumber.

We walked in silence, and I tread on my feelings as much as my feet.

This was the last time I would walk in this place. This was the last time I would be in the afternoon light. Each breath, filled with every scent of the world: the grass, the leaves, the dirt, even my clothes. They still smelled like clothes from a store.

What a mess I'd leave in this world. Dead and Jessica to clean up the mess. Would Mary help her go through my things? Would Jessica know to let her?

I'd have to write a letter.

There was just too much to do, and I wasn't done just breathing.

There was so much I wanted to say—so many questions. I tried to move to Mary, but as I shifted in the group, Mary shifted away.

Was it because Phyllis was wrong and now Mary didn't want anything to do with me? My whole chest ached. By the time we made the escalator at the metro station, I stopped trying. Gods, what would I say if she confirmed she didn't feel that way about me? Besides, what could I say in front of Jessica?

We rode the train in silence. Unable to make way for my feelings, I packed them and attempted to absorb the meaning of my life on a subway ride.

Chapter Twenty-One

The room was small and clean, two beds and a couch. Phyllis and Mary stayed with Horace, a thinly veiled attempt to give me time to make peace with my granddaughter. After we got food, she called the emergency babysitter, talked to both her kids, then called the apartment complex, making plans. She reported her findings like a corporal trying to impress a captain. She found comfort in routine. I no longer felt comfort.

My heart beat more slowly, as if it knew it was close to the end of its run. Soon it would rest. One hundred and forty-four years of perfect, pristine service. Two pandemics, and all of it just to end like this? Winter would come for me as she gathered her soldiers to march across our planet. I wonder if she'd use real warriors or if she'd just start throwing crazy storms. What would DC look like under fifteen feet of snow in May?

To distract myself, I fussed with my phone as Jessica moved about the small room. One of the articles suggested to me talked about stars. I don't know why, but I clicked on it.

Massive Star Explosion May Have Triggered Nebula Collapse Leading to Formation of Sun.

Huh. Sometimes these damned phones were prescient.

I read the article talking about how the nebula where our sun formed would have definitely formed next to other, more massive stars, whose life cycles are much shorter. It suggested our star would have formed close enough to experience the backwash from a nearby Super Nova as the sister stars in the stellar nursery were still in the early stages of formation.

Something nagged at the back of my mind, but it was all too much. I was too close to dead to worry about things like beginnings. I needed to focus on how to end out my life with dignity and...and what? Honor? I had none. I hadn't lived one of those great lives. Sure, I'd done great things. The mark of my life on humanity would be unknown but definitely felt for a very long time. But was it a good life?

Assuredly not. I had lied and stolen, cheated and double dealt. And worse, I'd done this to people I'd loved. Lies came easy, but the truth was too much. It came with a weight that broke through all the carefully crafted scaffolding of my fake life.

I tried to sleep, but knowing how soon I'd die took away all desire for dreams. I pretended to be asleep long enough for Jessica's breathing to go to the even rhythm of slumber before I got out of bed and watched the city. Our room faced west, giving us a view of the city and the impossibly full moon. It hung thick in the sky, fuller than I could ever remember it. I desperately wanted to be anywhere but this big city.

It called up memories of moonlit nights. How my stomach had swooped the first time I kissed Dorothy under the full moon. When we'd crossed a German field under the light of the moon breaking through clouds as we made our way to the Source. Mary's face as she pulled water from the air to spread it on the plants to hide our tracks and the silver light sparkling up like a million diamonds. The moon hanging over me the first night I called fire. The first time I knew I was a witch, and I wanted to be one. When the other mages had made me an initiate—if only I'd kept my robes. Fire mages are to be burned in their robes when they die. Not that anyone would know. I hadn't shared my rank or our rituals with anyone besides Dorothy. It was supposed to be a secret.

So many secrets, the biggest one that magic had even existed.

The pit in my stomach grew from the seed of regret. How many potential mages had been born and died during a time with no magic at all? Seven decades was a whole lifetime. So much talent completely denied to our world. Mages weren't that common, but our longer lives meant we were usually able to find each other. Inadvertently, my choice to hide magic away may have denied hundreds of people the chance to live the lives of mages. Had they always known and wished for more? What right had I to deny them their truest selves?

And worse, what about the children who discovered they had powers just before the end of the war? They would have grown up knowing they had had something special, and no explanation as to what it was or why it left.

No wonder our world degraded into chaos. All those untrained mages, knowing deep down, but unable to do anything about it. What had happened to them? Had they turned to art or science? With no reason why it had left, I could have easily turned to darkness when my magic was gone, much like Adolph and not making it into that art school in Vienna. Of course, he had the benefit of living in a world with magic and systems in place to find the mages and train them. Perhaps magic wasn't a very strong driving force in the depravity of humanity.

Who ever thought Nazis would come back? And now my time slipped away. I wouldn't be there to see this round of greed and racism get cast back. *If* they were defeated.

The clock ticked to five AM. Only a few hours until the moon was fullest. I'd checked and rechecked, and if there was one thing Winter would do was follow the letter of when the moon was fullest, even if it wasn't in the sky at my location at its very fullest. I sighed at the clock. There wasn't even enough time to watch a fantasy trilogy. If Winter was the timely sort, I'd be dead before I was offered airplane food.

Small favors.

I got dressed in the new clothes we'd picked up. Jessica had insisted on sleeved shirts on account of all the time in an airport and air-conditioned airplanes. We'd settled on a tight, long-sleeved shirt and a jacket vest that had been on sale. I didn't want to be any more of a burden than I already was.

I slipped out the door, carefully pulling it shut behind me, trying not to wake up Jessica.

A slight intake of breath from the hall caught my attention. Mary sat in the hallway leaning against the wall.

"What are you doing?" she asked.

"I couldn't sleep."

She snorted. "Imagine, your last hours on this earth and you didn't want to spend them snoring."

A smile tugged at my lips. "Maybe all insomniacs are just scared they're going to die."

Mary smiled back. "Not likely." She played with the carpet where a thread had pulled free. "About what Phyllis said—"

I held up my hand and shook my head. "Mary, I'll be gone by noon. Winter has always wanted me, she has dogged my steps for years. If I had the Source, it would be a fight, but I don't, and we have no clue where it could be." I took a deep breath. "I don't want you putting yourself in a position to be beholden to Winter. She's going to keep coming at us. You, Phyllis and Horace will have to find the Source and give it back to the world."

Her brows came down low over her eyes. "But how?"

I shook my head. "I don't know. If I had more time, I'd start looking into a more powerful scrying tool for Phyllis."

Mary got a sly look on her face. "Or we could just slip some Adderall into her coffee."

"You minx," I chuckled at the image.

"I'm just trying to save the world here." Mary pulled at the carpet with more determination.

"You guys are going to have a lot of hard work ahead of you. Is there anything I can do in the five hours I've got left?" I asked.

"You don't really think Winter will come that quickly."

I snorted. "Winter is never late." I stretched my fingers and yawned.

Mary yanked the edge of the carpet up to tear it in her fingers. The tuft of synthetic fabric cut across her timeworn fingers, and blood sprang up. I pulled a tissue from my pocket and offered it over. Silently, Mary wrapped her finger.

"It can't just end like this," Mary said. She twisted the tissue around her finger. "This is just ridiculous."

I shrugged. "I made the bargain a long time ago, and there are only a couple conditions that would nullify my contract.

Besides, nulling my contract is worse because it's kept her from attacking the human realm for decades."

Mary held up her finger. "Which is a very interesting point. I've been thinking about it. If she could attack all of humanity, why hasn't she? I mean she has clearly had plenty of opportunity before. Why now? Why make that particular bargain with you? She likes a deal, but she can't really pull together a war, can she?" Mary leaned toward me.

"Whatever she brings to bear, you and Phyllis are going to have a heck of a time fighting her off."

"You'll be with us," Mary said.

I shook my head. "No, Mary, I don't think I will. Even Phyllis said I'd die."

"She said you'd die if you met Winter again. You could run."

A puff of a laugh escaped my lungs. "Leaving you to stand in her way? No. The thing Phyllis's Seeing didn't mention was how many other people die when we meet. There's still time for Winter to create a swath of death and destruction as she's trying to get to me."

Mary scowled.

I kept going. "Can you even imagine how Winter would make sure I stopped running? The bodies of Jessica and her kids haunt my dreams. Which is why it's imperative that you and Phyllis and Horace start seeking the Heartstone as soon as possible. Without it, humans will never stand on equal footing."

"No, Ruth," Mary said, shaking her head.

I took Mary's hand and squeezed. "It's time for this adventure to end. Door-to-door service, remember."

"You're an idiot," she said, a tear escaping down her cheek.

"I am. I am an idiot, but this I know: if I go to Winter, she'll be too occupied with me to care about what you and Phyllis do. There are others—there have to be—find them and train them. Find the Source and train as many people in the way of magic as possible. The only way you all are going to stand against the Queen of Winter is if you can manage to find the Source and build the ranks."

Mary shook her head. "I don't want to do it without you!"

My heart froze over. I swallowed. I couldn't do this. My shriveled heart only beat because it was too dumb to know how broken it was.

"I—" my voice cracked.

"No, you listen to me, you crabby old witch. I have followed you through war zones—into the den of the lion!—and not once have I said the things I meant to. I love you!"

"What about Henry?" I asked.

Mary's face cracked, and she took a long breath. "Henry was a wonderful man."

My heart ached. I'd struck low. She should have yelled at me. Instead, she just pulled on her cheek as she wiped at her eyes.

Mary turned back to me, her wistful smile spreading. "Henry really was a wonderful man. Kind, handsome, so very thoughtful. And having kids and raising a family was so very expected. And then we couldn't have kids. He blamed himself, and I'd sworn oaths: 'till death do us part. My magic had had so little power, I couldn't risk oath breaking on top of that. What if magic had ever come back and I'd broken pacts? And Henry was right there, warm and kind, and..." Her voice cracked on a sob. "And then he was gone. Don't you dare leave me too!"

"What do you want me to do, Mary? It's not like I can go back in time and rewrite the contract!" I asked. "You wanted it! At the time, you said it was the best bargain. And it stopped a war! How could it have been a bad thing?" I paused for a response.

Mary just shook her head. "No."

I closed my eyes, searching for the strength. "Yes. I made a bargain with the Queen of Winter, and now it's time to pay up. She wants my life and if we don't hand it over, she will kill everyone I have ever loved." My chest fluttered with the vague attempts of my heart to keep a steady beat. I cupped her cheek with my hand, rubbing back a stray lock of hair.

My heart clicked into place, knowing she loved me, and suddenly I knew I loved her too. "How could I live with myself if my actions led to your death?"

"But you don't have to face her alone!"

"You are the last water witch. Who will teach the next generation? Who will make sure that the next group of idiots doesn't make dumb bargains with fae?"

She shook her head. "Why me? Can't we trade places? I'm so very tired, Ruth. I don't know if I can carry on without you."

My heart swelled. The cruelty of time and missed opportunities seemed to crush down on me. If I was going to die, then I wanted to have loved. I leaned down with every intention of kissing her.

The icy reality of my impending death stole into my heart, and I paused. If I folded into this feeling now, would that make it harder? Would it hurt her more to know I loved her back?

My back caught. The spasm ran up from my toes and all the way to my scalp. Pain shot through my body. "Agh!" I cried out.

Mary quickly got to her feet. "Ruth? Are you okay?"

"My back! Oh, damn it! I was in the middle of something, you mutinous body!"

Mary smiled, a wicked glint stole across her face. "I could kiss it and make it better."

The door to her room opened, and a sleepy-eyed Horace stood in the doorway. He rubbed at his eyes with one hand. "Not to put too fine a point on it, ladies, but I'm a bit tired at this point." Then he caught sight of our position. "Well, go ahead, kiss and get it over with."

I rolled my eyes. "It's not that simple."

Mary pulled back from me. "It isn't?" Her eyebrows folded in over her brow.

"Life is messy and complicated," I said.

Her face crumpled, and she turned away. My heart broke over the rocks of my idiotic decisions.

This would protect her from Winter. If she went into this with feelings, it wouldn't work. Death was coming for me, and she happened to have the power to level all of civilization.

Mary huffed. "Yeah," her voice cracked. "Life is messy." With that she slipped past Horace back into the room. The glint of light off a tear on her cheek was the only sign I had of how much I'd hurt her.

Horace looked at me, shaking his head. "Women," he said.

"Women," I echoed as if I hadn't just broken Mary's heart. I was such an idiot. I would be dead in hours. She didn't need to live with the pain of lost love. I'd already carried on through that particular issue. It hurt like nothing else.

Alone, hobbling, I went back to my room. If I sat in the dark, maybe I would ruin less before meeting my demise.

Chapter Twenty-Two

"Crap! We're late!" Jessica said, bolting out of the bed. "Why didn't you wake me up sooner? Damn jet lag!" Jessica rushed to grab her pants and jacket. She hadn't traveled with much, and the only luggage I had was the beach bag, stolen from a pharmacy in Nevada.

I shrugged as she rushed from one end of the small hotel room to the other. It didn't really matter to me if we missed the plane or not. I had a different arrangement. I tapped my freshly painted nails on the strap of my bag, waiting for Jessica. I had already pulled the clothes into my bag.

Jessica cursed as she put toothpaste on a brush. "Are you all ready to go?" she asked around the brush sticking out of her mouth.

"Yes."

"I don't want to miss this flight." She made half an attempt at brushing her teeth before spitting violently into the sink and rinsing it down with a quick swizzle of water. Instead of brushing her hair, she ran her fingers through the water and then ran them through her hair.

I raised an eyebrow at her hygiene routine. She'd be ripe as a daisy by the time she set down in California. She gave me an apologetic shrug as she wrestled with her bra.

"Why didn't you wake me? We still have to catch the shuttle!"

With a swat of my hand, I dismissed her worries. "It's a weekday, there'll be one every five minutes. I'm sure we'll be on time. Let me pay you back for the tickets when we get home."

"Let's not talk about money at this point," she said, grabbing a backpack that looked suspiciously like her teenager's. "Let's just get to the airport and catch this plane."

Without another word, she pulled open the door into the hallway. Phyllis, Mary, and Horace all stood there waiting.

Phyllis, dressed in black pants and fresh makeup sharp enough to be lethal, raised an eyebrow at me. "Cold feet?" she asked.

I shook my head.

Mary took a step toward me—somehow she always had a blue shirt, and today's was no exception. She must have bought it when Jessica was forcing me into a clean set of clothes as well. Mary fussed with my collar, the smell of department store clothes thick in the hallway.

She swiped my collar down with her hand, letting it linger on my shoulder for just a second longer. She caught my eye and nodded. "Chin up then."

My friends had turned out to walk me to my death. I couldn't imagine a better procession than my best friends. So little time, and so much to say. Instead of words, I led us off, heading down the hall while Jessica fussed with the door, darting back into the room one last time.

With each step punctuated by a cane, Jessica caught up to us before we made it to the elevator. The awkward silence stretched as we waited. The doors parted on a mostly full elevator. We crammed in, saying our pleasantries to our new co-occupants.

"Your first time in DC?" one couple asked Jessica.

"Yes, actually." Jessica's words were clipped with the hint of not wanting to talk about it.

"What did you see while you were here?" the woman asked.

Horace smiled. "The Smithsonian. Amazing museum."

"Really, we didn't get to see it all, they closed the part with that big diamond yesterday." She shrugged.

"It gives you a great reason to come back next time," I said.

The elevator doors opened, releasing us from our forced politeness. We stepped out into the morning air, crisp and filled with dew if not frost. The wind slipped through the edges of my jacket, and I shivered.

Winter was going to murder me.

The hotel had been chosen for its convenience and nearness to the airport. The shuttle to the airport was filling with people, and we all piled in. I clicked my seatbelt into the buckle, a funny habit knowing that it was Winter coming for me, not a car crash. I had a reckless moment where I considered not wearing it. After all, I was on my way to my death.

Ah, but Winter could come for me at any time, and there was no need to give her such an easy target as me in a van with other passengers and no seatbelt. She would kill everyone around me.

I checked my watch. An hour. There was one hour before the moon would be perfectly full. One hour until I was no more. What even came next?

The man driving the hotel shuttle checked everyone's seatbelt then rolled the side door shut with a crash. He went around to the driver's side and hopped into the seat like a man who made this trip every day for years. "Alright, everyone buckled up?" He made one more show of checking people. "Which airlines are we taking today?"

Horace unbuckled and grabbed the door. "Wait! I forgot my shaving kit back up in the room!"

"Just leave it," Phyllis said.

"Not a chance! It's my favorite one!"

He grabbed my arm. "Go ahead without me. I'll catch the next one. Get me checked in and all that. I'll be right behind you!" And with that, Horace pulled open the door and rushed back to the hotel.

The attendant drew his lips together in a thin line of annoyance as he walked back around the van. He checked the door before getting back in on the driver's side. "Anyone else?" nervous laughter chased his annoyed words, and we were on our way.

The morning traffic had thinned, but like every airport ever, there was more than enough traffic in the loop around the terminals. I watched the cars going by and couldn't help but notice how alive an airport was. Business travelers moving along with nothing but a briefcase and a phone, moving through the crowd like the world was made for them alone. They danced around the families gathering for some vacation, burdened by small mountains of luggage.

I checked my watch: fifty minutes until the fullness of the moon. Far too short.

The van pulled to the next terminal, and Jessica tapped my shoulder. "This is us."

We piled out of the van, and I searched the traffic for the next shuttle porter. If I was going to die, it would be best if Phyllis and Mary had as much support as they could get dealing with my body and my granddaughter.

The thought of them wrestling with my suddenly dead body filled my vision, and tears sprang to my eyes. What a needless waste. Even in death I would be a terrible burden to people. And my death would be such a complete failure. I was the last of my kind. The last mage with enough power to stand against Winter. And now the world would have to navigate the terrifying new world of fae invading after they'd been held back by the council for centuries before we lost the Heartstone. We were the last-ditch effort to keep Winter and Summer from plowing over humanity.

And now we didn't even have the Source.

We never should have locked it away. That had been so stupid.

I followed Jessica to the ticket counter, and she fussed with the kiosk. I watched the world pass by me, all the travelers going somewhere. My eyes blurred out for a minute. The sun streaming through the windows slanted down to the ground, splashing light onto the ticket counters. A dust mote caught in the sunbeam, swirling down in a lazy spiral.

If I didn't know any better, I'd say it was a message from Summer. In sunlight, everything held magic, even the dust.

A memory of Summer leapt into my mind:

You're travelling with the Source.

I thought she'd misspoken. I thought she meant to say *to* the Source. But there were few things in all of magic truer than the fact that fae love word games. They never made slip ups. People had lost their souls over misspoken words.

A queen would never misspeak. Never.

If she said I was travelling *with* the Source, she meant it.

I scoured my brain for other clues.

Winter had said, *You're no closer now than when you started.*

I had thought she meant that metaphorically, but suddenly it made sense. The Source had already been stolen, and I'd been travelling with it.

"Ruth, you okay?" Phyllis asked, her voice pitched low for kindness.

"Oh gods, we're such idiots." I grabbed her hand. "Winter was trying to tell me all along. It was never there."

"Why would Winter help you?" Mary asked, butting in.

Ahead of us, Jessica hurried toward security, we hung back a bit.

I pointed at Mary. "Remember at the rest stop in Nevada? Winter said I was no closer. But that couldn't be possible, we were hundreds of miles closer."

"Unless the Source wasn't in the museum when we were travelling," Mary said, finishing my thought.

Phyllis shook her head. "But where, then?"

As if it had always been waiting just beneath the surface of my mind, just waiting for me to take a moment to think about it, Horace's voice rose in my mind: *No one ever checks the shaving kit.*

I shook my head. "No, it can't be."

Phyllis caught my gaze, and her face dropped three shades of color. "No!"

"Are you ladies coming?" Jessica asked, exasperated.

"Coming!" I hollered, and we moved faster.

Mary squinted at us. "You don't think Horace has it?"

I nodded. "I do. He tried to sabotage us at every step. He forgot his blood pressure medicine, but he usually keeps it in his shaving kit. The Source was only ever unveiled when we were stopped. That's a mighty coincidence, don't you think?"

"But he's on his way here? Right?" Phyllis asked. She looked around as if he'd be walking around the corner any minute.

Mary grew still, realization dawning as she watched the travelers around us. "No, he won't be on his way."

Phyllis looked from Mary to me. "You two are crazy. I can't believe you, standing here and accusing our closest friend of such wretched betrayal. Think about what you're saying."

"I am! Has he seemed upset at all? No, because he's going to have the Heartstone and with it all the leverage that comes with it. He can strike a new deal with Winter, or—or anything!"

Mary shook her head. "As the sole owner of the Source, he could heal his whole body, be young again—control people without feeling the way it ate at him."

"Right? You thought my Order was bad, his was like a constant assault on his mind—on everything that might have been his. He told me once that he never really knew if he was himself or if he was just an amalgam of what they wanted—"

"With the Source, he'd never have to guess again," Mary finished for me.

Phyllis scowled at the ground, her face bitter with doubt.

I checked my watch. Forty minutes. "If you don't believe me, take one of those pills we liberated from the pharmacy."

Phyllis narrowed her eyes at me. "No way."

Mary's eyes grew wide. "Yes, then you'll be able to find him. He only has to avoid Ruth long enough for Winter to do the deed. Then he can go anywhere with the Source."

"Depending on the deal he's made with her," I said. They both stopped to look at me. "Well, he's going to need a deal with Winter if he has the Source. Otherwise, she'd just come and take it from him."

Jessica stood in the walkway some twenty feet ahead of us, glaring back. "Is there some particular reason you're determined to be late?" she asked, hands on hips.

"I have to go to the bathroom!" I cut away from her, heading to the nearest facility. Jessica sighed and followed.

As we stepped through the door, I caught Mary's eye and nodded. We all filed into our stalls. The flush of toilets covered all other sounds. I fussed with my door long enough to watch Jessica go into a stall with a huff.

Then as quickly as we'd gone in, Mary, Phyllis and I bolted from the bathroom.

"You're insane," Phyllis said.

"Take a pill and you'll know the truth of it. And if Horace is just late, you'll be able to See it easily."

We walked as fast as I could with my cane, scuttling along like a limping crab. Mary dug through her purse and produced a bottle from the pharmacy without a label on it. As we scuttled away, she pushed the cap down and twisted.

"Damn things. Why do they work so hard to make this so damn impossible to get into!" She paused just long enough to really dig her hands together. "Ha! Stupid child-proof mechanism won't defeat me today!"

Phyllis looked at us both, a scowl etched onto her face. She shook her head slowly, indicating that she had no intention of taking the pill.

"Please," I begged. "I don't have much time."

Phyllis rolled her eyes at me and took the pill from Mary. "I hope you feel like a real piece of work when I see Horace sitting in the hotel shuttle."

She took the pill and crushed it between her teeth. Her scowl turned to a grimace, but she swallowed it.

"How long 'till it works?" Mary asked.

"Not long," I said. I checked over my shoulder for Jessica, but she hadn't emerged from the toilet yet. "Just to be safe, we should probably get a move on."

I grabbed a corner of Phyllis's jacket and pulled her toward the double doors leading to the roundabout. The glass swooshed open. As we stepped through, I caught a glance of Jessica stepping out of the bathroom and looking around.

My heart clenched. At the first opportunity, I broke ranks and ran? She would kill me if we ever made it out of all of this. I ducked the three of us behind a pillar so she wouldn't be able to see us. I kept an eye in her direction. "How's it going?" I asked.

"I mean, it's really hard to tell." Phyllis scowled as cars drove by, magically finding their people and moving on. "We should get closer to the trash can. My tummy is—oh shit!"

"What?" I asked.

Mary grabbed Phyllis's arm. "Do you see something?"

Phyllis weaved on her feet. "I see something alright! Ruth, you're an idiot! He's in the shuttle on his way here—wait, I thought the airport was called Reagan."

"He's heading to the wrong airport?" Mary asked.

I cut her off, waving to get Phyllis's attention. "His shaving kit. Does he have his shaving kit?"

"Of course he has it, why wouldn't he—oh gods..." Phyllis stepped back like she'd been punched. She wrapped her arms around her stomach.

I scanned for the nearest trash can. It sat at the next pillar to our left. I started dragging Phyllis toward it, but she weaved again. Mary caught her under the arm and between the two of us, we directed her to the can.

"Oh gods, why? Why? Ruth! How did you know?" Phyllis asked, clutching onto the edge of the trash can.

"He has the Source with him," I said.

"Yes! In his shaving kit!" She leaned over the can but didn't lose her breakfast.

Mary's face hardened. "Well if he has it, then we need to get to him." She turned to me. "What do we do?"

"We steal a car and get to the other airport," I said. I glanced at my watch. There wasn't really time.

"I'm driving!" Mary declared.

"Blue car!" Phyllis called out.

I cocked my head to the side, trying to understand what she meant.

She pointed. "Blue car," she said again, coughing. "Ugh, this isn't gonna be pretty."

Through the glass Jessica spotted us and made a beeline for the doors. Mary and I grabbed Phyllis under her arms and started moving in the direction Phyllis pointed. As we hobbled our way to the curb, a man driving a blue car pulled up.

He opened the car door, and someone got out of passenger car. Neither shut their doors. As we hobbled over, the man pulled bags out of the car before heading over to the luggage carts. His passenger grabbed the nearest bag and started schlepping.

Without rehearsing or directing, Mary broke off and headed for the driver's side. I opened the door and Phyllis climbed into the back seat. I slipped into the passenger seat, and Mary hit the gas before my door shut.

The acceleration slammed the door, and I scrambled for my seat belt.

Mary sent the car up over a median to get out of the traffic circling the terminals. She smashed the gas, the acceleration pushing me into my seat.

With thirty-four minutes until the moon was at its fullest, we tore down the highway to the Washington Dulles airport.

Chapter Twenty-Three

I checked my watch. Ten minutes passed while Mary drove like a demon down the highway, blowing through tolls and breaking the speed limit.

"So much for the honeymoon," Mary said, taking glances in the rearview mirror.

"Oh gods, I don't know if I can do this!" Phyllis moaned from the back seat.

Gripping the car door, I half turned back to her. "It's not looking like you're going to get much of a chance to get out!"

Mary swerved suddenly, jumping lanes of traffic. She pulled the steering wheel over hard as we slid onto an on-ramp. On pure instinct, I abandoned the car door and reached for the oh shit bar, but the car didn't have that all-important handle.

"Check to see if he's unleashed the Source," Phyllis said before covering her mouth again.

I opened my channels. I felt something, but it wasn't the full, unfettered Source. I let the magic trickle in, concentrating on pushing it into a useable amount.

"Got anything?" Mary asked.

"Only small things, why?" I asked.

Mary pointed with her thumb behind the car. "Just wondering what we should do about that!"

Three cop cars tore down the road behind us.

"You'd think we were in LA!" I said.

"This is no time for jokes!" Mary yelled over the roaring engine. "Have you got it, or should I swerve?"

I pulled on the power, small though it was, and focused it. The biggest problem with fire was you needed a lot to do anything really destructive, right up until you're working with technology. Once you were dealing with tech, the trick was not to blow up the whole system. "They have to be closer! I can't feel the fire from here."

"You wanna be closer?" Phyllis yelled from the back. "That sounds like a terrible idea."

I nodded. "Probably!"

"Closer it is!" Mary yelled, slamming on the brakes.

Phyllis rolled off the bench, slamming into the back of my seat. The seatbelt caught me in the gentle embrace of a brick wall. The two cars in front swerved around us. The third car smashed into the back of our car, throwing me back into my chair.

"Phyllis? You okay!" I asked.

"Just cast!" she yelled back.

But now all three of the cars were close enough for me to feel the fire inside the engines. The tiny sparks blasting into little explosions driving a crank shaft, all perfectly timed. Timing was everything with all technology.

I dipped into the tainted bits of power, feeling myself slip away with the magic. I pulled it back, holding it for a breath. Then I cast the tiniest bits of fire inside the engines, all at the wrong time.

The results were instantaneous, rods and pistons broke in the engines, and the cars lost their power like someone had flipped a switch. Mary put the pedal to the metal and our stolen car accelerated away from the three suddenly fading police vehicles.

My heart skipped as the spell wavered. The tight pain filled my chest, and my whole world started to black out. I couldn't die yet. The moon wasn't full!

Miraculously, as if called back to life by my thought, my heart beat. It pounded through my chest like a hammer. First one strike, then another and another until it beat against my ribs, filling my throat. I gasped for breath as the world faded in and out of black. I clutched the door handle as if it could save me from the spinning sensation.

Then Mary slammed the stick shift down, pushing the car.

"You still with me, Ruth?" Mary asked as she wove through the sparse traffic. The speedometer climbed ever higher.

"I'm here," I said one hand wrapped tight across my chest, the other digging into the door armrest.

"You have to stay awake to take out Winter!"

"Gods, you sound like Summer," I said. "Phyllis! You alive?"

She groaned from the back. "For the moment, yes! What happened to you?"

"Digging too deep. Not enough power, and the old ticker doesn't like that."

Mary braked as she took an off-ramp, driving on the shoulder of the road. "So, we're flying to Winter and we've got no guns? Jeez!"

I laughed. "When have we ever been well prepared?"

"There was that time in Milan," Phyllis said.

"We don't talk about Milan," Mary and I said at the same time.

Phyllis groaned again. "We're all gonna die, and you still won't talk about the one time I was the hero."

"You're the hero today," Mary said. "This car is in great condition. I really hate driving it over the curbs."

At just that moment, Mary slowed down and jumped the curb. I fell forward as the car crunched down on the far side of the boulevard. "We're almost there," she said. "Phyllis, where are we heading?"

Phyllis wobbled in the back seat, but put her hands to her head as if she could pull the Sight right out of her skull. "I'm not getting anything." She wobbled in a vague circle as Mary took another curb, taking us to yet another lane of traffic.

The highway peeled away, then added more lanes as signs proclaimed our approach to the airport. Cement barriers corralled us until we were swooping toward the terminal. We passed more traffic signs proclaiming the airport and which lane we should be in to drop passengers off. Phyllis shook her head as we came to the first of the overhangs. "I can't concentrate when the car is moving like this."

"You need it to slow down? Fine!" Mary threw the parking brake and slammed the wheel. The whole car flew into a drift, and Mary threaded the needle, cutting across five lanes of circling traffic. As we skidded across, the eyes of the people in the other cars shone like beacons, whites rimming irises everywhere. Our car hit the edge of the curb with the tires on the right side of the car at exactly the same time. The car rocked in the direction of the momentum, tipping up dangerously.

"Whoa, girl!" Mary called like she was riding a horse and not driving a car. The car, obliging nothing so much as gravity, fell back to all four tires. Mary put her hand on the back of my head rest and leaned into the back. "That still enough for you?"

Phyllis held the door in one hand and seatbelt for the middle seat in her hand, as if she could stretch it across herself for more protection. "What is wrong with you? I could have—"

She broke off suddenly, her eyes rolling up into her head. "Red and blue ticket counter." She shook her head as if to clear it. "Oh no." She bent over at the waist and started to be sick in the car.

"We've gotta go," Mary said, pushing out of the car. "Can you move?"

"Go without me," Phyllis said. She heaved again, and I didn't wait for the next response.

My clock was ticking.

I pulled my cane out of the car, and started running, not even bothering to use it. It wasn't like I'd be paying for this tomorrow. Tomorrow, I'd be dead.

Mary and I scuttled into the terminal, looking right and left. I found a ticket counter with red and blue logos. Then I found another.

Then another.

"Oh gods, he could be anywhere!" Mary said.

"You go right, I'll go left!" I had already turned to the left and started down the row of airlines. I scanned through the people checking for Horace in his black coat. One man, I just had to find one man. A friend. A traitor.

I paused to scan the crowd, propping myself up with my cane to see over the heads of the other people all hauling their luggage to the counters and weighing them. The mass of humanity clung to the lines, standing like islands sending sacrifices to the gods at the desks.

A shift rippled through the crowd, and I spotted him. Horace stood at counter, a bottle of medication on the top of the counter on one side of the luggage gap. His shaving kit sat on top of the other side of the scale. I strode for him, hanging my cane in the crook of my arm. By god, I would face the betrayer without leaning on my cane.

At the fifth step, I took the cane in my hand. Besides, what if I needed to hit him with it?

I caught snippets of his conversation.

"I can carry this on? Right?" he asked the woman behind the counter. Then it hit me. It was his blood pressure medicine, all neatly packaged in a bottle with his name and address on the bottle.

He hadn't forgotten it. Of course, he had just been trying to slow us down.

"What's in the bag, *Horace*?" I lent the full intensity of my caught-by-mom voice.

He spun at the sound of my voice, backing into the ticketing counter. He clutched his hand to his heart, a boarding pass tucked between his fingers, the medicine bottle in the other hand. "Oh my word! Ruth! Ah... I mean— wow, what are you doing here?"

I raised an eyebrow at him and speared the ground between my feet with my cane. "An excellent question. What are you doing here, *Horace*?"

He looked to the ticketing agent, who drew her head back like a turtle retreating into its shell. He took another step back, bumping up against the ticket counter. "I mean, it's so good to see you, Ruth! I thought the moon would be full by now."

"I'm not dead yet." I watched him squirm under my level gaze.

His body shifted from backing away to suddenly loose, opening up and ready for the next scam. "Ruth, I was so worried I wouldn't get to see you again. Do you know, this young lady was just telling me I went to the wrong airport? Can you believe that?" He used his loosened stance to casually grab his shaving kit, but he held it like a shield, as if it could save him from me.

The Heartstone pulsed with its proximity in a way it should have at the museum. It was close, so near, I could taste it on my skin, like standing in an electrical storm. "What's in the bag, Horace?" I asked again.

He shook the bag, as if my words had travelled directly to his hands, causing them to act without his permission. He swallowed, fiddling with the slider on the zipper. "I was so worried Winter would, ah, you know."

The slider popped down one set of teeth, but it was enough. The power of the Heartstone leaked through. The Source of mankind's magic sat in a shaving kit in Horace's hands.

"Oh, Horace." My voice cracked. I shook my head slowly. "Why, Horace? Why?"

He choked on his first attempt at words. The corners of his mouth turned down until his face was like a caricature. "You have no idea how hard it is, Ruth!" He shook his head. "I've never been anyone. I could be someone, really *be* someone. And have you seen our world?" He held his hand out as if he could serve evil up on a platter.

I tilted my head to the side, hearing his words with disappointment. "You would steal the power of all mankind? Just so you could be someone?"

He took a step forward, holding up a finger. "Now you listen to me, Ruth. You might be full of righteous sanctity, but if these last years have taught me anything, it's that our principles will never win."

My chin quivered as I shook my head. "Our principles are all that's left of us."

"We've stood our ground, lauded ourselves for our choices—the choices of children!—and what has it gotten us?" His gaze swept the line of people, now watching us. "You think hiding magic away was the right answer? You said the Source was too much for one person? Well, I've proven you wrong, haven't I? I've had it for days."

"And look at what it's done to you in that time? They never gave it to one person! That was the whole reason we had to get it back from Hitler! You saw how he used it! Don't you remember the bodies?"

"Don't talk to me about Nazis, Ruth! Have you seen this *great* nation of ours? I burned my papers to come here. I had a homeland, and I traded it for this one." He drew a breath and narrowed his eyes. "Have you seen what they've become? Nazis, Ruth! They have Nazis! It's like everything we fought for was *nothing* to them. These ungrateful idiots prance around wearing god damned Swastikas and marching with Nazi flags like it's some damned parade!"

I stared at him, torn inside. "We should have done something with the stone. We should have used it as leverage or something against the government—or at least let them know what a resource they had. No one regrets more—"

"You're wrong! I regret more! I never should have listened to you and Phyllis and Mary. All of you are just weak. I should have known all along you didn't have the heart for it." His face set, he started to open the bag.

The power of the Source poured out into the ticket lobby, drenching the world in the power of magic. Utterly unfettered, it blossomed in my heart, spilling power to everyone around us. All eyes turned to us, reflecting the power of a star that died before ours was truly awake.

The pieces of truth fitted together in my mind. The heart of a star. Summer wasn't an embodiment of a season, she was that which was most influenced by the sun, because she *was* the sun.

And Winter was the star that had exploded to make our nebula collapse. She'd escaped to our world with the dead heart, as a guest of Summer. She wanted the Source, the Heartstone of a star, because it was hers. It *was* her.

My channels filled even as my heart skipped a beat. That knowledge, so deep, slipped into the place where the deep truths live. The glow of the Heartstone cast the airport in a golden glow, like it was brighter than every other light.

The power crackled along my hands, swirling around some people in line. I tried to meet his gaze. "Horace! What are you doing?"

He reached into the bag and grabbed the Source with his bare hand. Thrusting it over his head, he held up the power of all magic, enough magic for every human mage to never run dry. The heart of a star glowed, filling the lobby with power and heat, like unleashing all the heat from a single explosion at once.

The scent of burning flesh filled the air, but Horace did little more than grimace. "Winter! You said you would end the problem with Nazis! You said you would rid us of the bad people, the greedy and the self-centered! I call on you to fill your side of the bargain! And in return, I will bear the Source!"

The world cracked at his proclamation. He'd cast a spell into it. Horace had already signed a contract with Winter, and the power of it broke through me as my contract died with the fulfillment of Horace's. Reality stretched, and the power of Winter broke through the fae realms, flooding the earth in a power so cold, it stole my breath. So cold, because it was from a place where a star had grown, shined and died, and now nothing warmed that part of the universe that Winter had called home. Her cold was the literal cold of deep space.

Chapter Twenty-Four

After the heat from the Source, the burning cold felt like falling into ice water. Frost sprung up along the counters, and a thick fog descended through the airport. Shadows jumped and moved with a sinister purpose, and somewhere, the bells of a sleigh grew louder.

The lobby containing the ticket counter seemed to elongate as Winter used her magic to meld reality with her realm, drawing the airport—at least a part of it—into the realm of Underhill, where her power would dominate. Snow fell inside, and ice climbed the glass walls, creating a barrier between us and the rest of the world, completing Winter's circle of power. It happened so fast, the other passengers didn't have time to react. They gawked at the suddenly changing scenery, now party to whatever happened next. As the first startled yelps erupted from the crowd, Mary squeaked through the edge of the demi-realm, circling around the gathered passengers.

"What the hell?" an irate passenger called out over the din of concerned murmurs.

The sleigh bells grew louder, until one of the portals to the security lines grew spikes of ice crystals. The spears of ice cracked as they grew, covering the whole opening in a giant spiky sheet. Something grew behind the ice, a shadow that moved, getting closer and closer. A white horse broke through the sheet of ice like football players jumping through a banner on game day. An instant later, two horses flanking the first on either side broke through the bar between the worlds, pulling a troika. The fae beasts only looked like horses, but their sharp teeth betrayed their true heritage. They were monsters designed for killing, not for pulling a sleigh.

Cries of surprise pulled the other passengers together. They pressed into the center of the area as both sides of the crowd realized this wasn't some sort of trick. I tried to interpose myself between people and monsters, but we were in Underhill now—everything here was ready to murder. One of the creatures darted forward, and the crowd split in a torrent of screams, scattering around the baggage check area. People dove behind counters and pushed into the edges, pounding around the outside margin of the demi-plane. But Winter held her realm, and we were all caught in it.

The Queen of Winter stood on the bench of the sleigh. Above her, a spell floated in the air, swirling with the power of winter, promising death to any who touched it. She pointed, and the white spell of death spun into the crowd.

The pounding hooves echoed through the ticketing area as the first screams from the crowd rang out. Without hesitation, I delved into the power of the Source, pulling it around me and into my channels. I hadn't battled with magic in years. I was rustier than a 70s era Chevy in Detroit.

Mary zinged a sprig of water off the white ball of death. It turned to ice, but Mary's spell protected a family huddling in the remains of the ticket line, their luggage now scattered around their feet.

Winter shot another ball of ice into the crowd, determined to start her reign of terror here at the airport. I shot a ball of raging fire at her second spell, and the whole thing unraveled like a snowball in April. Sticky bits of unraveling magic splashed into the kiosk with the blank luggage tags. The labels blew into the air, drifting down like confetti at a party.

"Come forth my treasures! My beauties! The Winds, I call on thee! The very air shall kill at my command!"

Instantly, a powerful gale stole through the ticketing area. Papers flew, adding to the chaos. People huddled down, but some broke from the group. Those who chose to run slid and slipped as the floor had turned to ice. They fell, some with the sick sound of breaking bones. Others crawled away on the ice. I twisted around to face the troika, but my footing wasn't giving purchase, and I nearly fell to the ground.

The wind continued to strengthen, until I had to lean into it to be sure to keep my feet at all. Something else rode in the wind. The sting of snow, like a thousand tiny razorblades slitted through the wind, slashing and burning with cold. I leaned into the wind, shielding my eyes with my hand. My nearly bare arm took the brunt of the burn, but there was nothing to do but accept this pain, my price for not having enough brains to figure out Horace sooner.

I reached into the power of the Source for a second time, calling up a fire spell. Instantly, everything flammable caught fire and burned, raging against the onslaught of ice crystals. The ticket desk exploded in Formica and fire. Luggage raged with great, leaping flames, as if the clothes of the passengers knew they needed to keep their owners warm one way or another.

As I struggled against the power of Winter, feeding all the power the Heartstone could give me into fire to keep everyone from becoming frozen people-cicles, the depth of it all, my failure, my loss, all of it welled up inside me. How many years had I given away to not having power?

With my moment of doubt, the spell frayed around the edges, like a thread unraveling. I pulled the strings of the fraying spell together like the twine holding a roast together. It beat like a melodramatic bird flapping against a cage. I should have known my heart would betray me. Always my heart brought trouble on me, first falling in love with a person with zero magic, then doubting myself when I knew what was right. I knew what I had to do. There was one spell every mage could cast, but the cost was everything. It had always been there, lurking under the surface, and I'd been afraid to use it.

Around me, polar bears from Winter's realm formed. They had long white snouts that ended in bouquets of teeth, all as pearly and white as fresh fallen snow. Their fur was so white, blue highlights shown through it, like shadows were something for another realm. Their eyes glowed with the same blue as a glacier, but their claws promised to give us another color.

They shifted into existence around me and the passengers still tried to run away. I cast about for anything resembling a defensible position, but only the ticket counter and lobby in front of this one airline had been partially pulled into the realm of Winter. The destruction would be limited to this small demi-realm, but she'd trapped all the people from the lobby in here with us. A rumble with ample civilians.

The gale tore at my clothes, pushing them tight against my skin.

I pushed more power into the fires burning nearby, and they flared, but the spell threatened to split in two. I stopped feeding the fires. The magic would kill me as surely as bears.

"Grab anything with iron!" I yelled to the people huddling together in the center of the room.

Winter circled on her troika, her hell horses taking swipes at passengers. A woman took her umbrella and returned the favor. Where she hit the horse, a column of smoke rose from the beast. The creature unleashed a wretched howl of pain, and everyone flinched, trying to cover their ears.

Winter turned on the woman and shot a spell straight at her heart. I sent my own ball of fire to deflect Winter's onslaught. The two spells met with an explosion. Wind and light sped away. Winter's head snapped to find me, her team of three beasts still trotting around the passengers. The gale stopped suddenly. Snow fell in thick flakes, collecting in my hair, and numbing the skin on my arms.

The nearest polar bear turned its burning blue eyes on me. I stepped back, my foot squishing into a pile of snow. It swung its enormous paw at me, but I popped it on the head with the butt of my cane. It blinked and turned away from me, moving toward the next nearest target, Horace.

When the beast turned on him, he dropped the Source. "What's this?" he asked. The creature took a step forward, and Horace took one back. "Winter! We had a deal!" He bent over his hand, clutching it to his stomach. "You said it would be mine!"

Winter's troika stopped. All her creatures stopped, frozen in place as she cocked her head to the side to regard Horace. She stepped down in front of the huddled passengers. Her power warped the very ground around her, pushing apart the line of people cowering at her feet. The aisle that opened at her feet grew spikes of crystalline ice, glittering with the power of Winter. She walked like a stalagmite, rigid and made of stone. She stared down her nose at those she passed, and only barely regarded Horace.

Finally, she turned her attention on him, and the world turned cold. "Is this not what you wanted? Did you not ask that the world be returned to the greatness it once had? The integrity, you'd said, had been disrupted." She leaned her head to the side, narrowing her eyes. "You cannot even hold your side of the bargain."

Horace leaned over, his hands burned and blistering. The Source could not be held by just anyone. And he knew it. He crouched so low, he could have been bowing to Winter, but it didn't matter. He could never bear the Source for her. As much as he'd tried and tried, he had only ever mastered illusion and distraction. He could no more hold the primal force of magic than a cat could fly to the moon.

A person from among the huddled passengers stood. His business suit and the briefcase at his feet gave him the costume of a business passenger, but the set of his shoulders and jaw told a different story. In a practiced motion, almost mechanical in its deliberateness, he pulled a gun from his underarm holster and removed the safety. "US Air Marshall! Put your hands in the air where I can see them!"

Winter rolled her eyes. "Stupid humans, when are you going to learn that lead merely annoys us."

With a flick of her hand, a crystal grew up out of the floor and engulfed the grip of the gun. He pulled the trigger as the ice grew over his hands, but the barrel had already warped. The gun misfired. He pulled the trigger again, but no bullet would make it out of the warped chamber. The Marshall blinked at his gun for only a second before reaching for his next weapon, presumably in his shoe.

White and blue magic shot from Winter, swirling around the Marshall. The power of the wind pulled at the windows, sending snow into the counters. My fires all diminished in the onslaught of snow and wind, hissing instead of cracking.

When the man hovered ten feet over the floor, the spell evaporated, and he fell. The Marshall did not get up.

Winter turned her attention to me. "What are you doing here? I thought you'd be smart enough to at least avoid me for a time." She tilted her head slightly, holding me in her gaze. "It could take me weeks to fit you into my schedule."

"So you're not worried about the Seeing?" I asked.

Winter hissed at me. "You think I should fear some pathetic human magic? I was here before the first of you knew how to strike two rocks together to make fire."

"I know," I said.

She stopped and blinked.

"You were the other star. You are the Source, aren't you?"

She hissed at me. "You are a fool, child."

I nodded. "But you'll die, too."

"I am as constant as the air, as the water! I am the wind through the rocks, and the wave that crashes on the shore." She took one menacing step toward me. "I am the eternity of cold and dark that fills the voids between the planets."

The cold radiating from her increased, burning my skin. Her power sizzled in the air like an electrical storm. My jaw chattered, and the wind stole my breath away.

Behind the fae queen, Mary slipped through the crowd, building a spell. The heat of the water caused steam to rise from the ball. I'd seen her cast it before, Mary's own mixture of science and magic: superheated water. She finished the casting and launched the ball of scalding water. "Eat Thermite, bitch!"

The water slowed and stopped, freezing as it touched Winter. She pursed her lips as she turned, examining the newly frozen water. One droplet hung in the air next to her, and she tilted her head, extending her hand to the droplet. It grew into a jagged spear.

My heart pounded in my chest, but my limbs had stopped obeying me. Mary stood there, still as a statue when her spell did little more than distract Winter. Mary's hand still stretched out toward Winter, and she belatedly drew it back, wiping it on her pants like it might have been covered in jam.

"Well?" Mary asked. "What are you waiting for, bitch?"

I shook my head, trying to communicate to Mary. This was pure madness.

"Do you want me to kill you, mortal?" Winter asked.

"You swore not to harm humanity until your contract with Ruth was up. The contract is still in effect."

Winter hissed at her, stepping forward. "That's not how it works!"

Mary cocked her head to the side. "Oh really? Is he dead?"

The Air Marshall's chest still rose and fell with a steady rhythm. He lived.

I checked my watch. There were less than three minutes where we could play this game of cat and mouse. Three minutes till the moon was fullest. It wouldn't have mattered if Horace had been able to hold the Source, but when one contract fails, it resorts back to the most recent contract. Three minutes might be long enough to get everyone out of Winter's striking range.

I scanned the crowd and found it. On the far side of the people previously in line for the ticket counter, Phyllis—still green around the gills—quietly gathered people and directed them through a door. Doors were always weaknesses in Fae conjurations.

"You think you know how it works?" Winter asked. "You think you can tell me when I can and cannot be deadly?" She twirled, ice spear in her hand, and threw it at me.

I didn't have time to move. I watched in slow motion as my doom sailed through the air at me, speeding right for me. My heart gave a beat in my chest, and I measured it for my last. The cold spear burned with power, my death written across it. By the grace of some burst of air, it only skimmed me in a frigid kiss across my cheek.

My heart beat again, and the relief flooded through me. I lived. Mary was right. Winter couldn't take our lives for another two minutes. This could work. This could really work.

The spear thudded into something soft behind me. The icy breeze pulled at my hair, and I already knew. I dared to hope it couldn't be true even as I turned. Horace stood behind me. His burned hands clutching the ice spear embedded in his chest. The air went out of me. I hadn't been her target. She had never been aiming for me.

Winter's voice filled the air around me. "That's what happens to those who fail me."

Horace locked eyes with me. He let go of the spear with one hand, showing me the burns. The ice, smooth and slick, swayed dangerously. I turned my back fully on the queen of Winter, occluding her view of Horace. He pointed. The flesh on his hands turned blue as the power of Winter drove his body into temperatures colder than the Arctic. He made no noise as he stopped moving, the ice forming around him, holding him up until he looked like a statue encased in Lucite. But the power of Winter permeated everything.

I drew breath, and the exhale fogged so thick around me, I could barely see. I spun on my heels: The Queen of Winter was behind me, and only fools and dead people gave her their backs.

The scene waited for me, almost identical to what it had been moments before. Winter stood between the people cowering. Behind her and to the left, stood Mary, her pale face ghostly in the mist rising from the breath of all the terrified witnesses. The horses pulling the troika had stopped, and watched like curious dogs, their glacier blue eyes piercing the mists. The polar bears still walked, but now it was clear, their movement had only ever been to corral people. The fires I'd lit to keep the temperature from dropping too low sputtered out, plunging us into the cold.

"Still think I am incapable of killing people?" Winter asked.

As she focused on me, my mind raced. She would kill all these people to get to me. I checked Phyllis's progress, but there couldn't be more than a minute until the moon entered its fullest phase, the moment it was truly farthest from the Sun and most completely illuminated. Plans were always so easy for me, but I couldn't see a way out of this one that didn't kill a lot of people. And soon I wouldn't be alive to help anyone.

I stole a glance behind me. Ice covered Horace, catching him in the moment when he pointed at something, one last chance to communicate. One last shot at not being the bad guy.

I followed the line of his last gesture to the snow drift where he'd dropped the Heartstone. I stared at it as Winter took a menacing step closer to me.

"Our deal is clear, your time is up. Bear the Source for me, or I will unleash my power on your people."

Like a puppet, I bent over to the Source of Magic. It pulsed beneath the snow, glowing through with the power of ages. I scoured my brain for any answer, any way to win this.

The power had been given to mankind because Summer didn't trust Winter. They might be sisters, but that didn't make them friends. What would Winter do with it? Would she use it to destroy all of mankind?

"I can kill you as easily as your friend."

I nodded and took a deep breath before touching the ice. The cold bit into my hands before numbing them. Slowly, I searched for the glowing stone hidden in the pile of snow. I pulled at my thoughts, there had to be another way. This would be the end of all real power in the world. Humans would stand no chance if I gave her back the Source.

My hand encountered the Heartstone. Lightning flashed through my body, searing the mark of the Source onto my aura. It lit up every bit of my body, every ache and pain, every injury blurred away under the blazing power coursing through me. On the heels of the power, knowledge flowed through me.

The knowledge of ages poured through me, grinding information into my mind. Scenes passed so quickly, my mind couldn't process it. The smells pouring through the memories of previous bearers drowned my senses. The memories of a thousand sensations spilled across my mind like a waterfall, soft but hard. Everything from the feel of a sword puncturing my guts to the slip of satin over a shoulder, all of it soaked into my mind like water into a sponge, instantly changing me.

I didn't gasp, but the rush of power came with one certainty: I could never carry the Source for more than a second or two. I could never bear it. My heart thundered in my chest, unable to contain the power pouring through me. Even if I weren't so delicate, anyone holding it would be overwhelmed by the sheer power and information flood.

And in that flash, I realized something much bigger: Summer had thought I'd called her. Summer thought I'd sent a dragon to fetch her, and she came. Why would one of the fae queens come when I called? There were so few things the fae really treasured, and one of them was integrity.

Oh sure, they'd lie in a heartbeat, but if they put blood to their name, they saw it through to the end of time. Any loss of their integrity would spell disaster amongst their courts, constantly at war with each other.

And Summer had come when I'd called because she thought I had some sort of proof. She had thought I knew something. And I should have. Winter had violated our contract when she'd double dealt with me against Horace. With the contract broken, there was nothing to keep her from running her armies across the planet.

My back creaked as I stood, and I put a hand on the curve just above my butt. The cold had made its way into my very bones. I shook my head and hissed as each joint reminded me of each and every year since my youth. "Whew! You know, my back hurts like you wouldn't believe."

Mary blinked at me, her eyes bulging. She mouthed to me silently, *What are you doing?*

A valid question.

"Bring me the Source before the full moon has passed!" Winter pointed at me. Ice extended from her fingers as if she could lengthen her authority as easily.

"It's all this cold! It's not really my thing. A nice summer afternoon would be nice though."

Winter hissed. Her skin had faded to an even lighter color, powder blue and highlights. "What are you talking about?

Now is no time for you to wax poetic about your mortal body!"

I rolled my eyes. "Oh please. 'Mortal,' you say it like you can't come to an end."

"I already told you, I'm as old as time. I fill the void between the stars. I am the long pause between life and death. I am eternal, not something that can be killed with a bullet."

I nodded. "Funny, I hadn't really thought about it, but dragons aren't either, are they?"

Winter scowled at me. "Why are we talking about dragons? I see yours abandoned you."

"It occurs to me, now that I've reached the end, that I never really understood how it works. A dragon can't really die because they aren't really alive, are they? Brigid said you broke their eggs and they can lay no more. Sure, they can be banished from this plane, but they are smoke and fire. You are cold. The space between life and death, right?" I asked, but kept going without waiting for an answer. "I can't really kill you, but I could send you away for a time, is that right?"

She crossed the space between us so fast I couldn't be sure she took steps. The sharp points of her ice-crusted fingers extended, pushing into the bottom of my jaw. "Be careful what you hypothesize, human." A gleam in her eyes swirled, as if a greater power sensed the turning of the Earth and knew that she only held sway when the other pole pointed toward the sun.

As she held me with her ice knives, I reached into my pocket and drew out the parchment with our magical contract. I held it up, and the ice knives sublimated into the air around us.

"Because you're right. I could kill you, and you'd be back by the next Yule." I stepped back from her, holding the contract between us like a shield. "But does your reputation come back like a phoenix, too?"

Chapter Twenty-Five

Winter stepped back from me. I frowned at her, but took a step back as well. "I mean, you and Summer battle it out every year, right?" I pretended to be curious. "She told me about how the power is rekindled every year when certain stars..." I hesitated. "To be honest, I didn't catch all of it, but you two haven't had your annual fight, am I right?"

"Summer cannot touch me, stupid mortal."

I nodded. "Agreed, actually, I'm about as bright as a rock, or at least that's what you must think of me considering you've been suckering me for weeks if not years, and I had no idea. To be fair, you do have all the power of a star, and I'm just a human." I watched her shift uncomfortably. "Which reminds me, I have always wondered, what's up with you and the El Nino event? How does that even work? Is that just you losing to Summer?"

"Enough of this talk! You agreed! Your life is forfeit! You belong to me now!" Winter drew in her power. "And I forbid you from ever speaking of this ever again."

The binding spell hit me like a net, covering my body and seeping into my bones. I moved to hand her the Heartstone. My back seized, and I cried out.

"What's the matter now?" Winter asked.

"My back!" I cried.

"What do I care if your back hurts? Your weak bodies are why we're in this mess!"

The compulsion hit me, and my back tensed again. I cried out.

"Stop it!" Mary pushed past Winter, turning her back on the Winter Queen. "You're hurting her!" Mary put a hand on my arm, and the warmth of a healing spell stole through my whole body. The magic coursed through me, but it lifted the edges of Winter's compulsion. Mary's magic, weak though it was, slipped between the spell Winter had cast and the place where my power pooled. She took the extra time to rend the binding. It broke from me like breaking the surface of water after holding my breath for too long.

I paused, bent over with my hand on my back and checked the progress of Phyllis's rescue operation. She had one half of the ticket area completely empty. People were passing children out first, staying low to keep from drawing the attention of Winter. I caught Mary's eye, then looked deliberately over to the Air Marshall. He might not have his gun anymore, but he might have a knife.

Mary gave me the shortest nod.

"Bring me the Source, mortal," Winter said.

I stood to my full height, shaking my head. I thumped my cane down as if it could give me strength. "No."

She narrowed her eyes. "I see, you want to bargain. I can understand that."

I thumped my cane down again. "I said, 'no.' That was no mistake."

She frowned at me, her whole body moving at awkward angles as if my words hurt her.

For a third time, a rapped my cane on the ground in front of me. This time, there was power behind it. Power in the magic number. Power in the wood. Power in the very ground.

"I call on you, Lady of Summer, great Queen of the Sun and Fire. Your sister has broken her word!"

The world around us changed instantly. My fires erupted into conflagrations. The snow and ice melted into a mist that clung to the ground. The light in the room spun into a blinding white. The creatures called by Winter all turned their faces from the light. The giant polar bears tried to cover their eyes with their paws. One fell over in its attempt to shield itself from the light pouring into the ticket lobby.

The barrier holding everyone captive flexed, and the rest of the world outside became briefly visible. The sun shone in through windows, and vines grew up out of the ground. Pollen and flowers filled the air, catching in the beams of light. The diffused light reflected off everything, turning the airport lobby into a forest meadow.

The southernmost fire turned suddenly golden and red with hints of green and orange. The pillar of flame reached higher and higher until the flames parted, emitting the Queen of Summer. Attending her like a puppy walked a great white stag. The antlers of the stag had forked so many times it resembled the branches of a tree.

"Do you have proof?" she asked as if she hadn't just come from another realm.

Winter hissed.

It was a small spell, a tiny thing. Summoning an object to hand with which you are very familiar, as if knowing it made it easier to call it. I released the spell and the scroll containing my contract with Winter appeared in my hand. I held it up to Summer. "Written in her own blood."

"No!" Winter cried out. "It's all lies! Sister! You cannot possibly believe this mortal over me!"

Summer turned her burning gaze on her sister. The wave of heat that came off Summer sweltered through the lobby. The air rippled, a visible thing. When it hit me, it slipped by, cooking my clothes to impossibly hot. Winter screamed. The horses at the troika neighed in pain, and many of the polar bears vanished.

"Do not tell me what to do, sister!" Summer yelled.

Her voice raised the hackles along my back. Despite how this had panned out, the two Queens were monsters, both just as likely to kill all of humanity, just for different reasons.

I stood there, holding the contract out to Summer like a kid waiving the proof that the bully had really been mean to me. Winter's cold hand crushed down on my shoulder. She snatched the contract from my hand.

"Stop!" Summer cried out.

Winter altered reality and appeared in front of a fire.

A fire cast by my own hand.

Winter reached into the fire, burning her own hand as she destroyed the contract and any proof that she had sullied her reputation. The fire burned white and blue. Sparks of magic shot through the flames. The moment the contract lost its power snapped through my soul, as if a string inside me had been snapped.

Summer's gaze went from Winter to me. All around her, the vines of her power grew, covering the floor. She stepped onto a mat of growing greenery, as if she couldn't bear to walk on ground tilled by human hands. Her sigh came with a sudden wave of heat, but Winter pulled her hand from the fire and ice suddenly formed along many walls.

No warmth lived in the smile Winter shot back to her sister. "And now you only have the word of an old human, nearing death with every minute."

I sought Summer's gaze, but she shook her head. When she looked up at me, the yellow and gold of her eyes were almost sad.

Sunlight dimmed as something cast a shadow across the windows. "There is no proof," she said.

"No proof! She destroyed it! Why would she destroy it if it didn't have proof of her lies?"

Summer shrugged. "Alas, I cannot bring to bear any consequences against my sister without real evidence." She paused, looking at me from under her eyelashes. "More evidence than that of a dying mortal, at least."

"Horse shit!" Mary said.

"Exactly," I said. "She has threatened my people. I call grievance!"

Summer looked to her sister. "What say you? Have you threatened her people?"

"Not recently, and we had resolved our differences with a contract. She owes me her life, actually," Winter said.

They traded a look, and I knew it. They would team up against us in a heartbeat. I caught Summer's eye sliding to the Source, and felt the world shifting, the power tilting away from me. Neither of them could be trusted.

"You just burned the proof that I would owe you my life," I said, smelling the rules of the game too late to play to my advantage.

Summer nodded, catching her sister in her gaze. "True, can you not settle your grievances with words? Perhaps there is another way to fulfill the contract."

"She burned it!"

Winter stretched to her full height. "In the contract, she agreed to bear the Source for me. It is the only recourse I will accept."

That bitch.

Summer nodded. "Very well, I have noted it. Mage, what portion of the contract do you recall that you wish to file a grievance on?"

Ice ran through my veins. This was some sort of renegotiation that we'd use to determine the prize for our fight. I took a breath, giving myself a moment longer to consider my demand. "She said she would never bring her armies against humanity if I stole the Source from Hitler, which I already have."

Winter's gaze darted to Summer then back to me. I raised an eyebrow as distinctly as a middle finger.

The Queen of Summer considered my words before nodding. "Yes, these do sound like the terms I recall hearing about. Though, some details appear to have been lost." She met Winter's gaze and mine. "You are now both bound by the demands of the other. As the neutral power, I shall determine the victor."

I began gathering the power to me, casting as she spoke. The more I spread out the power, the less likely it would tear my failing heart. If I pooled enough power beforehand, I might get two spells, and I'd need everything I could to protect the Source from the fae queens.

The future of humanity would be determined by my actions.

"Do you both agree to the terms?" Summer asked.

"Wait! What terms?" Mary grabbed my hand and pulled me back.

Summer regarded her with the same curiosity most people reserved for a fly already missing its wings. "If she wins, my sister agrees to not march her armies against mankind forever more. If she loses, she will become the bearer of the Source, and my sister will own her. It's very simple."

"The hell it is!" Mary pushed forward, but Summer held up her hand. A magical force grabbed Mary and flung her away from me. She came to a rest next to the Air Marshall.

"Prepare yourselves!" Summer's voice rang through the lobby like a church bell, reverberating from every direction so there would be no way to miss what she had said.

A swirl of a storm welled up around Winter, and miniaturized lightning struck out from her. Her stark blue eyes shone through the gathering storm. Her glee at having beaten me already spread through her. She knew she could beat me. I knew she would beat me. I put the finishing touches on a big spell and gathered the power to start another.

But this was war, and I'd been through two. There was one thing you learned from war: it wasn't about beating them; it was about making sure the other side couldn't win.

"Begin!" Summer's voice came to me through my very bones.

Even with my spell fully formed and ready to go, Winter reacted faster, as if Summer had given her sister a warning I couldn't hear. The storm hit me like a hundred knives. The shards of ice cut my clothes and hands. My face remained free of damage only on account of me sacrificing my hands to the storm to shield my eyes. A magical trap wound through the wind, stripping power from me with each piece of ice.

My spell slipped from my hands, torn free by a merciless wind. I put every ounce of my being into a magical shield. The spell sprang to life, and the force of the wind pushed me back. I poured magic into the shield, and my heart gave a thump-thump. I slipped and fell to my knee. That was it. If I cast a single thing stronger than a simple shield spell, my heart would go for good.

"No!" Mary yelled.

Debris flew around the lobby, and Mary shielded herself with her hands as best she could. Summer stood still as a statue, showing no sign of the wind whipping through us. Papers whirled along in the wind, but also visions. The moment I discovered I was a witch slithered past. I watched the moment I stood before the great elders, begging for Dorothy's life. How bitter they'd been without their magic. Of course they were.

We fought diseases, built miracles. Magic had saved all of humankind on more than one occasion. The plague would have killed every European if not for the hard work of witches and wizards. And I was losing all of that for humanity. I was the weak link.

The little voice of fear whispered down my back. *Living is more important. It won't be so bad to bear the stone for Winter. And maybe over time, some could be siphoned back to the rest of the world.*

No! Winter would never allow something she thought was hers to be shared. This was all or nothing. Either I did this one thing, this one thing to bring back magic, or I'd be a living husk. A puppet.

The shield pushed on me, and I slid on the floor of the ticketing lobby, dragging a row of stanchions with me. The power of Winter's storm pushed me into a ticket counter, still burning from my first spell.

Everything I needed.

Knowing this was the end of me, I dug into the power with reckless abandon, flooding my channels. With the Source so near, the power came like trying to sip from a fire hose. My whole body vibrated with the power, and I fed it into the fire behind me. The flames raged, roaring like a living thing. The more fire, the stronger my dragon would be.

I released the full spell, driving it deep into the earth and the fire. The power shredded through me, and I felt the spell Winter had cast to ruin my heart tighten around me. My chest constricted as the whole world burned with the power of my fire. Red tinged my vision as flames reached all around me, even hotter, and hungrier than before.

"Brigid!" I called, hoping I'd put enough power into the spell to call my dragon back from the realm between worlds.

As I waited, draining my power into the summons, my chest seized. I couldn't breathe. The pressure on my back, like Atlas stood on me, still holding the world over his head. The whole world faded, narrowing to a tunnel.

As if I watched the world through a pipe, I saw her. Brigid burst through the fire like a great wyrm, pushing open the flames like curtains. Now fully formed, the connection between us flared, flooding my mind with gold, even as my body faded into the realm beyond.

Winter's glee fell from her face like laundry falling in a high wind. She frantically cast, trying to guard herself against a giant dragon, suddenly formed and full of all the strength my magic could give.

But Brigid didn't attack the Queen of Winter. Instead, she went straight for the Source. Just as she'd been trying to do this whole time. Dragons had always been the bearers of magic for humans. They were from Winter's first world. Humans could touch the power but never hold it. Dragons were from the power, tied to it. The bright red lacquer covering her talons contrasted the dark floor as she bent over and simply swallowed the Source.

The moment it disappeared down her gullet, the change radiated through her body. Where she had been nothing more than fire and ash before, scales, bone, and horns grew out of the fire. Her form filled my entire vision.

My heart sat dead in my chest, but I closed my eyes on the world knowing I'd saved it from another seventy years without magic.

Chapter Twenty-Six

Darkness covered me like the night between stars. Cold but firm. Oddly comfortable.

Then somewhere a strip of gold slipped in and around me. It pulled at me. I desperately wanted the comfort—the finality—of the darkness. I was so tired. My very bones had grown weary. I had never wanted to give up on anything. Stubborn enough for a team of mules, Anne had said once.

Gods, Anne. I almost never thought of her. If I was dying, she should be here. My daughter who went before me because I had been a coward. At least I could stand before my ancestors and not feel ashamed to do so. I had stolen the Source out from under those Queens' noses, in front of witnesses and everything.

The gold thread tugged at me, annoyingly.

There was something else. Something I hadn't finished.

Somewhere, something pounded.

It couldn't be my heart, that had stopped beating. My whole body didn't even exist anymore. I thought. Maybe.

I couldn't even tell.

The gold thread pulled at me more specifically, and I heard the rushing sound of water like static from hundreds of untuned radios.

"Damn you, Ruth Westings! Don't you dare stay dead! I have fought too hard for you to die now!"

A soft keening sound pierced the static just afterward. <Come back!> I heard in my head.

Mary bent my head back as she performed CPR on me, and breathed air into my lungs. Air and a potent spell. The power of it hit the bottom of my chest and spread out through my whole body, filling me with a shot of warmth.

The warmth faded to the cold reality of lying on the floor in an airport with a storm conjured by the Queen of Winter dying around me. I shivered and my whole body hurt.

I opened my eyes to Mary leaning over me, and Brigid's dragon head hovering just behind her. "I love you!" I blurted in case I didn't get a chance to, in case my heart gave out again.

Mary didn't say anything, she just pulled me up into a crushing hug. I returned her hug, but my body felt impossibly weak. I had been dead. Bouncing back from the flatline brigade takes time no matter the means of return.

Brigid hopped with joy, flaring a row of flames down the length of her back. <*You're back! I have it! I found it! It is so shiny and pretty, and you are shiny and pretty, and I want to keep you!*>

I smiled at the enormous creature as she shrank down to a black cat. "Yes, you can keep me, beast."

She purred, filling the link between us with the power of the Source.

Summer clapped slowly, drawing everyone's attention back to the queens.

Mary released me, standing with her fists clenched. "If you take one more step, I'll—"

Summer held up her hand. "I just wished to congratulate the winner of the duel." She caught my eye and tilted her head to me in respect. "Well played, Madame Magus. I look forward to the return of the Council."

"Wait!" Winter marched toward us. "You can't give it to her! She cheated! That wasn't in the rules."

Summer moved to touch Winter, and Winter backed away. "I was given the right to judge, and you have to admit she outmaneuvered you," Summer said. "Besides, it's hard to argue with true love's kiss."

"No, she cheated!" Winter said. An icicle formed in her hand, and she moved to strike Mary.

I scrambled for power, something to protect Mary, but almost as suddenly as Winter moved to attack, she paused. Her face contorted in pain. She caught me in her piercing gaze. The hate in her eyes seemed to devour me, but then, the very top of her head flowed like water until her whole body splashed on the floor of the airport to reveal the Air Marshall holding a knife. His suit coat dripped up to the elbow.

He blinked at the puddle on the floor around him, his chest heaving. "What was that?"

I pushed myself up to sitting. "Dash it all, you'd think she'd have the decency to die without getting my trousers wet!"

Summer smiled. "She is highly inconvenient."

And without another word, the Queen of Summer faded into the motes of light burning through the windows. The last barrier that pulled this world into the realms of fae faded. As if called back, all the fae creatures turned and disappeared, slipping between the veils of our worlds.

The Air Marshall stood before us, eyes wide. "You saw a dragon, though, right? I didn't imagine that."

Mary and I exchanged a glance. With the constant flow of power through the link between my dragon and me, I had enough energy to try standing. He offered me a hand just as I started to get my feet under me.

All around us, people moved to find loved ones. Miraculously, the only casualty lay on the ground not far from us. Nothing marked Horace's body. No hole, no sign of the fact that Winter had ended his life. The price of breaking a deal with her.

The Marshall saw Horace on the ground. "I'll call 9-1-1," he said, running off.

Phyllis ran over to us, out of breath and shaking her head. A tear sprang from her eye to track down her cheek. "Damn you, Horace! You knew better than to trust the fae!" She knelt down beside him, and ever so gently, she smoothed the hair from his forehead.

Mary laced her fingers between mine, and together we took a knee next to our fallen comrade. Over seventy years of loyal friendship only to have one moment of weakness. I folded his hands onto his chest to hide the burns while we waited for emergency services to arrive.

Mary watched the Marshall as he started to control the scene of emergency respondents. "What are we going to tell him?"

Phyllis rolled her eyes. "A Marshall? What are you going to tell Jessica?"

I chewed on the inside of my cheek. "The truth."

Phyllis hissed. "That's not going to be easy. You've spent seventy years living on lies."

Mary squeezed my hand. "She'll have help."

ACKNOWLEDGEMENTS

While it seems like writing a book is a singularly solitary pursuit, it turns out that many people have a hand in the making of a book. This book was written in the off moments of 2017, an odd year full of odd moments. Thanks go to my mom who read a very early version of this book and said she loved it. She continued to ask about it even after I'd given up on it finding a home. Thank you, Dad, for being my number one hype man. Thank you, Ben and Tracy, without your early tutelage I wouldn't have started school far too early or played with as many Hot Wheels (maybe that's why there are so many car chases in my books). Thank you to Akesh and my daughter: knowing the proper care and feeding of a writer is a delicate business, and you've both done admirably.

A hearty Thank You to my friends and critique partners. Thank you to indomitable Lizzes without whom my writing journey would have been much lonelier. Thank you, Caitlin, for all the feedback and the memes. Thank you, Sarah, for the encouragement even when I thought all of this was possibly a waste of time. Thank you to the many writers full of encouraging words in the Inklings Discord Server. Your support and guidance has been much needed. Thank you Space Wizard and Bill for taking a chance on an odd book where old people get to do things. I am forever grateful.

ABOUT THE AUTHOR

Like most mad scientists, Rena Rocford (she/her) has made an art form of living seamlessly among the normals. Today the bills, tomorrow the world. With a long history of shady labs and government projects, Rena now creates nerdy art and enjoys rolling polyhedrons at imaginary monsters with her family and friends. Her previous publishing exploits include the YA fantasies, *Acne, Asthma, and Other Signs You Might Be Half Dragon*, and *Prom, Magic, and Other Man-Made Disasters*.

Please take a moment to review this book at your favorite retailer's website, Goodreads, or simply tell your friends!

www.ingramcontent.com/pod-product-compliance
Lightning Source LLC
Chambersburg PA
CBHW032229050726
47591CB00001B/323